TRIPLE TAKE 2:
CHAMPAGNE'S KISS

Y. BLAK MOORE

ALSO BY Y. BLAK MOORE

Triple Take
The Apostles
Slipping

Second Printing: 2018
ISBN 978-1-387-48768-4
Elemental Ink Publishing
Chicago, Illinois 60619

Ordering Information:
Special discounts are available on quantity purchases by corporations, associations, educators, and others. For U.S. trade bookstores and wholesalers: Please contact Y. Blak Moore at Tel: (773) 850-5779; or elementalinkpublishing@ gmail.com.

DEDICATION

This book is dedicated to the readers and book clubs that have been down with me since day one. The only reason that I wrote this was to give you some more of the crew's lives which you loved so well. Thanks a million, zillion for making this wild, bumpy, ride that I can call a literary career well worth it. Just to hear you guys talk about one of my characters like they're really alive let's me know that I'm doing something right.

CHAPTER 1

In the rear of the Military Police car, JoAnn Wells hung her head as the white, crew-cut rocking military police officer parked in front of her non-descript house on the military base. She slowly shook her head and grumbled under her breath as the MP who was driving put the car in park.

"Hey! One of you guys got some gum?" JoAnn asked as she tasted the beer on her breath.

"No," answered the light-skinned, freckled, short MP in the passenger seat. "You're only 17. That's underage, you shouldn't have been drinking."

"Whatever," JoAnn grumbled. "Let's get this over with."

The MPs helped JoAnn from the rear of the car and marched her up the walkway to the front door of the house. At 17, she was already taller than one of the two policemen, and close to the other one's height of six feet. Though it was after 1:00 am and her drill sergeant father had to be up at 5:00 am, the porch light came on as they drew nearer.

"Shit!" JoAnn exclaimed under her breath. "Here we go."

As they stepped up on the porch, the wood groaned under the weight of all three of them. The front door opened and JoAnn's father stood there in the doorway with a storm cloud expression on his dark chocolate face. He stood six feet six and looked terrible to behold even though he was wearing a bathrobe and slippers. His cleanly shaven face was a terrible storm cloud as Master Sergeant Anthony Charles Wells stepped out onto the porch.

"Officers," he said gruffly. "Master Sergeant," returned the MP to JoAnn's left. "We found JoAnn hanging out in the park near the canteen well after her curfew. She was with some other kids. They obviously brought some beer from the canteen and drank it, then got a bit rowdy. We received several reports about their unruly behavior. Several of the suspects fled from the scene and JoAnn nor the other girl we caught would give us any information on the perpetrators who fled. We didn't want to *write this one up so we thought we'd cut her some slack by bringing her home and letting you mete out any punishment."*

JoAnn's father pushed open the front door and motioned for her to enter. She did and he closed the door behind her. He stepped up and shook both of the military policemen's hands in a huge, hand-crushing grip.

"Thanks a lot, officers. I really appreciate that you brought her home for me. It would really be a good thing for her and myself if this little incident never sees the light of day."

"No problem, Sarge," the MP said as he and his partner stepped down off the porch. "Let's just say you owe us one."

The two military policemen didn't see the Master Sergeant's face as they headed back to their vehicle, but they wouldn't have liked what they saw if they had. He didn't like being called "Sarge", and he didn't like owing anybody anything. As the MPs left, he stormed into the house, slamming the door behind him and went directly to his daughter's bedroom. Without knocking he flung open her room door and thundered in her room.

"What the hell is wrong with you!" shouted her father. "Are you trying to get us thrown off the base?"

JoAnn was lying on her bed. This scene had played out many times before. Her father was all bluster and no muster. He would yell at her and threaten her with restrictions, but he wouldn't touch her. She knew just how to play this scene.   "I didn't do anything," JoAnn said. "That's these do-gooders on this base trying to stop everyone from having fun because they're the Army's slaves."

"You didn't do anything? What do you call underage drinking?"

"I had a beer. I'll be 18 in two months then I'll be grown. You've got your nerve talking about somebody drinking. Every weekend you drink until you pass out. I'm sick of this base and everybody on it. I'm sick of these goody-two-shoes always sticking their noses in everybody else's business. They're a bunch of hypocrites and you're just as hypocritical as

the rest of them."

"I'm the one that has taken care of you while your slut of a mother does whatever she damn well pleases. I'm the one that made sure that you had a home. Me, the hypocrite. Your mother didn't care, she would have dumped you in an orphanage and kept right on whoring. But this goody two shoes made sure that you had a place to live and food to eat. I've cared about you."

"All you care about is your wife," JoAnn retorted. "You've never given me any more than what I needed to get by, but you jump through hoops for your wife and her son. Every time I get into any trouble, do anything that you don't like, the first thing you bring up is how my mother was a slut. I'm not her. She might as well have dumped me in an orphanage; that would have been about the same. You don't even pretend like you care. Oh that's right. If you have somebody around that's an even bigger screwup than you are, then you don't have to take a real look at yourself."

"You are more like your slut of a mother than you think," her father said much more calmly. "Just like her, you blame everybody for you not being happy. More to the point, you blame me. Everything is my fault. Forget all of the things I've done for you, just blame me. Every time you get into trouble and I try to correct you, then I'm the one that's wrong. No matter how you try to tarnish what I've done, I've been nothing but a good parent to you. Something that worthless mother of yours never was."

JoAnn threw her hands up. "See that's exactly what I was saying. My mother, my mother, my mother. That's all you bring up. You still love my mother or you wouldn't have anything to say about her. Do I bring up your wife every time we talk, or your perfect stepson, who's following in the footsteps of his perfect stepdad? Are you still mad that I'm not like James, the kiss-ass who doesn't have a single thought of his own in his head? I'm so sorry that I couldn't toe the line, Sir. If you only knew just how perfect your stepson is."

"We're not talking about James," fumed her father. "This has nothing *to do with James. James knew how to follow the rules. You almost make me wish that he was my son instead of you being my daughter. Of course I'm proud of James. He listens to me. You don't listen."* JoAnn kicked her shoes off and flung herself backwards onto her bed. *"James, James, James. Your precious James. You're always throwing him up in my face. If you only knew your precious James couldn't keep his hands or eyes off of me. I used to have to kick your precious James out of my bed. I would wake up and he would be in here on me trying to put his thing in me. When I kicked him off of me, he would play with hisself until he did his business and then he would sneak back to his room. Bet you didn't know that about your precious James."*

Her father released a harsh, cold mocking laugh. *"That's just the thing I'm talking about. Because James has his life together and you can't get yours together, now you want to lie on him. I suppose he tried to rape you. I know that didn't happen, because you're just like your whore of a mother, you would have given it to him without him asking. You're probably the one that was sneaking into his room and he threw you out."*

JoAnn gasped and then burst into tears. She pulled a pillow onto her lap and smashed her face into it.

"That's right," continued her father. *"Do what you always do. Cry about it. I've tried to do the best I could by you, but now I'm tired. You've almost destroyed this family with your lies, deceitful ways, and general whore-mongering. I've had it up to here. Not long after your 18th birthday, I'm being stationed overseas and I've decided that I don't want you to come with us. After your 18th birthday, I'm no longer legally responsible for you. I've had to take care of you as a lying, promiscuous, deceitful child, but I refuse to contribute to your life once you've reached the legal age."*

"What am I supposed to do?" JoAnn sobbed. *"Where am I supposed to live?"*

"I don't care. Look up your slut of a mother for all I care. Whatever you do, after I leave, I don't want to hear from you unless you've straightened

out your life. If that never happens, so be it. So for right now, I suggest you spend the few remaining months getting yourself together."

"Why are you doing this to me?" JoAnn wailed. "Haven't you messed up my life enough? You chased my mother away. You brought a boy into this house who tried to rape me over and over again and now you're saying that you're leaving me here when you ship out overseas? What's wrong with you? What kind of father are you? No wonder my mother left you." Her father walked to the door and looked back at her. "I don't feel bad about doing this. I taught you everything you need to know to survive." "You taught me things you wish you could have taught your son!" JoAnn screamed. "I didn't want to go on hunting trips and to the gun range. I didn't want to learn how to catch and cook a fish. I wanted to be a girl. That's all. A girl..."

"Well now you'll have your chance to be whatever you want to be," her father said before closing her room door behind him.

JoAnn leaned across the bed and picked up the princess telephone on her nightstand. She dialed a number with a Detroit exchange and waited for an answer.

The telephone rang twice. "If you got some dollars, my hoes will make you holla. This is Frito, who this?"

She shuddered before asking, "Is my mama there?"

"I don't know, who is yo mama?" Frito asked in a harsh tone.

"Theresa, Theresa Wells. Is she there?" "Is this little JoAnn?" Frito asked in a smoother voice. "You sound all grown up now. How you been doing, baby?"

"I want to talk to my mama," she stated through clenched lips.

"Now hold on there. You ain't got to be like that baby. We just ain't heard from you in so long and now you sound all grown up. Did you fill out yet? Please tell me that you look like yo mama used to look?"

"What??? Frito put my mama on the phone if she there."

"Hold on now, sweetheart. You can't go around giving pimps orders. It don't work like that. Pimp is the one that give orders, not the other way

around. Here it is I'm being all concerned about yo well-being and you acting like you ain't got no sense."

"Frito, I don't have time for this. Let me speak to my damn mama!" she shouted.

"Baby bitch, you better watch who in the fuck you talking to like that! I'm a motherfuckin' pimp and you gone respect me. I was trying to be nice to yo ass, but I see you ain't got no understanding of the hierarchy of this pimp shit. That's okay though, baby bitch, because when you come crawling to D-town begging me to let you stable up, I'm gone kick yo ass but good first for all the disrespect you've shown me. Now if you want to talk to yo mama, you need to ask politely, because remember while you over there with all that attitude, she over here with me, and I will spend the rest of the evening kicking her ass for the disrespect you've shown."

JoAnn looked at the telephone receiver in her hand like it was a venomous snake. She started to respond with an even more disrespectful torrent of words, but she thought about Frito's threats to her mother's health and safety. "I'm sorry, Frito," she said reluctantly. "I'm sorry for being so disrespectful. May I please speak with my mother?"

"That's much better, baby bitch," Frito said with a hint of triumph in his voice. "The fact that you can adjust your attitude when directed to do so by a pimp is gonna look good on your hoe application. I'll definitely consider you for hoe employment at a later date. Now I must go."

JoAnn thought he was going to hang up the telephone, but she could hear him shouting in the background. "Theresa! Bitch get the motherfuckin' phone and don't be on it all night!"

"I'm right here, Frito, you ain't got to holler," JoAnn heard her mother say. "Who is it?"

"Bitch, get the fuckin' phone!" Frito yelled. "I'm not yo motherfuckin' administrative assistant!"

"Who is this?" Theresa asked into the telephone seconds later. JoAnn was choking back tears at this point. "Mama, it's me," she said in a pitiful voice.

TRIPLE TAKE 2: CHAMPAGNE'S KISS

"Girl, what's wrong with you?" Theresa asked.

"Frito was talking to me like I was one of his prostitutes."

"Oh, that's all," Theresa said dismissively. "Don't take that personal. He talk to all womens like that, that ain't no big deal."

JoAnn looked at the telephone in disgust. It wasn't the first time that she'd been a victim of her mother's total disregard for her as her daughter. Tonight though, it had even more of a sting on the heels of her father's announcement of her pending eviction.

"Mama, my daddy just told me that I have to get out after my 18th birthday. I want to know can I come there and live with you?"

Theresa laughed. "Not the high-and-mighty daughter of the sergeant. Girl, this is a cathouse. If you want to live in a cathouse, you got to sell pussy. You ready to sell pussy?"

"Hell no!" JoAnn stated, appalled at the thought.

"Well, I don't know what to tell you."

"What if I come there and we get an apartment somewhere? I can get a job and help out with the bills."

Theresa's laugh was cold and harsh. "You sound just like yo square ass daddy. What kind of job do you think you could get that would take care of the both of us? I shole in the hell ain't working. I'm going to do what I was doing when yo father met me, sell some pussy. That's what I do and what I'm good at. I told him over and over again, and now I'm telling you, I don't want to live no square ass life. So you..."

In a blind fury, JoAnn slammed the telephone receiver into the cradle. She flung herself across the bed and sobbed for awhile, but soon the tears dried up. Before she went to sleep in the bed in which she knew her days were numbered, a look of resolve replaced her anguish.

CHAPTER 2

JoAnn "Champagne" Wells walked into the conference room of the penthouse condominium. She took a ripe, blood red plum from the tray of fruit on the table, and a bottle of water from the ice filled bowl next to it. Her long, brownish-red hair was pulled back into a severely tight ponytail and a towel hung around her neck. Her Adidas workout clothes showed signs of a serious workout.

At the head of the table sat Champagne's man, Jonathan "JC" Collins. She kissed him full on the mouth before taking her seat. JC's bald fade and thin goatee were perfectly trimmed, but his clothes were grimy looking. He was wearing a pair of scuffed, black, suede, Tims that had seen better days and his Champion sweatshirt and work pants were punctuated with paint and other miscellaneous stains.

Across from Champagne sat Shaunna, her best friend and business partner. Shaunna was wearing a pin-striped business suit and her short hair was spiked in a crazy, new wave hairstyle. The steam from the cup of tea Shaunna was sipping made her sea green eyes look even more striking.

In one of the comfortable, high-backed, leather conference room chairs at the other end of the table sat the group's business manager, Ronald Fortson. Ronald was wearing a stylish suit and tie, and a pair of square framed Versace eyeglasses. In his ear lobes were a set of tastefully sized, but extremely clear, princess cut diamond earrings. Ronald tapped his long fingers on his alligator briefcase as he sipped from a bottle of water.

Champagne opened her bottle of water and gulped half of it straight-a-way. She wiped her mouth and face with the end of her towel and took a bite of her plum.

"Okay, where's Rat?" Champagne asked between bites of her plum. "I swear he always late to something."

"I don't know," Ronald answered. "I called him three or four times, but he isn't answering."

"Did he know about the meeting?" JC offered. "He probably didn't know about this meeting."

Champagne rolled her eyes. "Like that makes any kind of difference. He knows about every meeting, but he still always manages to have his ass late. You quit trying to make excuses for that damn man, J. Shaunna, where is your man?"

"I was gone all morning taking care of a few things, but when I left he was still upstairs in the bed. He came in pretty late last night from the studio. He comes in late every night from that dang-gone studio smelling like a pack of squares and weed. Let me check and see if he's still in the bed."

Shaunna left her seat and walked to the condo's intercom system on the wall. She buzzed the intercom to the huge bedroom she shared with Rat. She knew that unless he was dead, the buzzer of the intercom would awaken him. Sure enough, Rat's sleep-filled voice came over the intercom.

"Yeah, yeah. What is it? I'm trying to get some fuckin' sleep. I had a long ass night."

"Well, we're in the conference room waiting on you," Shaunna said into the wall box.

"You better come on. You already late, and you know Champagne don't like it when nobody's late."

"Tell her I'll be down in ten minutes," Rat replied.

For the next twenty minutes the group talked among themselves, until Ronald looked at his watch.

"Hey, twenty minutes have passed and Rat still isn't here," Ronald announced.

"I think that someone is gonna have to go and wake him up."

"You know what, Rat is on some bullshit," said Champagne. She left her seat and got another cold bottle of water from the bowl of ice on the table. She was on her way out of the conference room when JC stopped her.

"Chammy, what you finta do, girl?" he asked, but he already knew the answer.

"I'm about to go get Rat out the bed."

"So what you need that bottle of water for?" JC asked with a smile.

"Oh, this is for Rat," she replied innocently. "When I wake him up he might be thirsty, so I'm just taking him something to drink, you know."

JC couldn't help but smile as Champagne left the conference room and went up the large double staircase to the second floor of the penthouse to the bedrooms. The door to the bedroom that Rat shared with Shaunna was partially open and Champagne peeked into the room to make sure that Rat was decent. He was sprawled across the bed wearing only a pair of basketball shorts and some white ankle socks. On his chest was a long, white gold chain with a bull charm covered in diamonds that sparkled even in the semi-darkness of the room.

Walking over to the window wall, Champagne pushed a hidden button that noiselessly opened the heavy, expensive drapes covering the ceiling to floor windows. Even with the room now flooded with sunlight Rat didn't awaken—he simply flipped over onto his stomach.

Shrugging her shoulders, Champagne took the top off the water bottle and prepared to dump the cold contents on Rat. She hesitated when she noticed his 40 caliber handgun, within his reach, on the nightstand next to the bed. She moved the wicked looking, black and chrome pistol to the dresser and returned to the side of the bed. With a good squeeze, she managed to get most of the water out of the bottle and onto Rat's shirtless back.

"What the fuck!" Rat yelped as he jumped up and reached for his gun. As his hand came away from the nightstand empty, he looked up and focused on Champagne. She was still standing there holding the half empty water bottle with her hand on her hips.

10

TRIPLE TAKE 2: CHAMPAGNE'S KISS

"Damn, Chammy!" Rat bellowed. "Girl, what the hell is wrong with you coming up in here throwing ice cold water on a motherfucker!"

Champagne leaned over and slapped Rat on the back of his head. "Stop cursing at me!"

"I ain't cursing at you. Chammy, you must be losing yo damn mind!"

Champagne popped him on the back of the head again. "I said stop cursing at me."

Rat cut her a frustrated look that made her pop him again.

"What you do that for? I didn't even curse that time."

"Don't look at me like that neither. Now get your butt out of that bed and come downstairs to the meeting."

Rat climbed down off the bed and went into his bathroom. He called out, "You ain't have to throw no water on me. When you wake somebody up, you don't throw water on them. You call their name or shake their shoulder until they get up. You don't throw no cold water on them."

"Whatever, Rat. You should get yo butt up when you know you're supposed to be. Don't nobody have time to be wasting coming up here to get you out of bed."

"I worked late last night," Rat complained as he came out of the bathroom. "I don't have no nine-to-five. If you was at the studio all night, then you wouldn't be up neither. You up in here trying to act like this meeting can't happen without me."

"We're all partners and everybody needs to know exactly what's going on. Being there firsthand means that somebody doesn't have to try and explain to you what's happening. You are part of a corporation now, not just some back alley crack house deal. To be in business you have to know what's going on with your business."

Rat pulled a fresh white t-shirt from a dresser drawer and shrugged it on. "I know what I need to know about what I do. I make music. What I don't know I'm learning in the studio every day. I talk to Ronnie when I need business advice and he get the lawyer to look over any contracts and stuff so I'm covered."

"Yeah whatever, boy," Champagne said. "Now come on."

Grumbling slightly, Rat followed Champagne downstairs to the conference room. Everyone's eyes were on them as they entered and took a seat.

"Young Gun, I see you woke now," JC said with a smile.

"Fuck you, Killa J. Yo damn woman came up there dumping water all on a motherfucker and shit. She lucky I couldn't get to my pistol, I mighta kneecapped her ass."

Champagne tried to pop Rat in the back of his head again, but this time he ducked under her swing.

"I wasn't even talking to you, Chammy," Rat said.

"You was talking about me though."

"Get yo woman, J. I'm telling you."

"You better tell his ass something, Shaunna," Champagne said.

Shaunna and JC both laughed.

"You two can leave us out of it," Shaunna said.

"Alright you two, that's enough," Ronald said.

"It's time to get down to business. I started to hire a stenographer for this meeting, but I'm glad I didn't. Are you two through so we can get started?"

"I've been ready all morning, "Champagne snipped.

"Certain people have to have a personal invitation to meetings, but I'm not one of those people."

"Let it go, Chammy," JC commanded. To Ronald, he said, "Alright let's get this show on the road. I've still got to get out to one of the properties to check behind the contractor to make sure his guys ain't laying down on our dime."

Ronald pulled several files from his briefcase and opened them.

"I have several things for you guys to consider. I know that we've been talking about diversifying and I think I've got some things that'll be really good."

TRIPLE TAKE 2: CHAMPAGNE'S KISS

"We already diverse as fuck, Ronnie," Rat commented.

"Gotdamn, what you trying to make us into the United Nations or some shit. Shit, we got real estate, Shaunny and Chammy got the lingerie stores opening, we got eight of them dollar stores, I got the studio and we just one single away from going platinum in the bitch. Shid, it's about to open up for Chicago and the Midwest coming real soon. I can feel it. We finta get this money."

"Can he finish Rat?" Champagne snapped.

"Damn, you already late to the damn meeting and now you won't let Ronnie do his job!"

"As I was saying," Ronald continued after giving Rat a look.

"We're looking into diversifying and I've got a few hooks in the water. Right now the most promising is a tow truck business. One of my mother's old boyfriends has had a tow truck business here in the city for close to thirty years. He's an old guy and his health is bad so he's looking to get out of the business before he ruins it. Seems he's ready to head to Arizona or Nevada, one of those states that is ridiculously hot to just relax and work on his health. I've been crunching the numbers and he let me peek at the books and walk through the business. Right now it's hemorrhaging cash, but that's mainly because of lack of management."

Ronald passed each of them a set of papers from his folders to look over. Rat had a befuddled look on his face while everyone else studied the facts and figures in front of them.

"Ronnie, what is this shit?" Rat asked.

"You know gotdamn well I don't read this shit. Break the shit down for me, man. That's what the hell we pay you for."

"Alright. Basically what I see is that this place could be a real gold mine if we bring it up to speed. I recommend we buy out the owner and give the business a quick cash infusion. A few new trucks, grease the right palms and this place will turn a profit in six to seven months of solid operations."

JC's ears perked up. "Ronnie, it sounded like you said that in six to seven months this thing could turn a profit."

"That's what I said. Using the old guy's contacts, with new equipment, and the right management this place could turn a buck in as little as half a year. The towing business is extremely lucrative if you're covering all the bases. I already got a line on some new trucks and I've got a guy that knows the tow truck business inside and out. He would be willing to work directly under Rat to get the business going and he's really psyched about it."

Rat sat up in his chair. "Whoa there, Ronnie. It sounded like you said something about me and this guy working together. He must be able to sing or be some new hot ass rapper if me and him are going to be working together!"

"I was getting to that," Ronald said.

"I don't want to hear it, man. I ain't running no gotdamn tow truck business. I don't know shit about no tow trucks. The closest I been to a damn tow truck is when my gotdamn car broke down and they came to get my shit for me. Man, I'm a motherfuckin' CEO of a record label not no damn grease monkey."

Champagne held up her hand. "Let me take this Ronnie. Okay, Rat how many records have you sold to date? No, no better yet. How many records have you completed?"

"Aw man, y'all trying to gang up on a nigga. I ain't just trying to put anything out there. Me and my artists have a lot of stuff recorded but we taking our time putting together a album. We want nothing but hits for our first record out the gate, that way we'll solidify our place in the industry when we come out. Plus I rent the studio out and the clients we've got pay for keeping the doors open."

"You've got to be fucking kidding me," Champagne sniffed.

"You niggas done recorded a thousand songs and still ain't put a damn album together. What you think that equipment down there run off of? Weed smoke. The electricity bill, heating that big raggedy building the studio is in, and the mortgage eat up way more than that studio makes every month. Plus you let the people who use the studio pay you in weed, watches, and features on your songs so you don't never really make any money in the first place."

"Killa J, you see this shit. Yo woman and them teaming up on me, JC. What you think about the studio, man?"

JC chose his words carefully. "Well, I look at it like this. If the studio was a self contained unit then it wouldn't be a problem. If the place was paying for itself at the least then it wouldn't be a problem. But, in all honesty, Young Gun, whenever something is taking up that much of your time and money with no return then, to me, it's a hobby. We didn't get in this shit for it to be no hobby. Let's just say that you are one hit record away from the big time. That's cool, but if you didn't have other things that made money how would you keep the lights on?"

Rat grabbed a plum and a handful of plump strawberries from the bowl on the conference table. He shook his head in mock disbelief.

"Aww, man. They done got to you too, Killa J. Man, what I'm doing is my dream. Y'all was all for it in the beginning, now I done hit a dry month and y'all ready to sell the place lock, stock, and barrel."

"Dry month," Shaunna interjected.

"Baby try dry years. That place never reached its potential and we all told you that it was a long shot from the jump. Initially we bought the place to tear it down and make a parking lot since it was close to the Loop. We could have been making a bundle by now on a parking lot, but no! Have you seen the money they're getting for parking spaces downtown?"

Rat threw his hands in the air. "Not you too, baby. This cuts me deep. Even my woman is against me. Now I know how Jesus musta felt at the last dinner. My own peoples shredding my dreams. That's cold, baby. Downright cold."

"I don't believe that you get to play the victim in this one, so you can get down off the cross and cut the theatrics," Champagne said.

"We've been telling you this all along and you didn't want to hear it, now you're on borrowed time. Ronald tell him what we're gonna do."

"Well, first of all I'm sorry Rat if things aren't going so well in the record business. I told you when you had me do the research two years ago that it could be rough going and hundreds of labels go under long before they ever break a record. Mortgage and utilities on the studio building are killing us."

"Damn, Ronnie it's that bad?" Rat asked with a bit more willingness to listen to reason.

"I knew that we was just barely afloat, but I didn't know that it was that bad." Ronald pulled more papers from his briefcase and slid them in front of Rat. The papers were punctuated with red slashes and negative balances.

"Yeah, it's that bad. That place is really a money pit. Now since I knew that it's your dream to do this, I came up with what I think is a viable solution."

"Now that's my man," Rat exclaimed as he broke into a wide grin.

"That's why we pay you the big bucks."

Everybody laughed. "This is my plan," Ronald continued when their laughter subsided.

"Let's say we do this tow truck deal. It's sweet as Johnny Gill. Rat you would take over at the truck yard."

"Here we go with this tow truck shit again. I done already told you I don't know shit about no tow trucks."

"Rat, would you shut the fuck up and let Ronnie lay this shit out, man," JC whooshed. "Gotdamn, we'll be here all damn day."

"Rat, just listen to what I'm saying. The tow truck business comes with a yard. It's a rather nice sized place, close to a whole city block in a non-residential area. Along with a huge industrial garage there are several more, smaller structures on the property. Also a trailer, I think. If we get the business we can redo a space in the yard for your studio equipment. Hell we can build you one with them prefab buildings. That way we can kill two birds with one stone. What do you all think?"

16

"Sounds good to me, Ron," JC said. "But the question is what does Rat think about it?"

"What if I don't like it?" Rat asked challengingly. "Tell me what happens then."

"Well, I don't know how to put this," Ron started. "Just give it to me like it is."

"Well, because the studio is so personal to you and you know that it's a drain on the corporation, and you still won't dump it, then we would cut our strings. The corporation would divest itself of the studio."

"Hold on, hold on," Rat said. "What ya mean divest? You making it sound like I'm South Africa or some shit. We are the corporation. I mean I'm a board member of the corporation."

Ronald held up one finger. "That's true, but when any member of the corporation knowingly continues behavior that hinders the corporation financially with any endeavor, the corporation can exempt itself from fiscal responsibility from that endeavor."

Rat waved his hands. "In English, Ronnie. English, motherfucka."

"Let me interpret for him, Ronnie," JC said.

"If you keep making a move like keeping that bum ass studio open and that's fucking up our money, and we tell you to stop and you don't, then we ain't got to fuck with it. That means that the corporation can charge you rent for the studio space, which will have to come from wherever you get it. And still in the next few months you'll receive an eviction notice because we're tearing that raggedy ass building down and making it into a parking lot."

As what JC and Ronald said began to sink in, Rat tried to appeal to his friends and business partners.

"JC, Chammy, Shaunny. Y'all just gone let this shit happen? What about my dreams? I'm putting together platinum shit that will more than pay for the studio."

"And you can put together a platinum album right up there at that tow truck yard too," Champagne said.

"And instead of losing money, the place where the studio is will be making money. Ronnie, let's move on to the next thing. We're spending too much time on this." "Sorry, Rat," Ronald said. "It's just business. All in favor of buying the tow truck business?"

Everyone raised their hand, even Rat, though his hand came up a little slower than his friends and partners, and he was grumbling under his breath too.

"Good, good," Ronald said as he made a note in his files. "Moving on. The next thing is the grand opening of Champagne and Shaunna's stores, "Intimate Imagination". The opening of the first one in the North Riverside Mall is right upon us, followed closely by the opening of the location in Westfield Mall, and then the one in River Oaks. Everyone is expected to attend the first grand opening..." Ronald paused and looked pointedly at Rat. Rat sat forward in his conference chair with an incredulous look on his face.

"C'mon now. What is this, fuck-with-Rat day? I'll be there."

Just then the door of the conference room burst open and two pint-sized versions of JC and Champagne scampered into the room. Hot on the heels of the twins was their nanny, Cynthia Penvale. Cynthia was in her early twenties, medium height with neat shoulder length dreadlocks in her hair. She wasn't traffic-accident beautiful, but was far from unattractive with her cinnamon colored eyes and shapely figure.

"Mommy, Daddy!" the twins shouted as they ran to their parents.

JC fielded his daughter Anaya and the boy, Kenton jumped onto Champagne's lap. JC leaned over and kissed Anaya on the forehead. "Naya, what are you and your brother up to? Are y'all giving Cynthia a hard time?"

Anaya looked up at her father, knowing that he was putty in her four-year old hands.

"Dad, we want to go to Gamma's house and Cynthia say we gotta go to the park. We want to go to Gamma's house and I know she want us there."

TRIPLE TAKE 2: CHAMPAGNE'S KISS

"Oh you know she want you two there?" JC asked with a laugh.

"Just how do you know that she want you two at her house?"

From his mother's lap, Kenton answered, "She want us there, 'cause the last time we was there she said that we could come back when we want to and now we want to."

"I'm sorry everybody about the interruption," Cynthia said.

"When I picked them up from the daycare, I brought them up to get a snack before we went back down to the play area. They were asking where everyone was, and I mentioned that you guys were in the conference room and before I knew it, they had busted in here. I'm really, really sorry."

"It's okay, Cynthia," Champagne said as she snuggled Kenton and gave him a tickling before setting him on his feet.

"We already know that they're some little monsters."

JC put Anaya down. "We'll call Gamma later and see if you guys can go over there for the weekend, 'Naya and Kent. But right now you two have to go with Cynthia."

"So you can talk busyness?" Anaya asked sweetly.

"That's my girl," JC answered. "So we can talk busyness. Now you two bums get a snack and get out of my house."

"Aww, dad, we aren't no bums," Kenton said with a huge smile.

"You always call us bummses."

"Cynthia... Cynthia...," Champagne had to say it twice. Cynthia and Ronald had been busy making moo-moo eyes at one another when Champagne called her.

Cynthia looked up to see everyone smiling at her and Ronald. "Uh, yes, Champagne. I didn't hear you."

"I think they're ready to get that snack and go out and they won't give you any more problems or no Gamma's house. Right?"

"Right," the twins answered in tandem. They grabbed Cynthia's hand and pulled her from the conference room, but not before she gave Ronald one last glance over her shoulder.

After Cynthia left, Ronald shuffled his files with feigned indifference, hoping that everyone in the room wasn't watching him.

JC spoke first. "Ronnie, you slick ass nigga you. What's up with you and Cynthia?" Ronald didn't look up from his files.

"What? I don't know what you're talking about. She's the twins' nanny. I see her around here."

"Man, you lying," Rat said.

"I can tell when a nigga lying and you is lying. From the way y'all two was eyebanging, y'all either done fucked or about to fuck. What you say, Shaunny?"

"Well, from what I see Ronnie, I have to say that for once Rat is right about something. There's something going on there whether it has happened already or not."

Ronald was adamant. "I don't know what you all are talking about. There's nothing going on between me and Cynthia. Now can we get back to business. I need everyone's receipts for their monthly expenses and Rat no more stuff written down on restaurant napkins. I need real receipts."

"Whatever lover boy," Rat said.

CHAPTER 3

"Nigga, we tired of playing with your ass!" Nathan "Nat" Johnson snarled from behind his black neoprene face mask. He shoved his tall, lithe body up from the love seat and strode over to where his victim was tied to a dining room chair. He smashed his pistol against the restrained man's jaw.

"Nigga, you better tell us where that shit is, before this shit get uglier than it is now!"

"Arrrrr!" the shirtless, shoeless man shrieked. He spit an incredibly large glob of blood and mouth tissue onto the floor. The man's bald head had several large lumps on it and his goatee was smeared with blood. His broad bare chest heaved in panic as he looked around the room at the three robbers in his grandmother's house. On the floor, tied with their hands behind their backs rested his two sons and his grandmother. Both of his sons were whimpering in fright, while his grandmother was lying totally still. The other two stickup men clad in all black, also wearing neoprene masks to conceal their identities, watched as Nat worked over their victim.

Nat sat on the man's lap and traced his jawline with his handgun.

"Jab, you got to be realistic. This shit is yo fault. You brought this shit on yourself. You brought us here, baby."

"Wh-wh-what th-the- f-f-f-fuck you talkin' b-b-bout?" Jab sniveled. "I-I-I ain't br-br-brought you h-h-here."

"I have to disagree, Jab my buddy. You brought us here to your grandmother's house by doing what you been doing. You the one that be up in the club with yo mink on. You got that red ass Caddy sitting outside on 22s. Nigga, the streets is hurting! You don't think that niggas is watching you. That's what we do nigga—watch fronting ass niggas like you, wait for them to slip up and then we take they shit."

"B-b-but I ain't g-g-got shit up in m-m-my grandmamma house, I swear," Jab stated weakly. "Y'all can ch-ch-check."

"Oh we know that," Nat said confidently. "We know you stupid, but we do give you some credit. Nigga, we done watched you. We know you don't come here to get yo shit when you take care of your customers. You pretty good about giving niggas the slip, too, when you going to get yo shit. Yo only downfall is we know where you lay yo head, dumb ass. "

"Now, so far we been light on yo ass, but now it's time to turn up the flames 'cause we ain't got all day. I'm sure that your granny there wanna get over to the church. I know you wadn't expecting to be getting robbed on no Sunday morning, but that's how this shit go. There's two ways out this shit. I'm gone give you worse case scenario. Granny and your sons go to the morgue this afternoon and you can spend whatever money you don't give us to bury them. We'll either cripple you or give you a shitbag or something but we'll leave you alive so you can think about how for the rest of your greedy ass life that you cared more about some money and drugs then you did your family. You listening, Jab?"

"Un-huh," Jab mumbled. "I hear you."

"Now the other way, you can patch yourself up after we leave and join yo grandma and sons at church today. There you can ask God to forgive your sins. All you got to do is take your phone." Nat motioned for the cell phone on the coffee table and one of his cohorts tossed it to him.

"All you got to do is tell me what number to dial on your phone so you can tell whoever you need to tell to bring that shit. All the money and all the drugs. Now what's it gonna be?"

"Dial 100 and push send," Jab said quickly. His mind was already working and he saw the end of this ordeal in sight. The robbers didn't know that giving up the money and drugs he had wasn't a problem--not in exchange for his sons and grandmother's lives.

"See how easy that was," Nat said pleasantly as he dialed the number and pushed send. As he waited for the cell phone to connect, he told Jab, "Don't say shit slick or code like on this phone or you gone have to put a wig on yo granny at her funeral."

As the phone connected Nat leaned forward and held the cell phone to Jab's ear and remained close enough to eavesdrop.

"Hey, Jab what's up Daddy?" a woman's voice said.

"Ain't nothing to it, Keisha," Jab answered. "Look, I need you to do me a big favor. I need you to put all that stuff I left over there together in a bag. Get that shoebox with that cash in it, too, and put that in a bag and bring it over my grandma house."

"Huh?" Keisha responded. "Why you doing that? What you ain't fucking with me no more?"

"Keisha, I ain't got time to explain what I'm doing to you," Jab said impatiently, then he softened his tone. "Keisha, I ain't through fucking with you, you my number one. I just need you to stand on this for me right now. I ain't got no time to explain, just do like I say, please."

"Okay Daddy. I'mma do what you say."

"Good. Now how long you gone be?"

"Give me fifteen minutes and I'll be there, Daddy."

Nat closed the cell phone and tossed it back to his partner. "Tell FEE outside that he got one on the way. A girl and she better be alone and carrying a bag." He turned back to Jab.

"Just out of curiosity, how much shit is she bringing?"

"It's about twelve thousand in cash and like eight ounces," Jab answered. Nat shook his head.

"I knew you was one of them fronting ass niggas. That's a damn shame. Big balling ass Jab. I guess niggas like you like to spend they money on shit people can see like cars and furs. Dumb ass shit. You is playing way too dangerous a game not to have no damn money, silly ass nigga."

"I pay bills and shit, man," Jab pouted. "And I take care of my kids and my granny, man. Plus you said it yoself, the streets is fucked up. Between the niggas getting knocked and tricking, plus I'm out on two bonds and paying lawyers that's where my money be going."

"I don't wanna hear that shit, nigga. Don't start whining now. You chose this shit. The same way you prey on motherfuckas, I prey on motherfuckas like you. Dumb ass nigga, you talking about the game fucked up, but you still be yo silly ass out at the clubs and shit drinking Remy like a don. Shit, the way things looking you better had of gave that shit up 'cause you ain't have enough to bury nobody. You woulda had to put both of yo sons in one casket, you broke ass drug dealer. Matter of fact, nigga where that fur at?"

"Aww, that's cold man, you gone take a nigga fur?" Jab asked.

I don't want to wear that gay shit. Nigga, I'm a thug, I ain't trying to wear no target, now where is it? And watch how you talk to me before I knock yo fuckin' teeth down yo throat."

"It's on the back of a chair in the kitchen," Jab said evenly.

"Go get it, FEE," Nat ordered.

The man covering Jab's grandmother went to the kitchen and returned with the black fur jacket.

"Put it on the floor," Nat said. He got up off Jab's knees and went into the kitchen. He returned a few minutes later carrying a gallon of bleach which without warning he dumped on Jab's fur coat.

"Now ain't nobody gone wear this bullshit. If you a broke nigga, start dressing like a broke nigga." Just then, they heard a piercing whistle from outside. One of the men moved over to the window and peeked out through the blinds.

"Broad out there parking, FEE," the man at the window said.

"She getting out and she got a bag with her."

"Well, go let her in, FEE," Nat said cheerily. "Give her a warm welcome. Don't nobody make no noise."

The man who was covering Jab's grandmother melted off toward the front door of the house. Seconds later everyone heard the screen door open.

"Jab, it's me baby," Keisha said loudly as she came in the house.

She was halfway into the living room when one of the robbers

24

stepped from behind the front door and slapped her in the back of her head with his pistol. Keisha pitched face first into the living room, slinging her purse and the bag she was carrying as she fell. Quietly and effortlessly, the man who hit her tied her hands and feet with plastic ties, and rolled her all the way into the living room. Nat picked up the Footlocker bag she'd been carrying and peered into it. The money and drugs were there.

Nat looked up at his partners. "It's all here, FEE. Let's ride. Thanks a lot, Jab and 'member if you get yo weight back up, we'll be back. Get out the drug game."

...

Nat walked into the living room of his house and looked at his fellow members of FEE lounging around on his expensive furniture and instantly became unhappy.

"What the fuck is wrong with you niggas?" Nat roared.

"What is you talkin' 'bout?" Kedale "Dale" Flint asked. "What you crying about now?"

"Y'all don't see this shit?" Nat asked. "Look at my motherfucking carpet. You niggas got guns on my antique wood table and this nigga, Mar, sitting on the arm of my fuckin' couch. Nigga do you sit on the arm of the couch at yo mama's house?"

Dale's younger brother, Kimar "Mar" Flint laughed. "It wouldn't make a difference if I did, that shit is raggedy as hell anyway."

"That's how the shit got raggedy," Nat said. "Get the fuck off the arm of my couch. Damn, Julie yo fat ass, did you even attempt to wipe off yo fuckin boots before you came in my damn house?"

Julius Cronell looked down at his muddy black Timberlands like he was noticing them for the first time.

"My fault Nat, but you the one that had me outside Jab's house. Nigga it was mud out there. I'm sorry that I stepped in the mud while I was watching y'all niggas' back while you was in the house robbing a motherfucka. My fault."

Nat just stood there with a look on his face like he couldn't believe the members of his stickup squad.

"You know what?" Nat said finally. "Get the fuck in the basement."

"Aw hell nall, Nat," Dale protested. "C'mon man, we'll move the guns and shit and Julie fat ass will wipe off his feet. Not the basement man. We'll get the carpet steam cleaned, and Mar will sit down like he got some sense."

"In the motherfucking basement now!" Nat stated adamantly.

"You grown ass niggas ain't finta be fuckin up my shit. Get y'all asses down in the basement with the rest of the damn dogs. I wish I had some cages for you niggas, too."

Mar grabbed the guns and Dale picked up the money and drugs.

"It stink down there," Julius grumbled as he followed behind the two brothers as they went to the basement door. Nat cursed under his breath as he followed the members of his team to the basement door. The minute Mar opened the door to the basement, the stink of unwashed dogs punched its' way into their nostrils. Julius tried to balk, but Nat pushed him forward.

"Get yo fat ass down them steps," Nat commanded. Julius covered his mouth and nose with his hand.

"Gotdamn, Nat! Them damn dogs stink like a motherfucka! Do you ever wash they ass?"

Nat prodded Julius again. "Hell nall. I wash them when, and if, I feel like it."

"Well you must never feel like it," Mar commented as they began to take seats on the ragtag assortment of furniture in the basement.

When the nine pitbulls that were caged in the basement saw their master, Nat, they went ape. They began barking and banging against their cages, spilling their food and water.

Nat was proud of his assortment of canine killers. "Niggas, them is pitbulls not poodles. They ain't got to smell good, just fight good."

"Well you need to hose they ass off once in awhile," Dale said. "These motherfuckas smell like the zoo. You need to move they cages too so I can get in here and finish that piece."

Dale was referring to the graffiti mural he had started on the wall before Nat put five of the dog cages on the wall in front of it. The mural so far was the acronym FEE in four foot lime green, yellow, and blue letters with Fuck Everybody Else shadowed in the foreground. He had started painting in several masked men with guns but that was as far as he'd gotten.

"Whatever," Nat said as he began divvying up their proceeds of the robbery. "Yo scary ass can move them damn cages yo'self. Look, Julie did you call Broke Dick Dave?"

"Yeah," Julius said, as he still held his nose.

"Dave said that he'd be here in about half an hour. I told him that we had eight ounces and he said five hundred apiece."

"That nigga know he be getting over," Mar commented. "He lucky he yo cousin or we would rob his ass too, Julie."

Nat tossed a pile of money in front of each of them. "That's three stacks apiece. When Broke Dick Dave buy that coke everybody will get a stack more. That there that's left over is seven hundred. I'm holding onto the seven. About a hundred of that should get my carpet cleaned and the rest will go for expenses."

"Expenses?" Dale balked. "What damn expenses?"

"FEE expenses, nigga," Nat snarled. "Shit, bullets and shit ain't free. Information ain't free. Gas for following these niggas around ain't free. Getting up in them clubs and drinking ain't free. The fuck..."

"Alright, nigga," Dale said as he picked up his cash.

"Don't get yo panties in a bunch, I was just asking. Man, we got to stop taking off these fronting ass broke ass niggas. This shit ain't no money."

"I know," Nat agreed as he sat back and lit a cigarette.

"This is some bullshit. The game so fucked up we ain't been getting shit from these bum ass niggas. But my friends, I have a plan in the works. It'll be a little different than the shit we're used to, but the payoff can be six figures at least for each of us."

"Now that's what I'm talking about," Mar said. "No more of this kiddie paper, I needs me some grown man money."

"For that much money it must be something heavy," Julius said with a hint of worry in his voice.

"We ain't gone have to kill nobody or hurt no kids for that much money is we?"

Nat looked at Julius, scorn evident on his face. "It don'tmake no difference, Julie. Fuck everybody else!"

CHAPTER 4

JC and Rat hurried over to the table in the food court of North Riverside Mall, where Champagne and Shaunna sat drinking coffee. JC was carrying a two foot pair of silver cardboard scissors. The pair of friends had been arguing in the car about whose fault it was that they were almost late to the grand opening of "Imagination Apparel", their women's newest venture. They both looked relieved that they'd made it with time to spare.

"Are you ready, Chammy?" JC asked as he placed the scissors on the table and leaned down to give Champagne a kiss on her cheek.

"I'm nervous as hell, J," Champagne replied. "I got butterflies big as Southwest airplanes in my stomach. I'm just glad that you made it. Oh believe me, you was gone hear it if you didn't make it."

Rat kissed Shaunna on the cheek too. "This time it wasn't my fault, Shaunny. I ain't gone say who fault it was that we was almost late, but this time it wasn't my fault."

"I'm with Chammy on this one," Shaunna said. "I don't care as long as you got here, but if you woulda missed it..."

Wearing an impeccably tailored suit Ronald joined them at the table. His telephone was plastered to his ear, but he still shook hands with Rat and JC and pecked Champagne and Shaunna on their cheeks before sitting down.

"Looks like everything is ready," Ronald said the moment his telephone conversation was over.

"Champagne, remember you're going by Ms. Wells and Shaunna, Ms. Foster. We've got a few members of the local press here and the crowd is looking quite nice. Champagne, you ready with the speech?"

"I feel like I might hurl first, Ronnie, but yes I'm ready. I feel like I'm back in fifth grade and I have to give a speech at the Black History month assembly. I've always hated public speaking. How do I look?"

Champagne stood up for them to inspect her smartly cut pinstripe business suit and Rat playfully slapped her on the butt and managed to avoid her return blow at the same time.

"Aww, Chammy you know you look good, girl," Rat said. "If I didn't know you, I'd be like, a baby what's up."

Everybody laughed.

"What about my glasses, you don't think they're a bit much?"

JC looked at the tortoise shell, square rimmed bejeweled Versace glasses Champagne was wearing.

"Nall, baby doll. Them there is fly with your hair pinned up and shit. I know a place that I'd love to see you wearing them. Matter of fact, keep them by the bed tonight. You know I like it classy and trashy."

Champagne was all smiles as she said, "Okay, Ronnie. Ready when you are. Shaunny, you ready?"

"As ready as I'll ever be."

Ronald stood up and picked up the scissors. "Alright let's do this, then."

In front of Champagne and Shaunna's flagship store a massive red ribbon had been draped across its' doors, as well as a glass podium that was connected to a small, but powerful portable sound system. There was a fairly decent crowd of about seventy-five women of various ethnicities, a few harried looking husband types, and several apparent members of the local press.

"Wow Ronnie, you weren't lying," Champagne whispered in Ronald's ear.

"You got them to come out. Thank you, you handle the busyness." Ronald winked. "It's amazing what gift bags and the leakage of a rumor that a certain female talk show host might be in attendance will do. Now get up there and milk this cow. You too, Shaunny."

JC and Rat moved into the fringes of the crowd and waited for Champagne to give her speech. Champagne stepped to the podium and cleared her throat as several cameras flashed. The second before she began her speech a slight panic crept in on her and she paused. Only because JC knew her so well could he tell that she was in terror for a brief moment. Watching his woman go through that discomfit for even a few seconds was like an eternity to JC. Champagne scanned the crowd in slight desperation until she spotted her man. JC gave her a broad smile and nodded to her. With her eyes on his, Champagne began her speech.

...

Champagne lay in the bed catching her breath. She was wearing a body stocking, high-heeled black leather boots, a pro baseball, fitted cap and her Versace eyeglasses. She looked up to see JC standing at the bedroom window completely nude. The window was actually the entire eastern wall of the penthouse condo, from floor to ceiling, and as he stood there bathed in the moonlight, Champagne got goosebumps. It amazed her that after five years she could still get excited just looking at her man. She was already wet between the thighs of her crotchless body stocking from the love she'd just made to JC, but she'd be damned if seeing him standing there wasn't adding a fresh wave of juices to her goodies.

"J, come over here," Champagne said huskily.

JC looked down at his woman. "No way. I know what you on. You gone try and fuck me to death. I done done what I can do for you tonight. We got to get up in the morning, so you better go take you a shower and lay yo hot ass down somewhere."

"Awww, c'mon J. You know you want some more. Look at your man."

JC looked down and saw that his man was already stiffening in anticipation of another round with his woman. He had to admit that the outfit she'd worn to bed was definitely doing its' thing. Her body was a marvel already, but the body stocking, boots, hat, and glasses were the icing on the cake. After she'd had the twins, Champagne had worked out obsessively to get her body back in shape and it had paid off. Her hips, thighs and ass were super tight, along with her flat abs and bountiful breasts she was still in the same shape as when she used to dance, maybe just 4 or 5 pounds heavier.

Champagne left the bed and slid up behind JC. She slid her arms around his front and tried to grab his growing hardness, but he took hold of both her hands. She wrapped one leg around his thigh and nuzzled his neck.

"J, what's up? You trying to hold out on me? What you doing? Saving it for someone else?"

"Yeah, I'm saving it for my other woman."

"Well, I'm sorry but your other woman gone have to get it the best way she can 'cause I need some more."

Champagne tried to break loose and get frisky again, but JC successfully maneuvered her in front of him. That wasn't any better because she started rubbing her behind against him.

"Girl, you better stop acting up before I get my cover and go downstairs and sleep on the couch."

"And I'm gone come right down there and get under them covers with you. I don't know why you trying to deny me, I feel your man breathing all on my ass."

Champagne lifted her face to JC and offered her lips. He gave her a long deep kiss and she squirmed in his arms until she was facing him. When he broke the kiss, she continued to plant moist passionate kisses on his broad chest.

"Champagne?" "Yes, baby," she said between kisses.

"Champagne, for real. Let me ask you a question."

Champagne heard the change in his tone and stopped nuzzling her man and looked up into his face. "What's wrong, baby?"

"Nothing. I just want to ask you a question."

"Shoot."

"Are you happy? I mean really happy."

TRIPLE TAKE 2: CHAMPAGNE'S KISS

Champagne thought about it for a second. "I never really thought about it, but yes I would have to say I am. Since I met you, it seems that my life has been nothing but better. With the exception of the time I got shot everything has been good. I'm doing things for money that I can hold my head high about. I've got my kids and a wonderful man. I've got the little brother that I'd always wanted to boss around and hit on in Rat and Shaunna, the best friend I've ever had in my life, is right here for me. So am I happy? I would have to say I am. I prayed to God many a night for things I have, things other people search their whole lives for. I've got family, love, success, and friends. It's kind of scary because people live their whole lives in search of what I've got and never achieve the same outcome. So yes I would have to say that I am happy; extremely. What about you? Are you happy?"

JC rubbed his head. "Sometimes I don't know. Sometimes I get scared because things are so good. I can't help but remember all the years I spent in prison and think about how different my life is from those times. Yeah at times I'm happy. Like when I'm at a silly kid movie with our two bums. Or when I'm working on a new deal that'll make sure my family has plenty to eat. Or when I can give some ex-con that couldn't get a break no where else, a chance to do some good, honest work to feed his family and keep himself outta trouble. Small things, seem like that make me the most happy. I thought after I got revenge on Zo and them other fools it would make me happy, but it didn't. If anything I felt empty inside. It took you, Rat, Shaunny, and the twins to fill me back up. I know I don't say it much, but I love you Chammy and you make me happy."

Instead of replying, Champagne forced JC back on the bed. She climbed on top of him and leaned down to kiss him.

JC stopped her and removed her hat and glasses. "This time I want to see my woman's face."

CHAPTER 5

On the stage of the strip club, a large breasted white woman moved rhythmically to the slow R and B song playing. She was wearing only a cowboy hat, cowboy boots, and gun belt complete with two plastic cap pistols. Soft looking strawberry red hair flowed from under her cowboy hat, falling to the middle of her back and it seemed to be keeping time with her dancing. Her perfect silicone enhanced breasts captured the attention of the patrons bellied up to the lip of the stage. The men, young and old alike hooted, hollered, and tossed dollar bills onto the stage as the white woman danced and twirled her nakedness in front of them. She took the cap pistols from her gun belt and ground her way to the lip of the long, narrow stage. She lowered herself to the floor and opened her legs, completely showing her womanhood. She used the cap pistols suggestively to build herself up to a supposed orgasm.

Her antics whipped the patrons into a frenzy and they showered her with dollar bills, as though they were barely able to contain themselves. Two huge, bouncers patrolling the stage area made sure that they did contain themselves, though. As the song drew to a close, the dancer scooted all the way to the edge of the stage directly in front of one gentleman wearing a long gold chain with a sparkling diamond charm, and holding a particularly large rack of bills. She put her feet on the bar on either side of the man's drink and sat up. He seemed entranced by her large breasts and the pouting lips of her pussy. She cocked her head to the side slightly and gave him a sexy look.

Grinning, the man stood up off his bar stool and tucked a twenty dollar bill into her money garter. He looked around to judge the looks of envy from the other patrons and noticed plenty of them. "Fuck y'all broke ass motherfuckas looking at?" the man asked loudly over the music. "Don't be mad at me 'cause I'm paid. You broke ass niggas better learn how to hustle. This is Chocolate City, baby. The money is out there laying *in the fucking streets!"*

The stripper holstered her guns and put her hands on either side of the man's head guiding his mouth to her breasts, to let him lick her hardened nipples. While he was sucking her breasts, she took his hand and inserted his index finger and middle finger into her pussy, when she took them out of her, she sucked both of them. Her behavior achieved the desired effect because a bulge instantly appeared at the front of the man's expensive looking jogging suit pants. When the song ended, he stuffed several twenties into her garter, grinning all the while.

Over the sound system, from the DJ booth, the DJ hollered into the microphone, "You motherfuckas better give it up for Cocaine! One of DC's finest! The white girl that you'll always want more of! Give it up, you motherfuckas!"

There were plenty of hoops and hollers as Cocaine bowed to the crowd. She took her cowboy hat off and used it to collect the scattered bills that had been tossed onto the stage. When she'd retrieved all of her tips, she came back to the man with the gold chain and leaned down to him.

"I'm just going to clean up, baby," Cocaine told him. "Then if you want, you can meet me in the VIP room."

"And what we gone do in the VIP room?" the man asked, still grinning.

Cocaine used her fingers to lightly stroke the man's jaw. "Aw, baby c'mon now," she purred. "You ain't new. You know what goes on in the VIP room. As long as you got the dough, anything can go. Now if you don't want no Cocaine, then I'm sorry you got me wasting my time."

"You ain't wasting yo time. You just like me girl, time is money. Hell yeah, I want to go to the VIP room. I ain't like these other broke ass motherfuckas, I can pay my way. Even while I'm up in here playing my money is still getting made out there. I ain't gone never run out of cash. It can't happen."

"That's good, sweetie," Cocaine said as she stood up. "Just give me a few minutes to freshen up and change my clothes. I want to be just right for my big spender."

Cocaine blew the man a kiss and disappeared through the curtains at the rear of the stage. Over the loud speaker, the DJ announced, "I'm gone give you hard leg motherfuckas a few minutes to get yo mind and finances together before we bring out the next featured dancer. I told y'all that I was gone get your pilot lights lit with our first featured dancer. You suckers better hold onto some of y'all money 'cause we got plenty more fine ass dancers taking the stage tonight. Please make sure you buy drinks as the club does have a two drink minimum. Also make sure to tip your waiter, you cheap bastards. Buy a couple of lap dances too. No fighting over the girls, there's plenty to go around."

Cocaine walked down the short hallway behind the stage curtain and into the women's dressing room. The dressing room of the club was well-lit and filled with women in various stages of dress and undress. Cocaine walked over to her locker and opened the combination lock. She began tossing parts of her costume in her large athletic bag and selecting pieces of lingerie. Before changing into the lingerie, she hurried into the restroom and quickly took care of her female hygienic process. When Cocaine returned to her locker, the tall, new girl with the locker next to hers was there changing into her first outfit of the night; a construction worker costume, complete with a hard hat and tool belt.

"Hey Champagne," Cocaine said cheerfully. "Girl, you know yo ass is late. You bet not let Misty dyke ass see you. She been stressing real hard on club rules lately. Talking about fines and shit for being late. I hate that old white bitch."

"I'm cool," said JoAnn "Champagne" Wells as she continued to dress. "I talked to Misty earlier and she said it was alright if I was going to be a little late."

"Uh-oh," Cocaine said. "Girl, you better watch out. The only reason Misty is nice is 'cause she be liking a bitch. Don't fuck around with her stalking ass, Champagne. Misty will drive a bitch to drink."

They both laughed, before Champagne asked, "How's it looking out there, Cocaine?"

TRIPLE TAKE 2: CHAMPAGNE'S KISS

"Same old perverts. It's a few dollars in the house though. Usually I hate being the opening feature, but when there's a few dollars in the house I don't mind. I already done caught me a sponsor. Some goofy ass dude wearing a lot of gold and shit. He want him some Cocaine and he got a big ass bankroll, so he gone get him some Cocaine. He out there fronting and shit bout all the money he got, but I love that 'cause it make the other dumb ass dudes in the room go into debt trying to prove that they got money too. Dumb bastards!"

Champagne looked up and around the room as they were laughing and she saw enough to make her stop. They were close to twenty dancers in the room and a nice portion of them were admitted lesbians. They, for the most part were all staring at her body as she dressed. She knew some of the fascination was because she was the new girl, even though she didn't go that way. She had thought that she would get used to it after a couple of weeks, but she still hadn't become accustomed to the brazen stares. Silently she cursed her body. As far back as she could remember it had always brought her trouble. Even when she was a little girl the boys couldn't keep their hands off her and adult men couldn't see past her big butt and breasts; couldn't see that she was a person with emotions, wants, and needs. It wasn't even a matter of losing weight. No amount of running, dieting, and exercising could diminish her thighs, hips, and bust. Throughout her life, no matter how much she tried to hide her dynamic body it always seemed to get in the way. That was the reason she decided that, for once, she would let it work for her and what better place than exotic dancing.

As she fastened her costume's tool belt around her waist, Champagne looked up again, shuddering when she received a provocative wink from one of the other girls. When the girl saw Champagne's reaction she went so far as to lick her lips slowly and suggestively. Champagne rolled her eyes and turned back to her locker. In truth she felt more comfortable dancing naked in front of strange men, than she did in the dressing room with the lesbians looking at her like a sandwich they wanted to take a *bite of.*

Champagne turned back to Cocaine. "Damn, Coke these dykes be up in here staring like crazy. I can't move without them eye-raping me."

"Fuck these bitches," Cocaine said loudly as she continued to dress in her lingerie. "Bitches act like they be starving for some pussy. If they want some coochie that bad all they got to do is buy some, they got money."

"I know that's right," a light-skinned green-eyed dancer named Shaunna said as she dropped her gym bag on the floor and opened the locker next to Champagne's. "These bitches act just like the trick ass niggas out there, so they might as well spend their money on pussy too. Hey Champagne, Coke."

"Hey, Shaunna," Cocaine said. "What's up with you bitch?"

"Nothing much, white girl."

Even though Shaunna's tone wasn't malicious, Champagne could tell that she didn't like Cocaine much. She couldn't tell if Shaunna liked her, she just seemed to look through you with her bewitching green eyes. Cocaine slammed her locker door bringing Champagne back to the present. Champagne watched as Cocaine took a look at herself in the mirrors on the opposite wall of the dressing room.

"Where you off to so fast, girl?" Shaunna asked.

Cocaine pursed her lips in the mirror and hefted her pricey bosom.

"I'm off to make that dough. Dollar dollar bill y'all."

"About to let some darkie fuck your mouth in the VIP is what you're trying to say," Shaunna said without much emotion.

"Damn skippy," Cocaine retorted. "And if his money is right, he can do it all night. Don't get mad at me 'cause they love Cocaine. It ain't they fault. They just addicted."

Both Champagne and Cocaine laughed, but Shaunna just shook her head. Shaunna took an outfit out of her gym bag and put the bag in her locker.

"Whatever you say, Cocaine," Shaunna said. "But we all know that most addicts get addicted to things that ain't good for you."

TRIPLE TAKE 2: CHAMPAGNE'S KISS

As Cocaine gave herself one last look in the mirror, she said, "Shaunna, it sound like you saying that I'm bad for men's health. Well that is true 'cause this white girl want to leave them just like the white girl that they put in they nose and smoke. I want to leave they ass, penniless and homeless, but don't come around if you ain't got no green if you know what I mean."

Cocaine laughed at her own witticism and slapped five with Champagne and two other girls who were watching the back and forth between her and Shaunna.

Well don't you sound like the happy hooker," Shaunna conveyed with the same emotionless tone.

"Well you can call this white girl plenty of things, but you can't call me broke. Shaunna, it's starting to sound like you're a little bit jealous. I would have never pegged you for an envious person. It's okay though. We all got gifts, you just keep on looking for yours. I already know mine, so don't hate the game, hate the rules."

Shaunna gave a cutting chuckle. "Cocaine, I thought so at first, but now you done proved it, girl. You are really delusional if you think that I'm jealous of you. I don't care how many Black babies you swallow in VIP. Actually I'm proud of you because I consider your dick-sucking a public service. Cocaine, you're actually good for the economy."

Cocaine stopped making faces in the mirror. "What you mean by that, bitch? That don't really sound like no compliment."

"My fault Coke. Let me explain. You save the taxpayers, the city of Washington, and the District of Columbia a lot of money. See you perform a public service for every baby you swallow. That way these no good bastards don't go out into the city and shoot that nut into some fertile pussy and beget another unwanted ghetto child. Because you perform ball abortions, you save taxpayers millions of dollars in social service, education, medical treatment, food coupons, and incarceration facilities for those unwanted babies. Really they need to give you a medal, Cocaine. They could give you some type of trophy for most nut drunk in a year or *something."*

Some of the other dancers in the room howled with laughter at Shaunna's acerbic wit. Cocaine's jaw dropped for a second as she searched her brain for a wicked comeback, but Shaunna had already gone into the bathroom to change by the time she thought of something to say. Instead Cocaine turned her semi-wrath on the peanut gallery.

"I don't know what you ho's hee-heeing and haw-hawing for. I know for a fact there's plenty of cum guzzlers in here. And free-fuckers. I don't give a fuck what I do in life but I ain't gone never be no free-fucker. You all some phony bitches. You sitting in here laughing at me and there's plenty of bitches in this room that'll be right in there in VIP with me, drinking some dick tonight and every other night, so don't try to play me. 'Cause I know for a fact that I'll be the one climbing into that cocaine white Saab in the parking lot while some of these broke ass free-fuckers will be on the bus stop, or trying to hitchhike home tonight. "

While Cocaine was saying her piece, Champagne took in the whole scene with an air of wonderment. A lot of this was still new to her, especially the tricking off in the VIP room part. She hadn't gone that far yet, but she had to admit that some of the offers were extremely tempting. She had been offered as much as a thousand dollars for VIP room services, but so far she'd declined. She'd heard that some of the girls made a thousand or more dollars in a night for their extra-curricular activities in the VIP room. So far she had managed to avoid that dark, curtained off area called the VIP room with its mismatched couches and their mysterious stains. But the stories the girls told were making her curious. The stories of how easy it was to make men part with their money was intriguing. From the way she'd heard it, nothing was off-limits in this world, especially when the dancers did private parties. Cocaine had already given her the low down on these private parties. She'd made them seem like the best thing going since sliced bread, but to Champagne they sounded more dangerous than anything. She had been assured by Cocaine, that one day soon she'd be more than ready to attend a private party, but as of now Champagne *didn't see it happening.*

"Champagne, I've got to go, girl," Cocaine announced. "I can't keep my sponsor waiting. Dollar dollar bill, y'all."

"Alright, Cocaine, I'll see you out there, girl."

While Cocaine went to make her VIP room appearance, Champagne finished securing her locker. When she stood up and turned around to leave the dressing room, the club's owner Misty, was standing behind her. Misty was holding her cane with its' golden cat head and a clipboard. She wore a pair of reading glasses and her white-grey hair in a severe bun making her look like a second grade teacher, but she was far from that. Champagne knew from the stories the girls told that Misty had seen it all and done it all in DC's underworld. Just the fact that she was a white woman who was well respected by the criminals, Black and white in DC said a lot for her.

"Champagne, how are you?" Misty asked innocently.

"I'm okay, Misty. How are you doing?"

"I'm well, my darling," Misty said after a small chuckle. "I just wanted to know if everything has been going well for you, and if it hasn't I would like to help you in any way that I can."

"Is that Misty?" Shaunna asked from behind the club owner as she returned to her locker. "That can't be the Misty I know. It sounded like I heard words of genuine concern coming from you, but I know that can't be Misty."

"Hello, Shaunna," Misty said in clipped tones.

"Now that's the Misty I know. The ice queen that only warms up when something new, hot, and sexy is on the menu. Better be careful, Champagne. Misty is hard on a girl like kids are hard on shoes. Ain't that right, Misty."

"Don't you have some customers to attend to, Shaunna?" Misty asked.

Shaunna spun the dial on her combination lock to make sure her locker was secure. "That's where I'm headed, Misty. See you on the floor, Champagne."

"I'm coming right now," Champagne said.

Misty put her hand on Champagne's arm. "You go on ahead, Shaunna. I want to talk to Champagne. Champagne, I want you to dance the next feature. The guys are really starting to ask for you on a regular basis. I usually don't let new girls dance so early in the night, but I want you to get out there early while the fellows still have some money."

"I don't know what to say, Misty. Uh, thanks."

Misty gave Champagne a light pat on her butt. "Don't mention it. I do that for the girls that don't give me problems. Now get ready because the DJ is about to announce you."

Champagne didn't say anything, but she didn't appreciate Misty groping her. She decided to wait until later to let Misty know she needed to keep her hands to herself. Right now she was reveling in her good luck at receiving an early slot on the featured dancers list. Everybody knew the girls who got on stage early got the most money. The girls who came on stage later in the night would have to work twice as hard to get less than half the money the early features would get.

As Misty went out of the dressing room to cue the DJ, Champagne gave her costume a final inspection, locked her locker, and went to stand behind the curtains that led to the stage.

"And now fellows get yo wallets out!" the DJ boomed. "I told you sucker motherfuckers that we was gone turn the heat up in here. The next dancer, oh shit. She bad than a motherfucker! She thick like a Luke dancer and prettier than Whitley offa A Different World. Y'all get yo dollars ready! It's time to celebrate with Champagne!"

As the DJ began blasting an uptempo song, Champagne took a deep breath and then strode through the curtain onto the stage.

CHAPTER 6

Champagne stepped off the elevator to the penthouse and unlocked the large double wooden doors. In the foyer she dropped her briefcase on the table and kicked off her stiletto-heeled shoes. She stepped into the sunken living room and wiggled her stockinged toes in the deep luxurious carpet. She looked up to see JC and Ronald staring at her smiling.

"What?" she asked as she pulled her scarf from around her hair.

"Chammy, how you feeling?" JC asked, still grinning.

"I'm tired and pissed off. I need a new administrative assistant and them doggone shoes I had on today damn near had me crying. Fuck Manolo Blahnik and them suicide ass stilettos. Those are made for them bony ass girls and you won't ever catch my big ass in another pair. Other than that I'm fine. I just want to sit on the terrace, drink me some green tea, and watch Law & Order until I pass out. I don't even want to see my little monsters except for to give them a kiss and tell them to stay the hell away from me."

"Good," JC said as he walked over and grabbed Champagne's arm. "Let's go then."

"What? Didn't you just hear me? I ain't going nowhere. Where you trying to take me?"

"I got to show you something, woman. Now come on."

"JC, I ain't playing. I'm tired boy. Don't be on no bullshit."

Champagne followed JC back to the foyer where he tried to hand her back the shoes she'd just kicked off.

"Oh hells no. You thought I was playing. Give me a minute." Champagne disappeared around the corner and returned minutes later wearing a pair of Adidas running shoes and ankle socks over her stockings.

"Now that's better. JC, I'm telling you, you better not be up to something. And why the hell are you grinning?"

"Just come on girl, "JC said.

After a short ride north on Lake Shore Drive in JC's maroon Porsche Panamera, he pulled into the Hyde Park section of the city. It was one of Chicago's oldest neighborhoods, brimming with ethnic diversity, and home to some of the city's oldest and wealthiest families. The 4-door sports car zipped up several streets lined with huge homes before coming to a stop in front of one of the more modern mansions--it was truly a marvel of glass and brick. JC killed the engine and they climbed out.

"Who lives here?" Champagne asked in amazement as she looked through the gated driveway to the huge home.

JC fished a set of keys out of his pocket and dangled them in front of Champagne. "We do if you want to."

Champagne was taken aback. "Huh?"

"I said it's ours, if we want to live here."

JC pushed a button on the remote that came with the keys and the gates of the house slid noiselessly out of the way. JC took Champagne by the hand and walked her up the driveway to the front doors of the house. He keyed open the doors and pushed in the temporary alarm code he'd been given. He switched on the lights and let the absolute beauty and charm of the place capture his woman. Champagne hadn't managed to close her mouth since he'd opened the doors and turned on the lights. The way she had her hand on her chest, JC was slightly worried that she was having a mild heart attack.

"Chammy, you alright?" JC asked.

"J, you got to be kidding me. This place is absolutely, totally, fucking nuts! How big is this place?"

"Seven bedrooms, five bathrooms. What they used to call servants' quarters, and an eight car garage with loft space above that. The basement has a full laundry facility, a home theater, and fitness center. Out back there's a huge deck, a big ass hot tub, and a pool. Minister

TRIPLE TAKE 2: CHAMPAGNE'S KISS

Farrakhan lives around the corner. There's great schools for the kids within walking distance. Private police patrol the neighborhood. That ain't even the best part, check this out."

JC led her around a corner slightly to the right of the foyer and there were the stainless steel doors of an elevator. He pushed the up button.

"No way," Champagne gushed. "This is a house and it's got a elevator."

They stepped on the elevator and JC pushed the button for the third floor. "You ain't seen the best part yet."

"I thought there were only two floors to this place."

"There is, but the third floor is the power center.""Power center?"

They stepped off the elevator on the third floor, it was only the size of a large bedroom, but there were several large machines in the room. The room had several glass doors that led out onto the roof of the house. When they went on the roof Champagne could see that it was covered with glass panels.

"Are those what I think they are?" she asked.

"You guessed it. Those are solar panels. It would cost a fortune to heat, cool, and power a place this size. The genius motherfucker who designed this crib had solar shit put in. It powers everything from the elevator to the toaster."

"Who in the hell even had a house like this?"

"One of the dudes that fucking helped create the atomic bomb or some shit. Some big brain scientist professor. He died a couple of years ago. His kids were grown and moved out and the wife wanted to get rid of this place. There's a few people interested, but if we want it, it's ours."   "I know we got some money, but can we afford this place? What's the price tag?"

"They're asking 3 for it, but Ronnie got them down to 2.6 in cash for it."

"All this for only 2.6 million, I'm sold. Do we have that much money to spend with all the investments we've been making?"

"It won't be no problem to get a loan from the bank with all the collateral our corporation has, but the sweet thing about this shit is our penthouse is worth 1.6 easy. That means we'll only need one mill in cash and you've still got your condo to sell which is another three or four hundred thousand. If we want to do it, we could swing it with no problem. I say it'll take us about two hundred maybe two-fifty to furnish this place."

Champagne put her arms around her man. "You got it all figured out, huh? How long you been working on this?"

"Well my man that got me the penthouse picked up the listing and I told him that I was in the market for a house for my woman and kids. He called me 'bout two days ago and told me I would have to move fast if we wanted it. Ronnie wants to buy the penthouse and your condo is gone the minute I tell him go. The only thing is getting your approval and seeing if Rat and Shaunny want to stay. If they don't, we'll give them your condo for a good price, but I really want this place. I know that Rat won't want to go nowhere, but I don't know what Shaunny will want to do."

"I know what I want to do," Champagne said as she led JC back onto the elevator. She let the door close on the elevator, but she didn't push a floor. She placed her hands against the wall of the elevator and bent over slightly. "I want my man to go under my skirt and rip my stockings so I can get me some in my new house."

JC smiled wide as he began to unzip his pants.

"I thought you was so tired."

CHAPTER 7

Rat sat at the desk in his office at Rathole Studios with his feet kicked up, watching the large flat screen plasma television mounted on the office wall. He was watching an episode of Law and Order: Special Victim's Unit, a television program that Champagne had started him to watching. When the intercom button on his desk telephone lit up, he sat forward in his chair and pressed the button.

"Yeah, Tina?"

"Fly Ty and Big M are here," announced Tina, the receptionist. "You still want to see them?"

"Yeah, send them to my office."

"And Auburn is here too?"

"Who?"

"The female singer. She's here with her producer. What studio should I put them in?"

"What's open?"

"Two and three. Quinine is in four and I know the Fly and G gonna want studio one."

"Alright give Auburn studio two and make sure you collect for their time down to the minute."

The door to Rat's office opened and his two artists strode in. They were carrying a bottle of Remy Martin and a twelve pack of Corona. Rat knew without asking that they had several bags of cush in their pockets. Both young men came over to Rat and showed him some love. Fly Ty was a medium built dark-skinned man in his early twenties. His long braids were always perfect like they'd just been done and he was always dressed in the latest of urban fashions. Big M, a huge light-skinned man, was exactly opposite. His wardrobe consisted of white t-shirts, wheat Tims, and Dickies. His hair was fashioned into a short, curly afro that he rarely combed.

Y. Blak Moore

"Rat, what's up baby pop," Big M said as he looked at the plasma television.

"This here SVU is my shit. I be getting my medical terms from that pretty ass medical examiner. I love this here shit."

"He ain't lying," Fly Ty said. "This nigga will sit in the crib and watch that shit over and over again. Don't let it be one of them Law and Order marathons, this nigga will watch ten, twelve hours of this shit. I came over his crib and tried to change the channel, this nigga went nuts."

"Alright, I didn't call y'all in here to hear about your choice of television programming. Sit y'all ass down, so I can tell y'all what's what."

"Yessum, Mr. Rat sir," Big M quipped. "I'sa so sorry, boss. I'sa gone sit my black ass down now sir."

"Man, shut yo ass up and listen fo I throw you out of here," Rat threatened, but there wasn't any trace of anger in his voice.

"Country ass nigga. Damn!"

"Nall for real, what's up Rat?" Fly Ty asked. "We want to hurry up and get in the studio so we can lay some verses and I want to bang out a couple of tracks."

Rat used the remote control to switch off the television. "Well that shit gone have to wait 'cause we're having a business meeting. Give me one of them beers."

Big M handed Rat a cold Corona.

After popping the bottle cap and pouring in a squirt of lime juice that Fly Ty gave him, Rat took a long sip of the cold beer and held it up. "To the business at hand. My fine fellows we have a few things to discuss. There's gonna be a few changes coming real soon at Rathole Records and Rathole Studios. First thing is roster changes. Currently I've got about eight rappers and one female singing group signed to Rathole. Six of them rappers is axed and them fake ass Destiny Child wannabes."

Fly Ty chuckled. "Now that's what I'm talking about. Them other niggas ain't no hustlers and them hoes couldn't sing a lick. Bitches thought they was gone be in videos with them stretchmarks and sagging ass titties."

"You wadn't talking that shit when the lead singer Shante was blowing on yo nuts and shit in the car out back," Big M said. "Or when you was fucking the short bitch by gassing her up telling her she should be the lead singer."

"And you was fucking the other bitch," Fly Ty retorted.

"Get off that shit," Rat said. "What I'm doing is cutting back. My business manager recommended I cut back and that's what I'm gonna do. I only see them other niggas once in a blue moon when they come in the studio and dick around for a couple of hours, when they feel like playing rap star to they homies or bitches, so fuck 'em. You two are my only artists as of today. If them other dudes step foot in Rathole Studios they better have some dough to pay for studio time. That's effective immediately too. Next, you niggas gotta get more focused. Everything you do from this moment on is about putting together finished product. I want you both to go through that fuckin' stockpile of songs y'all got, and I want you to come up with a complete album for the two of y'all together."

Fly Ty started to interrupt, but Rat held up his hand. "I don't want to hear it, Fly. I want a complete album from the both of you and two mixtapes. The two mixtapes need to be ready to get mastered by next month so I can get them pressed up. They're also gonna go to the promo team that I've hired at extreme cost to my black ass. I almost forgot, I want at least three to four radio ready, women friendly singles ready to go. I know, I know. Shut up. I don't want to hear it. I'm following the formula on this. Women shit on the radio; hard shit in the streets on them mixtapes. It's that simple and I ain't asking, I'm telling." Rat paused to let his directions sink in. "The second part is the studio will be moving soon. When we move the setup will be basically the same, but I'm gonna need y'all to step up. One in productions. Both of y'all produce and I'm gonna sign y'all as the inhouse production team for Rathole. That'll mean more money, but y'all gone have to stand on the busyness. Any questions?"

"Yeah," Fly Ty said. "Where the studio gone move to?"

"I don't know the exact location and it may be a couple of months, but it'll be the best thing for us all. No more business as usual. We been bullshitting for too long. I ain't in this shit purely for my love of listening to music, we got to make some money."

The buzzer on Rat's telephone intercom buzzed. He pushed it. "Yeah, Tina? What's up, I'm in a meeting."

"Rat, I think you need to come down here. There's a couple of guys here that say they need to talk to you."

"Give them the studio info and tell them to get back at me, I'm busy."

"I already tried to do that, but they're insisting that they have to talk to you now and they're not going to leave without talking to you or somebody in charge."

Rat shook his head and rolled his eyes to the ceiling. "Alright, I'll be down in a minute." To Fly Ty and Big M, he said, "I'm serious y'all, this is our time. I'm finta go downstairs and listen to these rappers in the lobby, and then I'm gone go in the studio with y'all and we gone start picking songs for them records. Gimme another one of them beers."

They all left Rat's office and took the building's ancient freight elevator down to the lobby. Tina, a young, white girl with a million silver rings on her fingers, midnight black and maroon dyed hair, and several visible piercings, including her ears, eyebrow, bottom lip, nose, and tongue was sitting behind the high lobby desk. Tina saw Rat and head-pointed him to the two twentysomething Black men seated in the lobby, thumbing through the rap and fashion magazines. Both men were dressed in black army fatigues, black boots, and black jungle hats.

"How yo brothers doing?" Rat greeted them.

"We all right," one of the men answered as they both put down the magazines and stood up. "Are you Rat, man? 'Cause we ain't got no time to be talking to no nigga that they left in charge while somebody went to the store or something."

Rat glanced back at Fly Ty and Big M before turning back to the two men. "Yeah, I'm Rat. If this is about getting signed, Rathole Records isn't currently accepting any new artists on the roster, so if you want just leave your demo, but I'm not promising anything."

"So you're Rat, the owner of Rathole Records and Rathole Studios?" the other man asked, the taller of the two.

"What is this twenty questions? I said I'm Rat. Y'all know my name, what are you dudes' names?"

"That don't make no difference," the first man said. "What's important is who we represent."

"And that is?" Rat asked.

"We represent the Concrete Click," the second man said proudly. "We're here on their behalf today to make arrangements with you."

"What is this about, studio time?" Rat asked.

"This ain't about no fuckin' studio time," the taller of the men rasped.

"We ain't here to pay you, nigga we here to let you know that you gotta pay us."

Rat turned back to Fly Ty and Big M again. "Is it me or do it sound like these two Black Panther rejects is trying to tax me? It sounded to me like some form of extortion, but maybe because I been listening to so much loud music lately that my hearing ain't so correct."

"Sounded that way to me too," Big M said.

"Okay, so I ain't going crazy," Rat said as he turned back to the two men. "Okay representatives of the Concrete Click is y'all losing y'all damn minds?"

Nigga, the Concrete Click own Chicago when it come to music. If you got a record label or a studio in the Chi, you gots to pay the Concrete Click. Since you got both, that means you gots to pay us double."

Oh, I do, do I?"

"Hell yeah, nigga."

Rat stood still for a moment and then he walked over to the two men with a huge disarming smile on his face. As he drew nearer, he quickly pulled his pistol from his waistline and pointed it at the two men.

"Lift them shirts real slow like and turn all the way around real slow," Rat commanded.

The two members of the Concrete Click did as Rat told them.

"What you niggas ain't got no guns? Y'all come up in here in my place of business on some gangster shit and y'all ain't got no guns? What kind of new space age goofy shit is this? To get on gangster shit with a nigga, you should have a gun. That is unless you think the nigga you on the shit with is a pussy? Did y'all think I was a pussy?" Both men shook their heads no.

"Now you Concrete Click niggas can't talk. A minute ago y'all was talking plenty and now y'all can't say shit. See, that ain't gangster. If it was me, I would still be talking just as much shit as I was before, but the only difference is I would have had my gun with me. You know what? Get over here nigga. You with the big mouth, mister-we-representatives of the Concrete Click. Get yo ass over here!" With a look of false bravado on his face, the shorter of the two men walked to Rat. When he was within arm reach, Rat grabbed him by his shirt and spun him around.

With his hand on the back of the man's neck, Rat said, "Little big mouth nigga, you must be fuckin' crazy coming up in here with this bullshit."

"I'm just doing what I was told to do," the man said stubbornly.

"And who the fuck told you to extort me?"

"That ain't none of your fuckin' business, nigga," the man said mustering up a slight bit of his former boldness.

Rat smacked the man in the face with his pistol. As blood spurted from the man's face, his knees threatened to buckle, but Rat wouldn't let him.

"Stand yo punk ass up, nigga! I asked you a motherfucking question."

TRIPLE TAKE 2: CHAMPAGNE'S KISS

"Fuck you!" the man shouted, showering Rat in blood droplets. "I ain't telling you shit!"

Rat began to furiously pistol whip the man. The other man had already begun easing toward the door the moment Rat's attention focused on his friend, and when he started beating him, he bolted out the doors. Big M and Fly Ty ran out of the building in pursuit of the second man. They came back a few minutes later empty-handed. Rat was over at Tina's reception station and she was giving him paper towels and trying to help him clean the man's blood off of him. The man was lying in the middle of the lobby in a pool of his own blood, moaning and groaning. Several of his teeth were evident on the floor in the pool of blood.

Fly Ty stood over the man and looked down at his ruined face. "Oh shit, Rat. You fucked mister representative up. You fucked this boy up."

"You and he told me what I wanted to know. The Concrete Click is headed up by some nigga named Con. I'm gone need y'all to find out what y'all can about this nigga Con."

"What you gone do with dude right here?" asked Big M.

Rat didn't even look up from his task of trying to clean his shirt. "Take that piece of shit out back and walk him down the alley a block or two and throw him in a dumpster. Then get y'all ass back in here so we can start picking those songs. I got to go get me a clean shirt out my truck, shit."

CHAPTER 8

Champagne sat in front of her locker uncrumpling all of the bills she'd just received for dancing on stage as a feature. There were only a few singles in the pile of money she had; most of the bills were fives, tens, and twenties. Several of the other girls in the dressing room looked at her pile of bills enviously. They knew that at the end of the night their garters would be much slimmer, mainly because they wouldn't be featured dancers. Champagne had quickly become a club favorite, attracting even the attention of other club owners. So far, she had guest featured at clubs in Philly, Baltimore, and New Jersey because of her growing notoriety.

After counting and straightening her money, Champagne went to the bathroom to freshen up her goodies before she changed into another costume. She didn't like this part of the night, but she was required by management to return to club floor after a feature to make herself available for lap dances and just all-around interaction with the customers. The VIP room was no mystery to her now, though she couldn't see herself going as far as Cocaine did. She had only gone as far as letting herself be orally sexed and fingered in the VIP room. She had even gained a few regular customers that she would let eat a light snack, one man would actually wear a napkin around his neck as he ate her out.

As Champagne prepared to leave the dressing room, she folded her money as flat as possible into three separate stacks. She tucked the singles stack into her garter and the other two stacks of higher denominations, she tucked into her high-top patent leather boots. Once she'd made the mistake of putting her money into her locker, only once. She returned to the dressing room later that night to find the door of her locker almost torn off the hinges and her money and portable CD player missing. She found out later that it was a new girl, an ugly little beast of a woman who averaged about twenty or thirty bucks a night because she'd do anything at all in the VIP room for a few singles. The new girl had given several *of the club's patrons gonorrhea and that got her fired. Champagne had actually been one of the few dancers that was nice to the new girl, so it made her mad as hell that the girl had stolen from her. Between the lesbians and the thieves, she had to be extra careful about who she chose as a friend. Her best friend was Cocaine. She loved that crazy white girl, mainly because she didn't give a fuck what anyone thought about her. Cocaine gave a fuck only what Cocaine thought. Shaunna had also become her good friend; though she still remained as standoffish as possible. Often Champagne had caught Shaunna watching her, but not in the way the lesbians did, it was more like she wanted to tell her something, but she never did.*

Some of the stories that the girls told made her wary of almost everyone. She had already adopted several rules to live by, as long as she was in this world. She would never do a private party alone. There was one girl who had accepted an offer to work a private party with another dancer, but at the last minute the other dancer backed out. The girl had greedily decided to do the private party and entertain alone. The drunken men at the party had gang-raped her and added insult to injury by mutilating her face with a razor blade. Also Champagne would never let anyone but a bartender hand her a drink and she'd never drink any drink she'd left unattended for any length of time. It wasn't just the date rape drugs and men trying to slip Visine and things in your drink, some people in the club would put things in your drink out of spite. There had been one girl who was beautiful but downright nasty to everyone. She left her drink on the end of the bar one night to give a customer a lap dance. She returned after the dance and finished her drink, but someone had slipped her a mickey. The girl wigged out and hadn't been the same since. It was rumored that she was still in a mental hospital.

Champagne slammed her locker and went out onto the club floor. It was a Wednesday night, but as always Misty's' was packed with men. Champagne was used to the way the men acted, boisterous and oversexed, but it still bothered her that most of the men she encountered had girlfriends and wives. By now she'd lost most of the respect she had for men. Night in and night out she witnessed them commit more and more depraved acts. She knew that she played a major part as an enabler to that depravity, but hers was strictly a business situation.

The club smelled like wet sex and the men were revving at the starting gate tonight. Like every other night, the drug dealers were trying to outdo one another, while the rich businessmen and politician types were trying to be a bit more discreet, not much more though. There were girls all over the club trying to interest the club goers in lap dances. The more popular girls had men waiting in line for a dance from them, or trying to reserve them for the VIP room.

Champagne had to almost beat off a particularly disgusting old guy with a fistful of singles as she headed for the bar. She wasn't the type to hound the crowd for lap dances. Her routine consisted of her sitting at the bar, sipping on small bottles of Mumms' champagne until an opportunity presented itself. Opportunity usually consisted of a man with a couple of hundred dollars who wanted a private session in the VIP room. Depending on the amount of spending he was doing, the more liberties he could take with her body. To her credit, she'd sent plenty of men home with sticky boxers just from her VIP room lap dances. Champagne sat on a bar stool and pulled out some money. To the bartender, she said, "Terry, give me a Mumms'."

"Fuck that Terry," a drunken young man slurred as he came up to the bar on Champagne's left. "This my girl here, Terry. Tonight she gone celebrate my birthday with me. Tonight she ain't drinking no motherfucking Mumms'. Her bad ass is drinking Moet's and shit. Give her one of them little bottles of Moet's, Terry. And don't be taking yo motherfuckin' time having my girl waiting."

Champagne smiled. "Why thank you. I definitely appreciate you buying me a drink on your birthday. How old did you make?"

"I'm twenty motherfuckin' one as of twelve o'clock last night! I can finally get up in the club! I didn't know that this is what I been missing!

TRIPLE TAKE 2: CHAMPAGNE'S KISS

And you! You the baddest motherfucka up in here!"

"Why thank you, I think," Champagne said, as she took a sip from the straw in her bottle of champagne. "Happy 21st birthday and many more. What's your name?"

"They call me Flow. You can call me Flow."

"Flow, I never heard that before. That's cool. What you getting into for your birthday, Flow?"

"I'm trying to get into the VIP room with you. My niggas already told me what was up with the VIP room and that's what I'm trying to do."

"I don't know, Flow. It sounds more like you ready to call it a night. Don't try to do it all at one time. You 21 now, so you can come back any time. Misty's is open every day and I'll be here."

Flow pulled a wad of money from his jeans pocket. "What you think I ain't got money? I ain't no young punk. I might have just made 21, but I been getting money for a long time. I got cash. I just want to go to the VIP room for a little private time with you. You know, for my birthday." "How much you talking about?" asked Champagne without taking her eyes off the money Flow was holding.

Flow peeled off some big bills and handed them to Champagne. "That's five hundred, baby girl. If you want more, I'll give you more. I'm just trying to be up in the VIP room, 'cause I'm a VIP. Now bring yo thick ass on."

"That's what I'm talking about Flow. That five makes you VIP room material. First you bought me some champagne and now you buying yourself some Champagne. Now that's what I like."

Champagne picked up her bottle of Moet's and followed Flow to the VIP room. It was dark in the VIP room, darker than the rest of the club. The only light streamed in from around the curtain covering the doorway. One of the club's loud speakers was located right outside the curtained off VIP room, so the dancers inside with their clients could hear the music. The number of songs played and the amount of money a man spent on a girl dictated how long they would be with that customer.

When Champagne's eyes adjusted to the darkness of the VIP room, she could make out several shapes on the couches. One girl named Exotic was on her knees with her customer's penis in her mouth. Another girl had stepped out of her dancing costume and was sitting on her customer's lap naked. The man whose lap she was sitting on was sucking her breasts like a newborn baby.

Flow had chosen a couch furthest from the door and had sprawled across it with his drink in hand. Champagne went over and took a seat beside him. She made small talk with him and sipped her drink until the DJ put on a new record and then she started dancing in front of him. At first Flow seemed content to just rub on her big legs, but as she continued dancing, he became frisky and began touching her everywhere. Halfway through the third song, Flow pulled her onto his lap and shook her breasts loose from the bikini top she was wearing. Champagne let him fondle her for a bit but then he started to get a bit rough.

Champagne put her arms across her chest. "Whoa, there Flow. Slow down a bit, baby. I ain't going nowhere. You got me for awhile."

"Oh shit!" yelled the man on the couch who was receiving oral stimulation. "I'm coming! Catch that shit! Catch it! Damn, Exotic you got some good ass head!"

"Yeah whatever," Exotic said as she spit into a napkin. "I'm going to get me some Listerine, man."

Exotic and her customer left the VIP room, leaving Champagne and the other girl behind. The other girl danced for one more song and obviously her customer's money had run out, because she left. The man lingered for a second watching Flow and Champagne and then he left. Flow was kissing Champagne on the neck and trying to jam his fingers into her.

Champagne resisted. "Whoa player. Slow it down. You didn't pay for all that. You got to ask me."

"Fuck that, bitch," Flow snapped. "Bitch, I done just gave you five hundred of my hard earned dollars. I'm bout to get some of this pussy."

"Some pussy, nigga. Is you crazy? I ain't say I was about to give you

no pussy for no little funky five hundred dollars. Let me the fuck go!"

"Bitch, you the one that's crazy! I know you ain't think I gave you that for no funky ass lap dance! Bitch for that much money I'm fucking yo big thick ass!"

Champagne tried to jump up off Flow's lap, but he tripped her and grabbed her hair at the same time. With his free hand, he punched her in the temple until she saw stars. He drug her around to the end of the couch and draped her over the arm of the couch on her stomach. He ripped her g-string off and dropped his pants and boxer shorts to the floor. He was prepared to enter her from the rear when Shaunna flung open the curtain of the VIP.

Shaunna walked over and looked down at Champagne. "Bitch, I thought you was different," Shaunna snarled before she noticed the glassy look in Champagne's eyes. "Here you is fuckin' niggas in the VIP room like the rest of these skank ass bitches. You ain't shit!"   "Bitch, you better get up outta here and mind yo business!" Flow threatened.

"I paid good money for this ho and you in my business, bitch! Get lost!"

"Nigga, fuck you!" Shaunna retorted.

"Shaunna help me," Champagne moaned. "Help me, he raping me."

"What you say, Champagne?" Shaunna asked just beginning to become aware of her co-worker's helpless state.

"This nigga raping you?"

"Hell nall I ain't raping this slut ass bitch! Bitch, I done told you for the last time to get out my fuckin' business. I done already told her and you, I paid for this bitch and she ain't about to renege on the deal. This funky ass stripper bitch is getting some dick tonight."

Champagne tried to push herself up off the couch arm, but Flow leaned his weight on her, pinning her in place. His hardness wavered around her butt cheeks as he prepared to push himself into her. As Flow concentrated to aim himself, he missed Shaunna scoop up Champagne's discarded bottle. He never saw the bottle coming, but he felt it crash into his eye as

Shaunna slapped him with it. She followed that up with a punch to his throat. When Flow grabbed his throat, Shaunna used that opportunity to kick him in the nuts. With all of his bluster gone, Flow dropped to his knees and threw up.

Shaunna helped Champagne up and out the VIP room. On the way back to the dressing room, she informed the club bouncers that a would-be rapist was in there throwing his guts up. Two of Misty's' largest bouncers promptly went into the VIP room and beat Flow nearly into a coma.

In the dancers' dressing room, Shaunna helped Champagne take a seat and went to get her a cold towel for her head. By then most of the other dancers had heard what happened and made their way to the dressing room either out of concern or curiosity. Cocaine elbowed her way through the crowd of women.

"Get y'all ass out my way!" Cocaine cursed. "Nosy ass bitches! Where was y'all at when that nigga was trying to rape my girl! Champagne! Champagne!"

Champagne held up her hand. "Cocaine, stop hollering bitch. My motherfucking head is banging."

Cocaine dropped to her knees beside Champagne. "Girl, tell me what happened. I'm gone have Black Mike and them come up here and fuck somebody up."

"Black Mike ain't gone have to do shit to that nigga," a dancer named Torture commented. "The way Big Tony and Mountain stomped his ass in the VIP room ain't nobody else got to do nothing to that nigga."

"I know that's right," added another girl. "They shoulda kilt his punk ass. Fucking rapist."

Champagne stood up and opened her locker. She pulled on a pair of jeans and a t-shirt and some New Balance running shoes. With tears in her eyes, she stuffed her dancing costumes in her bag and slammed her locker.

"Where you going, bitch?" asked Cocaine.

"I'm fucking going home."

TRIPLE TAKE 2: CHAMPAGNE'S KISS

"Wait up, girl. Let me get my shit."

"That's okay, gone finish your shift. I'm straight. I just want to go home and lay my ass down."

"Alright girl," said Cocaine. "Call me when you feeling better. Y'all bitches get up out her way."

Outside of Misty's in the parking lot in her Corvette, Champagne let her tears go full force. In the middle of her sobbing, someone tapped on her car window. Quickly, she tried to hide her tears, but the knocking persisted. She looked up and saw it was Shaunna. She started the car and rolled her window down.

"You alright, Champagne," Shaunna asked.

"Yeah, I'm straight. Thanks for looking out for me. I'm glad you were there."

"Don't worry about it."

"My head was foggy as hell from when he hit me, but it looked like you fucked him up."

Shaunna laughed. "Girl that's years of martial arts. You gone have to learn to protect yourself in this world."

"I'm an army brat so I know how to shoot somebody, but I want to learn how to do that shit you did."

"Girl that was actually some basic stuff. I can do way more damage than that, but I knew that the bouncers would want a piece of his ass too."

This time it was Champagne's turn to laugh which she did and it made her wince in pain. "Don't make me laugh, Shaunna. My head hurts like hell. I'm about to go my ass home, sit in a tub of hot water and bang back a few Tylenols. I'll see you tomorrow."

"Alright, Champagne. I think I'm out of here for the night too. See you tomorrow."

CHAPTER 9

"So you never said, do you like the house or what?" asked Champagne.

"I thought you could tell by the way I was acting when we was there," Shaunna said. "That place is so beautiful. I know that it'll be a nice place to raise a family. I can't get over how nice it was."

"Girl, I know. When JC showed me that place it made me horny. I made him give me some on the elevator."

"That's just too much information, Chammy. But, I feel you though. You gone have to give Killa J some for me too for finding a place like that."

"You don't think it's too big do you?"

"No, it's just the right size. That place says that we've made it. I mean it's huge as houses go, but it's not ridiculously big. I can already see some swings and stuff in the yard. Us relaxing in the hot tub or pool while JC and Rat burn up the food on that nice gas grill. Any kid would love to grow up in a place like that. I wish I could have grown up in a place like that."

Champagne took a sip of the water the table attendant had just poured her. "Yeah that place is a long way from those little ass slingshot houses the Army used to give my father for us to live in. The closets in the house seem like they're bigger than those Army base quarters. I used to hate living on base. It seemed like all of the places were exactly alike. When I was little all I wanted was to live in a house that looked different than everybody else's."

"Well you don't have to worry about that now," Shaunna said as she opened the Cheesecake Factory menu in front of her. "I haven't ever seen a house that looks like that one. Not one that I could see myself living in."

"So you and Rat are gonna stay? I was really hoping you would. I know we're partners and we work and live together, but I love that. Every since you came back into my life it seems like my stuff is going in the right direction."

"Of course we're gonna stay. We're not gonna break up the crew. I love having y'all as family, and living in a big house will make it even better. Rat told me he went over there with JC and he came home ready to pack up and move in."

"That sound just like that fool," Champagne said. "Well, I know that Ronnie is going to be glad that you guys are moving into the house because he wants to buy the penthouse. JC said that he was slobbing at the thought of buying it. To this day, Ronnie thanks his lucky stars that he was at work the night I got shot and helped you all carry me and that stuff into the house. He was just a business school student working part-time and now a few years later he can afford to buy close to a two million dollar penthouse. That can definitely be considered progress."

"Uh, yeah, now where the hell is the waitress?" asked Shaunna as she looked around the late lunch crowd for their server. "Whoever is serving us need to come the hell on."

"Dag girl, you just ate a big bag of Ruffles in the damn car," said Champagne.

"I know but I'm still hungry. What you about to get, Chammy?"

"Well, I'm going to get me one of those big ass salads so I don't feel guilty when I tear me up a piece of turtle cheesecake and wash it all down with a glass of their pink lemonade."

"Well I'm not going to feel guilty in the least when I rip up a big plate of this Cajun angel hair pasta with shrimp with a cherry vanilla Coke." "You're not having any cheesecake, Shaunny?" "I want a slice of banana cream cheesecake with extra bananas. I'll be having that first, as soon as this slow ass waiter come on. Do I have to whistle, because I can whistle."

Shaunna put two fingers in her mouth to whistle, but Champagne managed to snatch her hand down just before she let out a shrill blast.

"Shaunny, what's wrong with you?" Champagne asked. "Girl, are you losing it?"

"I'm fucking starving I keep telling you that. I've been craving some of this damn cheesecake. It's about time."

"I'm sorry for the wait ladies," said a tall, red haired waitress that stepped up to their table. "Things are really crazy around here because we're so short-handed. Can I get you ladies something to drink?"

Champagne and Shaunna were decisive as they ordered their food and drinks. In the short wait it took for Shaunna to get her cheesecake, Champagne tried to strike up a conversation with Shaunna, but she was too preoccupied watching other people eat their food. The minute the waitress sat her dessert on the table, Shaunna dove straight into it. She finished her dessert long before her lunch arrived and as soon as her pasta arrived, she dug into that too. Champagne ate much slower and marveled at the way Shaunna was putting away her food. A shrimp fell from Shaunna's fork onto the table and without hesitation she scooped it up and devoured it. Champagne's mouth fell open. It was like Shaunna had forgotten they were in public. She looked at the healthy rosy glow of Shaunna's cheeks, the slight thickening around Shaunna's middle, and how her everything seemed a little bigger, wider, and more voluptuous. It hit Champagne like a load of bricks. Catching Shaunna with a mouthful of pasta, shrimp, and garlic bread, Champagne spurted, "Girl, yo butt is pregnant!" Shaunna slightly choked on the food in her mouth and it took a second for her to clear her airway. After a gulp of water, she asked, "How did you know?"

"I didn't 'til now. Look at you though. You're eating like they ain't gone never make no more food. Your face is all aglow. And look at how big your legs and titties done got. I don't know how I missed it. Come to think of it, were you throwing up two mornings ago?"

"That morning and every other morning before that. I can't hold down nothing in the morning that's why I pig out all day."

"I thought I heard somebody throwing up in your bathroom, but I thought it was just Rat coming in drunk early in the morning. How many months are you and what did Rat have to say?"

"Going on two," Shaunna said bashfully. "I haven't told anyone yet.

I'm so doggone scared to tell Rat, I don't know what to do."

"Why? Girl, you know that fool Rat love kids. You see how he is with the twins. The twins love that fool too. Really he's just a big kid himself, that's why he gets along with them so well. He already takes care of his little brother and sisters so he knows what it means to be a provider."

"Well, he has so much going on with that studio and that record label, I haven't been able to find the right time. I hoped that he would notice the changes in my body and guess but he didn't. The only thing he said was Shaunny you getting thick as hell, girl. I know he loves kids, but I don't want to stress him out any more than he's already stressing with his stuff."

"Hold on," Champagne said to Shaunna. To the waitress, she said, "You can wrap the rest of this salad and bring my cheesecake please."

"Sure thing," the waitress said as she lifted the plate containing the remainder of Champagne's salad. "Anything else for you, ma'am?"

"Two more slices of banana cream, one to stay and the other to go," answered Shaunna. "Throw in a slice of strawberry to go too."

"Shaunny," Champagne said reproachfully. "Girl, that's just too damn much cheesecake."

"It's not for me, it's for Rat."

"It better be."

As the waitress walked off, two Black men obviously on lunch break from one of the many businesses in the area stopped at Champagne and Shaunna's table.

"Hey there sisters," the shorter of the two said.

Champagne looked him over. He was short, wearing a dress shirt and stained tie, could use a pair of new shoes, and he had food stuck in his teeth.

"How are you two lovely ladies doing this afternoon?" the man continued. "You two were looking so fine sitting over here all by your lonesome and since I didn't see no wedding rings, me and my friend thought we would come over and introduce ourselves. My name is

Frank and this is Carl. What are y'all names?"

"Shaunna, do you see this?"

Shaunna had already started maxing her second piece of cheesecake. She wiped her mouth with her linen napkin. "I see them."

Frank was persistent, though his friend was looking like he wanted to bolt. "Ladies, all I asked you was for y'all names."

"Okay," Champagne said. "My name is We Don't Wanna, and her name is Be Bothered."

"Okay, okay," said Frank. "I'm feeling that. You ain't got to be so mean though. You just missed out on taking a ride in my brand new Maxima. That's y'all loss."

Shaunna laughed. "You must have had too many drinks with your lunch, Frank. I drive a Cayenne S and she drives an Infiniti. Are you suggesting we park those and climb into your Maxima?"

"Y'all got big money, huh?" asked Frank. "That's what I like 'cause I can't stand no broke ass woman. Now if..."

"Look man, yo little short ass can't take a hint huh!" Shaunna snapped. "Get the fuck away from us! You need to stop eating out and take a lunch to work so you can save you some money and get you some new shoes. Them boys right there is leaning. Take the rest of the money you save and buy you a fucking clue! Now it was nice to meet you, and I got a feeling that Carl isn't as corny as you, but could you move around so we can finish our lunch."

"Come on, man," Carl said putting his hand on Frank's shoulder. "You always get yourself embarrassed."

Frank turned to walk away with his friend. "Carpet munchers," he coughed over his shoulder.

"Lame," Champagne coughed into her napkin. "Girl, his shoes was leaning so hard he have to lay down to put them on." They both had a nice laugh at the expense of Frank's shoes, paid the check, and left the restaurant with plenty of cheesecake in tow.

CHAPTER 10

JC stood on the terrace of the penthouse with his cell phone to his ear. "Yeah, okay... Dave and Buster's in an hour... I got it... No problem... We'll be there... Thanks for handling the business on such short notice... Of course... Alright then..."

He closed his cell phone and stood for a few moments looking out at Lake Michigan and a few golfers on the city's golf course, stories below. The dark green of the lake waters looked inviting and terrifying at the same time. He knew when they moved to the new house, the thing he would miss most would be this view. No matter the weather, he'd often find his way out here. He loved being outdoors. Maybe it was a by-product of being locked up for over ten years. He also loved peace and quiet, too, but with a young friend as wild and impetuous as Rat could be, often that peace and quiet would be shattered.

Tearing himself away from the view, JC left the terrace and went to find Rat. His young friend was in the game room, playing Madden football on the 72-inch plasma screen. Heavily JC dropped onto one of the room's overstuffed leather recliners and looked at Rat.

Rat looked away from his game. "What?" he asked. JC didn't answer, just continued to stare at him.

"What?" Rat repeated. "What, man?"

JC couldn't help but to shake his head. "Look man. I just got off the horn with Dante. After you told me about your little trouble down at the studio, I had a bad feeling about it, so I had Dante use a couple of his Apostles to put some feelers out in the street to see what was to this shit."

"Man, J!" Rat exclaimed. "I didn't tell you about that 'cause I thought I needed some help. I was just letting you know what had happened on GP. Fuck them niggas! I ain't thinking about no fucking Concrete Click! Man, fuck them bitch ass niggas! They tried to pull a power move without no power. That was some gay ass shit and I handled it accordingly."

JC rubbed his temples. "That ain't the issue. I didn't feel like you were running to me for help. I didn't feel like that at all. I just wanted to do some checking on the shit. I had a bad feeling about the shit, so I reached out to someone that could put me at ease."

"Put you at ease? I hate to say it, J, but you might be getting soft in yo old age. This wasn't no big plot or plan. A couple of chumps thought they could tax me and I let them know it wasn't like that. I ain't never even heard of no Concrete Click before the other day, so how serious could these niggas be?"

"You always manage to get shit twisted," JC said. "How the fuck do that make me soft 'cause I wanted to find out about the shit? I guess for me not to be soft I should handle any problem like you. Shoot somebody or beat their ass and ask questions later."

"I ain't saying that, but you have slowed down. Every since we got that chump Zo, you been on cruise control. You done got so used to tinkering around on them properties and playing landlord that you done forgot what kind of dude you is."

"How in the hell did I forget what kind of dude I am?"

Rat looked at JC closely. "Come on now, J. This is yo man talking. Keep it gully with me. I know you. I was in the joint with you. I know about the bodies you done left. Now all of a sudden you a maintenance man walking around in dirty khakis and shit. It's cool for a nigga to change up, but you can't never forget that gangster shit was what got you what you got. Them buildings you work on Mr. Landlord, you got them shits 'cause you got down and dirty in them streets, when it was time. If you ever got to go back to living by the gun what then? Wait on a lawyer or the police to solve a problem for you. It ain't like that for me and I know it ain't like that for the old Killa J."

JC threw his hands up in air. "How in the fuck did you manage to miss my whole point? I ain't went nowhere, I just prefer to think my way through some shit now. This is a thinking man's game out here. This ain't the joint and I'll be goddamned if I give the Department of Corrections another day of my life. You call it getting soft, I call it getting wise. Ain't nobody about to pull me off my square or have me jag off the rest of my life over no bullshit. I believe in the Art of War. Out-think yo damn enemies. You forget I got kids and I happen to want to be in their lives. I don't ever want to feel that feeling of being in them nasty ass joint visiting rooms, not being able to touch my babies. Gangster shit got me here, that's true. But gangster shit got me into way more trouble than it got me out of."

"You got to see my side, J," said Rat beseechingly. "Imagine if some nigga came at one of your buildings. Imagine him saying he wanted yo building and that was it. He ain't finta pay no rent, he ain't work to get you that building, he just want it. That shit is crazy. I can't never go like that. You know when we was in the joint, wadn't no nigga taking nothing from us but plenty of static if he got out of line. I don't care how old I live to be, I'm gone always think like that. Ain't no nigga taking shit of mine."

"Rat, when the hell did you hear me say that you was 'sposed to let somebody take anything from you? I didn't say shit like that Young Gun. All I said is that it could have been handled different. You done half killed one of this Con's men, without ever getting close to Con to find out what kind of stud he is. Whether he is a real threat, or just on some bully shit to see if you'll hand over your shit without a fight. So now without you ever being able to see who's behind this shit you already got him aware that you're a threat by what you did to his guy."

Rat rubbed his chin and sat back in the chair. "I didn't think about it like that. I ain't gone lie, I just got mad 'cause some punk ass nigga come up in my shit trying to tax me like I'm some bitch. Then all the time this Tough Tony ass nigga ain't real 'cause he couldn't even back the play he was making with his mouth. I know you mad, but I couldn't let it go like that."

"Young Gun, I ain't mad 'cause you whupped some punk ass nigga. I know a while back we would have slumped him, and the nigga that ran, but now we above board. When you trying to live legal, you have to understand that your every action is gonna be scrutinized and analyzed. You ain't no little kid no more. Another bit like your last time in the joint would take a lot out of yo ass. So next time please think before you do anything. Now like I was saying. I got Dante to cut into this nigga Con and set up a meeting. Dante said this nigga was talking real jazzy and only agreed to meet if the Apostles would secure it and mediate the negotiations. This is out of the Apostles control, so Dante is doing this as a favor for us. He said that if Solemn Shawn was alive he knows that he would have done the same thing. So go get yo ass ready."

Rat got up to go throw on some clothes. "Are we taking heaters?"

JC picked up the game controller and reset the game. "No heat in the meeting, but I ain't going without none. We'll leave 'em in the truck."

...

JC and Rat got off the escalator on the second floor of Dave and Buster's on North Clark Street. Dante, Murderman, and a few of their gang members were waiting on them. Dante had become the Head Apostle after Solemn Shawn's death. He and Murderman had grown even closer in the absence of their old friend. Dante was still in great physical shape and a few grey hairs in his short afro and goatee were the only sign of aging. Murderman looked exactly the same. His hair had grown longer and there were two tattooed tears with an S in each of them under his right eye, but he still looked like a lean jungle hunter. The Apostles exchanged hugs with JC and Rat.

"Rat, Big Ant said to tell you what's up?" Dante said.

"Yeah, what's up with his big buster ass?" Rat joked. "He still out there hacking the shit outta motherfuckas and calling that shit defense?"

"That nigga deep into them race cars," Dante answered. "All he be worried about is building some faster shit than the cars he already got.

70

They be going to the racetrack and running them boys for big money."

"What's up with Mumps?" JC asked.

His eyes constantly moving in every direction, Murderman said, "That nigga got him a couple of fighters. Some young cats that are pretty nice with their hands. If he ain't in the gym with them, then he in Vegas or Atlantic City or at one of the boats in Indiana. That's all that nigga do is gamble. It's a real sickness with that nigga."

"This way," Dante instructed them. "We got a pool table near the back where we can have some sort of privacy."

"Them cats here yet?" asked JC.

"Nall," Dante answered. "Not yet, but we got the street covered so we'll know the minute they touch down."

By the pool table, they took a seat in the chairs while they watched two Apostles play a sloppy game of eightball. A waiter approached them for their drink requests. Rat ordered a beer and enough hot wings for everybody. JC just ordered a beer.

"Dante give us a full rundown on this Con," JC said.

"Murderman is my info guy. Let them know what you found out about this stud, M1."

"I hear that he's from the East Coast, not from New York, but either from Philly or B-More. They say he came to town a few years back 'cause he was trying to get into the rap game, and Chicago was uncharted territory. The nigga got a rep real quick out in the Wild 100s where he landed. He would throw little talent shows and rap battles and niggas that beat his rappers out had a nasty way of ending up hurt. Once niggas peeped that, they started jumping on the band wagon. Plus the nigga talk real slick, I gather that's how he got the name Con."

"So what made this nigga think he could extort other niggas with studios and labels?" Rat interjected.

"Well, this nigga started seeing that Chi-town is really dry on that rap shit and he wasn't getting no success, so he had to switch his game up. Just like a hater he started blaming other niggas for his failure.

Thinking that niggas was in the way and putting out wack shit that had the labels not wanting to hear what Chicago was talking about. The way Con sees it, if he gorillas rappers and studios they'll either fold up and get out of his way or pay him. He thinks he can't lose."

"That's some slick ass shit," JC said.

"Yeah, but he got the wrong motherfucka," said Rat. "He can miss me and mine with that bullshit."

"Well, I got to tell you," Dante said. "The nigga really think he a heavy 'cause we reached out to him. Also you can't take this stud too lightly, he's a smart ass nigga and he got followers, so don't underestimate him." Across from JC, Murderman answered his cell phone. He listened for a couple of seconds and then closed his phone. "Con and his men are on the way up."

Minutes later, Con the leader of the Concrete Click and six of his followers got off the escalator on the second floor. Con was wearing green camouflage army fatigues from head to his custom painted green camouflage Timberland boots. Several Apostles greeted them and discreetly searched them for weapons. Finding no weapons, the Concrete Click was led over to the area where Rat, JC, Dante, and Murderman were seated.

When they were all being introduced, Rat had to control himself so as not to laugh because Con resembled an adult version of the kiddie rapper Bow Wow—the same height and all. Rat and JC towered over him as they gave him half-hearted handshakes. Con took his seat in the chair across from Rat and JC, and the meeting started.

"I'm glad you all agreed to come here to try and iron out this misunderstanding," Dante said. "As you are both leaders in your own right, it's only logical that you seek the most peaceful solution to any problems that may have arose between your groups."

"Man, this nigga sent his little messenger boys up in my place of business to try and tax me," Rat stated. "That ain't no misunderstanding on my part."

TRIPLE TAKE 2: CHAMPAGNE'S KISS

Con smiled, revealing his diamond covered platinum upper and lower teeth. "You got that right, son. That wasn't no misunderstanding. If a cat in the rap game in Chi-town, he gotta cough up that cream. That's what's real. If you own a studio in Chi, you owe me cream and I got to have mine. I got pussy bills to pay."

"Man, who you talking to?" Rat asked. "I don't give a fuck about yo pussy bills. That's on you if you paying for pussy anyway."

"That's beside the point, son," Con said. "Whatever I use that cake for, it's mine and I got it coming. Wadn't nobody trying to make no moves in this town until I got here and showed them what was happening. I came up in here and shook the trees and if you think I'm gone stand there and watch another nigga catch my fruit when it falls, you crazy son."

"I ain't yo son," Rat said rather irately. "Quit calling me that, rap ass nigga. I don't know what the fuck you think is happening, like you put Chicago on the map musically, but that lets me know you ain't got it all. Chicago still ain't on the map. You act like we trying to eat off yo plate by doing our thing. Nigga, you can't be all the fuck you think you is, 'cause I just heard of you. And what I hear ain't enough to scare me into not making no moves to feed mines."

"That's what you not understanding son," Con said. "Chicago is my plate. If you trying to eat here in the rap game, then you is eating off my plate."

Rat stood up. "Didn't I tell yo ho ass to stop calling me son, pussy. Now call me that shit again!"

Con jumped down from his chair. "Keep on disrespecting me!" JC, Dante, and Murderman stood up and got between the two men.

"Calm down, you two," Dante said. "Remember we're not here to start a war, but trying to reach a peaceful solution."

"This nigga better watch his mouth, yo," Con said.

"He will and you'll watch yours too," Murderman countered.

"The man keep asking you to quit calling him son. This is the

Midwest not out East. That shit ain't cool to us. Now everybody sit down so we can get on with this. I said sit down."

Both parties slowly took their seats.

"Can we continue," Dante said. "Con, being that these are friends of ours why don't you overlook Rat's operation just on the strength that I asked you?"

"Are they Apostles?" Con asked, his platinum teeth flashing.

"No, but they are close personal friends of ours."

"Well if they ain't Apostles then we don't have to go around them like they are. This is a business thing and Apostles understand that better than anybody. How would it look if I cut them some slack? A couple of my other clients hear about that and then they won't want to pay. That ain't the way it is or how it's gonna be. If you have a record label or recording studio in Chicago, then you pay the Concrete Click. The next time I hear from Rat, it should be to tell me when and where to pick up my cream or that he's shutting down."

That was all Rat could take, he leapt from his seat and almost got his hands on Con, but JC and Murderman held him back.

"Let me go, I'ma beat the shit out this short ass nigga! I'ma make sure he swallow them silver ass teeth!"

Grinning Con jumped down from his seat again. To his crew, he said, "Let's bounce, yo. This shit is over."

The Concrete Click exited leaving JC and the Apostles to restrain an infuriated Rat. He was so angry he was shaking when they managed to shove him into a seat.

"I'ma pop that nigga balloon!" Rat vowed. "That nigga is dead!"

"Rat, motherfuckas is looking at us!" JC fumed. "Calm yo ass down!"

"Man, fuck that, I'm gone... Nall it's cool. I'm cool. Don't even worry about it. I ain't got nothing else to say about it. My fault y'all."

An uneasy silence fell on the group as Rat pulled out a cigarette, lit it, and began to furiously puff away.

"So what are you going to do, Rat?" Dante asked finally.

"Don't worry about it, Dante. A nigga ain't never made me pay shit I don't owe, and I'll be damned if I ever start. I tried to talk about it, now I'm gone be about it."

"Well whatever happens, you know you've got some friends if you need the help. What are you gonna do now?"

Rat laughed, but there was no mirth in his laughter. "Right now I'm gonna eat up some of these hot wings. Then I'm gone win some money off you and yo guys shooting baskets over on the other side. I wish that Mumps and Big Ant was here so I could take they paper too."

"Well my man, I got a pocket full of money, and Murderman ain't no slouch, so hurry up with them hot wings so I can get me some of yo money," Dante said.

JC just looked on. He knew that Rat was trying to make light of the situation, but he smelled war. Whatever happened he would ride with his best friend, because his best friend would always ride with him.

CHAPTER 11

"See, now aren't you glad you came with us?" JC asked.

Hell yeah," Rat said, as he looked at the small screen on his minuscule video camera. "This is some great footage. I'm glad I didn't miss this."

Champagne punched Rat in the arm. "Are y'all laughing at my baby?" she asked. "Y'all better not be laughing at my child."

"I'm not laughing at Kenton," Rat said with a smile. "I'm laughing at every kid out there."

They were seated alongside the basketball court in the gym of the YMCA watching Kenton play in his first biddy league basketball game. Anaya was sitting on Shaunna's lap wrestling with her over a bag of cheddar cheese pretzels they were supposed to be sharing.

On the basketball court, Kenton and the other 3 to 5 year olds were providing the comic relief, by running in every direction with the basketball.

"Man, look at number four's shorts," Rat commented. "He got them boys pulled up around his neck. That got to be uncomfortable."

Champagne was smiling when she gave Rat a light punch in his arm. "Shut up man. They are so cute. I just wish they would get big old Number 8 out of there. His parents ought to be ashamed of themselves trying to pass him off for only five years old. He's got to be at least seven or eight. He's the only one out there that knows what to do with the ball."

Champagne was right, because Number 8 snatched the ball from a little girl's hands, sprinted for the basket, and tossed up a shot that almost went in the goal. The crowd gave up a collective groan. Kenton was standing in the middle of the court with several other players not paying the game the slightest bit of attention, as he jumped up and down. "Kent!" JC shouted, trying to get his son's attention. "Kenton, get in the game son! Get the ball! Go get the ball!"

TRIPLE TAKE 2: CHAMPAGNE'S KISS

Kenton looked up like he'd just discovered that he was in the game and spotted a teammate running with the ball. He streaked toward his teammate and when the boy stopped to shoot, Kenton dove on his back tumbling them both to the floor. Several other children dove onto the pile. While the coaches and referees were untangling the children, a little boy streaked off his team's bench, grabbed the basketball and raced out of the gym leaving the crowd breaking up in laughter.

"Nice tackle," Rat said. "I think y'all got my man Kenton playing the wrong sport. You see the way he hawked down little dude on his own team, I might add, and clotheslined him. Now that's skill. He should be playing linebacker instead of guard."

"I just know my baby better not be hurt," Champagne sulked. "If that big ole fat boy over there jump on his back one more time, I'm gone go down there and jump up and down on his fat ass mama's back."

"It ain't like she would feel it," JC said. "But you can't do that, Chammy. These are kids. This is basketball. It's okay. They're not big enough to hurt each other. Hold on. It's starting again."

The referees had managed to catch the little boy with the basketball and return him to the gym. The game play resumed without any more children escaping the gym, but it was just as hilarious. When it was finally over, Kenton's team logged their first loss. They lost by two points, but the total score was only four to six. JC took his son's hand and went with him to the locker room to change clothes. As he was helping his son into his jogging suit, JC gave him a few pointers on the game of basketball, but Kenton was more preoccupied with the fact that Rat had promised that they would go to the House of Kicks after the game for pizza and rollercoaster rides.

JC and Kenton left the locker room and joined the others in the gym. Champagne was apart from the others, over by Number 8's parents talking with them, as she slyly checked out Number 8. She joined her family and friends shortly.

"I told y'all Number 8 was older than five," Champagne said as they left the gym.

"Did his parents admit that he's older than five?" JC asked.

"They didn't have to. When I got closer I could see that that boy shaves and he had a few hairs on his chest."

Everyone laughed, but the twins. They were still laughing as they climbed into Rat's Infiniti QX56. The twins climbed in the rear of the truck and made a fuss until Rat turned on the rear DVD player for them and let them watch a kiddie movie. While the kids watched their movie, the adults chatted about the game as Rat drove to the House of Kicks.

At the House of Kicks, Rat and JC ran off with the twins to play video games and seemed more reluctant to eat than the twins when an hour later, Champagne informed them that their pizza was ready. They were totally engrossed in helping the twins play a game of House of the Dead, shooting zombies and monsters.

"Remember who is the grownup and who's the kids!" Champagne whispered forcefully to JC and Rat.

"Aww man," JC said. "Just a few more minutes. Me and Kent almost beat this game. We got just a few more zombies to kill."

"Please Mom," Kenton pleaded. "We're on level six, Mom. We've never made it to level six before. As soon as we finish, I'll bring Daddy and Uncle Rat to eat. I promise."

"What about you, 'Naya?"

"I'm going with you, Mom," Anaya said.

"Sell out," Rat said to Anaya as he took over her video game gun.

"I want some cheese pizza and then I'm ready to go." Anaya announced.

"What do you mean, you ready to go?" Rat asked over his shoulder as he assisted JC and Kenton in slaying zombies. "We just got here."

Anaya put her hands on hips. "The only reason I wanted to come was to ride the rollercoaster and it's broke. After I eat my pizza, I'm ready to go."

"You heard my baby," Champagne said as she took Anaya's hand.

"We're going to eat pizza. As soon as that game is over, Kent, you come eat too."

"Okay," Kenton said as he blasted a zombie's head off. "As soon as we're finished."

Fifteen minutes after Champagne and Anaya sat down to pizza at the table with Shaunna, the menfolk joined them.

Kenton was excited. "Mom, we finally won the House of Dead!"

"Almost used all the credits on our cards doing it too," JC grumbled. "Doggone dude at the end was hard to kill."

"Nall, Dad. The hardest to kill was that mole thing."

"Right," Rat agreed as he drug two slices of pizza from the box and onto his plate. "That thing was crazy. You got to shoot this thing in the feet while it's running around on the walls. I know I'm gone need another card 'cause I used most of mine trying to stay in the game."

"Don't get another one, you can have mine," Shaunna offered.

"Me and Chammy played a few games of skeetball, but I was through after that. I've been sitting over here eating ice. They have some crushed ice that's banging and I ate half a pizza, so I'm ready to go to sleep."

"That's all you do nowadays is sleep and eat," Rat said. "I swear."

"That's alright, 'cause you like it," Shaunna said.

"That I do, but don't be putting my business in the street," Rat joked as he pulled another two slices onto his plate.

"Hurry up, J and K, we want to get a couple more games in before these girls is ready to go."

"Don't encourage neither one of them, Rat," said Champagne.

"Don't neither one of them chew their food as it is. Kenton, put that pop down and eat some of this pizza."

"Daddy," Anaya said.

"Yeah?"

"You should buy this place."

"Why you say that 'Naya?"

"Because you would keep all of the rides and games fixed and I could help you with the busyness."

"Okay, baby doll. I'll have Ronnie check it out for me. Remember if I get it you have to run it."

"Okay."

"That means you gone have to quit school and start drinking coffee so you can get up early in the morning to run your busyness."

"Aww, Dad you crazy. I already know what I would do."

"What's that?"

"I would pay Kenton to get up early for me and go to school for me too."

The adults laughed at Anaya's kiddie logic, but Kenton didn't find it funny.

"I'm not going to school for you. I don't even want to go to school for me."

"Alright y'all take a emergency slice with you, 'cause I'm gone to game out," Rat announced. As the men left, Anaya sat with the women listening to their conversation as long as she could, but she got bored and went to find her father, uncle, and twin. Two hours later, an hour longer than the women wanted to stay they wrapped up the festivities and piled into Rat's truck. This time the twins didn't request a movie, mainly because they were asleep a few minutes after they left the parking lot. As they were driving home, content to listen to Anthony Hamilton's latest CD, Rat's cell phone buzzed.

He freed it from the clip on his belt, opened it, and held it to his ear.

"Yo, Tina what's up? What? What? Stop crying, I can't understand you... Okay, I'm on my way. Don't leave... Yeah, I'm on the way now... About 20 minutes."

"What was that, baby?" Shaunna asked.

"Just a little trouble at the studio," Rat answered guardedly.

"Nothing major. I just got to run by there real quick and check things out. You know how it is. When the cats away the mice will play.

Me and J will help y'all upstairs with the twins and then I'm gone ride down there."

Rat caught JC's raised eyebrow in the rearview mirror, but he didn't offer any explanation. He just kept driving and minutes later he was pulling into their building's garage. Rat jumped out to help with the twins, but Champagne stopped him.

"Me and Shaunny can get them. You two go and take care of whatever down at the studio."

"Thanks, Chammy," Rat said gratefully. He knew that she would be within her rights to read him the riot act about the studio, but she somehow recognized that now wasn't the time. "The minute we check things out, I'll get your man back to you safe and sound." "I'll be back baby," JC said. He kissed his sleeping daughter and son on the head before climbing back into the truck. They waited until the women got on the private elevator with the children before Rat peeled out of the garage. "What happened at the studio?" asked JC.

"I don't know the details. Tina, the receptionist called me blubbering and shit. She said that a couple of niggas in all black ran up in the studio. They was carrying baseball bats and they had a nigga backing them up with a machinegun. She said they kicked her ass and beat one of the sound engineers pretty bad. She said they broke up the equipment in the studios too."

"You got a gun on you?" asked JC.

"I keep a thumper. Hold on, here go Tina again." Rat answered his cell phone. "Yo, Tina. I'm on the way... No, don't call the police or nothing, I'll be there in a couple of minutes and then you can call... Well tell Bernie, he got to hang tight for a few minutes then he can go to the hospital... Five minutes, I promise."

"Who's Bernie?" JC asked when Rat hung up the phone.

Rat dialed another number on his cell. "Sound engineer. Tina says he's moaning about getting to the hospital. Hold up, J. Fly this is Rat. Them Concrete Click niggas just pulled a stunt at the studio... Nall, I wasn't there... They fucked up Bernie and smacked Tina around...Yeah, I'm pulling up now... Bring them jackhammers... Meet you there."

Rat pulled onto the block where the studio was located on, but he drove past it and slowly went around the block. They didn't see anything that looked out-of-place so Rat parked in the rear of the studio and they went through the back door of the studio building. In the lobby, Tina was holding a can of Pepsi to her eye as she righted a rubber potted plant.

"Tina," Rat said startling his receptionist.

"Damn, Rat you didn't have to sneak up on me!" Tina screeched. "Fuck! You scared the shit out of me!"

"Sorry. Let me see your eye."

Tina took the can down from her face. "I know it's got to be bad 'cause it hurts like hell. One of them, I know what he looks like. The one that hit me. While his partners was breaking the shit in studio 1 and 2, he was standing here the whole time with me, like he wasn't gone do nothing. The minute they was about to leave, he just said "lights out, white girl" and popped me one. When I woke up, they were gone. How's my eye, Rat?"

"Don't worry I'll buy you some sunglasses. My fault, Tina this is my man JC. JC, Tina."

"Nice to meet you, JC. I've heard a lot about you and it would have been great to meet you under different circumstances."

"Likewise," JC said.

"Tina, where's Bernie?" Rat asked.

"He's in Studio One lying on the couch. Near as I can tell his ribs may be broke or bruised and he's gonna need a few stitches in his head, but he'll live. He's whining like a bitch though."

"Think you could drop him off at the hospital for me?" Rat asked.

"Yes, it's on my way home, but he's going to need help to my car."

"Go pull your car up in the front and I'll be right out with Bernie."

While Tina went to get her car, Rat went to studio one with JC following him. From what Tina had told him on the phone, he'd expected the studio to be in shambles, but he still wasn't prepared for the way they destroyed his studio equipment. "Gotdammit, them motherfuckas!" Rat exclaimed. "Them fucking motherfuckas! I'm gone fucking kill them bitch ass motherfuckas!"

Slumped on the couch with a t-shirt swaddled around his head to stop the bleeding was the sound engineer Bernie.

"Hey Rat, stop hollering man," Bernie moaned. "My fucking head is pounding man."

"Sorry I wasn't here to help you, Berns," Rat said.

"That's alright man. I probably could'a got out of the shit without a scratch, but I had to let them young ass street punks know that they was wrong for coming up in your place of business with that bullshit. Young bastard slapped me in the ribs with that fucking bat. They don't feel broken, more than likely they're bruised. Then on top of that he gave me one to the nugget. I need to get to the hospital to get these ribs wrapped, and have them take a look at my head. Come help me up."

Rat walked over to the couch and helped Bernie to his feet. He was able to make it out of the studio and into Tina's white Solara under his own power.

Rat leaned down to the car when Bernie was safely in the passenger seat. "Tina, don't stop for him to get a beer or nothing. Take him straight to the hospital. Don't worry about coming in tomorrow to clean up."

"Don't worry, I wasn't," Tina said.

Rat pulled a knot of money from his pocket and peeled off a few hundred apiece for Tina and Bernie. "Bernie, take a cab home when you get out the hospital. Tina, you get you a good steak for the eye."

"Thanks," Tina said as she put her car in gear. "Now let me get out of here before Bernie bleeds on my leather seats and then you'll have to buy me a new car."

He stood for a minute and watched Tina zoom down the street and then he and JC went back inside the building. JC just stood and watched as Rat righted a few chairs in the lobby.

"Before you say anything J, I already know."

"I wasn't gonna say a word," JC said.

"I know, but if you were gonna say something it would have been about the fact that the studio is way more trouble than it's worth. Either that or you woulda said you told me so about handling the shit my way. I can agree with all that, but now these niggas is done pushed me too far."

JC picked up the office phone and placed it back on the receptionist desk. "So what are we gonna do now?" Rat righted another one of the lobby's rubber plants, when he straightened up he tossed JC the keys to his truck. "Right now, I'm going to handle the studio's business. I'm going to call the police and report a break-in, so I can give the police report to the insurance company so they can replace my boards and mics and shit. You can go to the crib."

"You sure you don't want me to wait for the police with you?"

"I know you don't want to be around the cops no more than I do, plus them motherfuckas might take all night getting here. Fly Ty and Big M is on they way, I'll make them stay with me and then drop me off at the crib."

"Young Gun, you sure? 'Cause I'll chill with you if you want me too."

"Nall, that's alright. Just let Chammy know what happened. I'm gone give Shaunny a call. I already hear her mouth now. Thanks for riding down here with me, J."

"Wadn't no thing," JC said as he walked towards the rear door. He stopped. "You know when you get up with these niggas I'm riding with you, right?"

"Look at you, Mr. Landlord, looking for some action. If your tenants could see you now."

"Fuck you," JC said as he pushed open the heavy steel back door. He walked out onto the small loading dock there as the door slammed behind him. He hit the auto starter on the remote as he walked down the stairs to the truck. As he rounded the back of the truck, the alley erupted in gunfire. Several slugs thwacked into the truck in front of JC, so he turned to run back to the other side of the truck. As he ran, JC heard the boom of the gun again and a slug drilled into the biceps of his right arm. Another boom and a bullet hit him in his hip. The next boom airmailed a slug into his back and he went face down in the alley, his hand splaying the truck's keys along the alley floor. As he lay there, JC knew he was hurt bad. As much as he wanted to get up and run, he just couldn't make his legs work. He heard footsteps approaching and knew it was his assailants coming to finish the job.

Just then the back door to the studio banged open and Rat rushed out onto the loading dock. He saw the two figures in all black with guns walking toward his truck. The two men saw Rat come out the door and opened fire at him. Rat returned fire and took cover. He threw a few shots the men's way and jumped down the steps to alley level. That's when he saw his best friend laid out in the alley. Firing blindly, Rat ran from cover to JC's side. The two men had taken cover deeper in the alley and were returning fire. In spite of his assailants' bullets, whizzing and zipping through the alley, Rat pulled JC behind the truck. The two assailants kept them pinned down behind the truck with strategic fire, managing to flatten both tires on the truck on the opposite side. Rat sent a few shots back at them, but the clip of his .40 cal was almost empty.

A car pulled into the opposite end of the alley and headed their way. Rat assumed that it was more ambushers and prepared to make his final stand. The ambushers shot at the car several times as it pulled adjacent to the rear of the studio and Rat's truck. Rat breathed a sigh of relief when he recognized the 22-inch rims on Big M's Chevy Caprice Classic. The Chevy slammed on its' brakes and the two front doors popped open. Fly Ty began spraying the alley in the ambushers' direction with a Mac 10. Big M's gun of choice was a .357 semi-auto and its' booming was terrifying alongside the staccato of the Mac 10. The ambushers' guns grew silent and they seemed to have obviously fled under the return of such firepower. After a few minutes of calm, Big M and Ty crept down the alley to make sure. When they returned Rat was sitting on the alley floor with JC's head on his lap.

Rat looked up at his two artists. "We got to get my man to some help. He's fucked up."

CHAPTER 12

Rat walked out of the emergency room entrance of the hospital and looked around. He spotted M and Ty over on a bench by the parking lot. He looked down at his clothes, they were covered in JC's blood but that was of no concern.

Ty and M stood up when they saw Rat approaching them. Rat waved them down and took a seat beside them. He bummed a cigarette off of Ty.

"How yo man looking?" Big M asked, his voice full of concern.

"Right now, I don't know," Rat answered, as he blew smoke into the night-time sky.

"He wasn't looking too good. Shit, I almost just got locked up. I'm trying to see about getting J some help and the police all in there asking a zillion questions. I told them motherfuckas I ain't know shit, that it was a driveby."

"Yeah, when I got shot, the cops was all in the ambulance asking me shit," Ty said. "I told them if you ain't finta stop the bleeding, then I ain't got shit to say."

"They wouldn't even let me stay with him," Rat mumbled.

Big M patted him on the shoulder. "Yeah, I know how that shit is. They kick you straight out the room. When my cousin was shot up, I was trying to stay in the room , but they threw my ass out of there. The saddest shit is when the doctor finally come out after you been waiting in one of them small ass rooms for like years and tell you that yo peoples is dead. That shit fuck you up. My auntie went crazy when they told us my cousin was dead. She started hitting me and scratching me like I got him killed. Shit, it was his girl's ex boyfriend that shot him up. I was just with him."

"Man, I 'member that shit there," Fly Ty said. "Yo whole family got into it over that shit. Yo mama was tweaking when she found out that yo aunt was trying to blame that shit on you. Believe it or not, the way yo cousin died is the reason that I don't trust no bitch 'til this day. Niggas be all in love with a bitch and the whole time she be riding some baby daddy ass nigga dick, still in love with the nigga and she'll set yo ass out. I'm telling you. I can't go. Not on no day."

Big M stood up and threw Ty a look. "Man, Rat don't wanna hear all that shit. R, is there something you want us to do, man? Rat."

Rat looked up. He had slipped into his own thoughts. "What?" he asked.

"I said is there anything me and Fly can do for you?"

"Nall, I'm good. Where y'all headed?"

Big M stretched. "Well, since you talking about police we want to get out of here 'cause we got them thumpers in the car. I was gone go over my crackhead ass uncle crib and pay him a few bucks to try and get that blood out my Chevy."

"If it don't come out, let me know and I'll get the interior done for you," Rat offered.

"Nall man, all that ain't necessary. The way my uncle scrub shit for a couple of sawbucks it should be cool. That nigga would get the dirt outta mud for a coupla cracks."

Rat stood up and gave his two young friends a half-hug handshake. "Thanks for coming through back there. I don't know what I woulda done without y'all."

"Ain't no thang," Fly Ty said. "You our mans. And we know you would do the same thing for us. If you need us, just bump us on the cell. Hope yo mans in there pull through."

"We gone keep an eye out for old boy you told us called this shit," Big M said. "I got family out in the Wild Wild that should be able to point me in that stud's direction. We'll see if we can't draw a bead on that nigga."

"If you get a line on that runt, don't touch him," Rat warned as he sat back down on the bench. "That nigga is all mine. I'll give y'all a call as soon as I hear something about J. Thanks again my niggas."

Rat watched his two artists head for their vehicle and get in the Chevy after a loud chirp of the alarm. Big M gave a soft toot of the car horn as they passed Rat and then he glided off into the night. Rat sat for a few more moments before pulling his cell phone out. He dialed a number and hesitated before pushing send. With one hand on his head, he pushed the send button and waited for Champagne to answer the telephone.

CHAPTER 13

Champagne and Shaunna hurried through the automatic sliding glass doors of the hospital's emergency room. Champagne's eyes were puffy from crying and Shaunna wasn't looking much better as they hurried down the hall to the nurses station.

"I need to know about Jonathan Collins!" Champagne demanded of the nurse on duty.

"Hold on one second," the nurse said without looking up from the medical forms she was filling out.

"I need to know right now, not in one second!" Champagne stated. "I don't have a damn second! I need to know what's going on right now!"

"Ma'am you're going to have to calm down. This is a hospital. We have other patients here, if you just give me a second."

"Bitch, what part of I don't have a second don't you understand!" Champagne snapped.

"Chammy!" Rat called out as he walked up behind them. He'd just come from the bathroom trying to clean himself up the best he could at the time. "Chammy, you got to chill, baby!"

"I am not about to chill," Champagne said with her voice wavering. "I want to know what's going on. I want to know how my man is doing."

Champagne crumpled against the desk sobbing. Rat and Shaunna guided her over to the waiting room area of the emergency room. When she was seated, Shaunna put her arms around Champagne and rocked her.

"What happened Rat?" Shaunna asked.

Rat took a seat beside Champagne and rubbed her back. "Well, by the time I got out in the alley behind the studio he was already down. Near as I could tell, he was walking to my truck and the niggas that tore my studio up was waiting out there to catch me slipping. They musta thought he was me and tried to put J down. I was inside trying to straighten up a few things and waiting on my guys when I heard the shots. I ran out there and got the niggas up offa him. My guys showed up and helped us out 'cause the niggas had us pinned down. If they wouldn'ta showed up our gooses would'a been cooked."

"Did you get a look at them?" Shaunna asked.

"Nall, but I know where the shit came from. Champagne, I swear if I woulda thought that JC could get hurt from this shit, I woulda left him at home."

"Like he would have stayed out of it," Champagne said, as she sat up and wiped at her tears. "Boy, you know how much he love you. He wouldn't have never let you fight whoever these bastards are by yourself. I don't blame you for nothing. You didn't shoot my man. I just want to know how he is. Did you talk to anybody?"

"Well the doctors wouldn't tell me shit. They just went to work on him. Then when I tried to get back there to check on him again, they gave me the immediate family spiel. I don't know what's going on and I don't want to think the worst, but I can't lie, Chammy, he was looking pretty bad when we brought him in. He wadn't moving and I could barely hear his heart beating and shit. I tried to stop the bleeding, but they were too many holes."

"Oh shit, what did they do to my man," Champagne cried out. Her hand flew up to her mouth and it was shaking. "How many times was he shot?"

"At least three or four," answered Rat softly. "That's near as I could tell, but some of those might be exit wounds."

"Exit wounds!" Champagne exclaimed as she jumped to her feet. "Somebody about to tell me something! I got to get back there and find out what's going on." Shaunna stood up and gently, but firmly pushed Champagne back into her seat. She said "Let me handle this one, baby. You're too worked up. I'll talk to the nurse and see what I can find out."

Champagne put up a struggle, but Rat held onto her firmly as Shaunna went back to the nurse's station. Shaunna returned shortly and took her seat.

"The nurse said she would find out what she could," Shaunna said. "She apologized if she seemed nonchalant, but she's gonna poke around for us. She's not promising anything, but she'll try."

"Thank you, Shaunna," Champagne breathed.

It was a long ten minutes before the nurse peeked into the waiting room and nodded them toward an empty hallway. The trio rushed to meet with her.

"I couldn't find out much," the nurse said. "They're still operating on him now. They stemmed the bleeding, but the nearest I can tell there must be a lot of damage to his organs. His vitals are real low, but at least they're there. I can keep checking in on him and updating you."

"Thank you, thank you," Champagne gasped as she hugged the nurse.

"Thank you so much. I'm really sorry for acting like a bitch, I just wanted to know what was going on.""It's okay, baby," the nurse said. "I've been an emergency room nurse in this city for twelve years so I've been called all kind of names and have run into attitudes way more intense than yours. Don't worry about it. The best thing you could do now is pray and cross your fingers. We've got some pretty good doctors in there working on him so they'll save him if he can be saved."

The nurse left and Champagne, Shaunna, and Rat returned to the waiting room. They took turns pacing, worrying, and praying for the next two hours. Finally the nurse came toward them with a smile.
"I just came to let you know that the worst is over," she said. "The doctor will come and talk to you in a minute, but for now he seems stable. I'm not saying that he's out of the woods yet, but they seem to have a handle on most of his injuries. They're going to do one more surgery and depending on how things look after that, they'll know which way to go. Now, I suggest you get you some coffee and dig in because it's going to be a long night."

The nurse squeezed Champagne's hand and hurried away, leaving

TRIPLE TAKE 2: CHAMPAGNE'S KISS

JC's friends to sweat it out for the next three hours. They took turns napping and worrying until finally a doctor came out of the emergency operating room and beckoned them into a small patient conference room. They followed the doctor into the conference room and took seats around the table. Rat and Shaunna both took hold of Champagne's hands as they waited for the doctor to give them the news.

"I'm Doctor Thayer and I just wanted to keep you abreast of what's going on with Jonathan. I have to tell you that the GSWs he received were pretty bad. It's lucky for your friend that he's a fighter. Right now he's in a coma."

Champagne gasped at the mention of the word 'coma'. "It's actually a drug-induced coma," Doctor Thayer said hurriedly. "We've found that when victims sustain injuries of this severity it's often best to let the body shut down all but the necessary functions, until the body's systems can begin to recover on their own. Also it allows us to manage the patient's pain without administering such high doses of the pain relievers. The biggest problem is that Jonathan experienced deep and severe tissue and nerve damage. He should recover just nicely from the majority of his bullet wounds, barring infection, but the bullet that hit him in the back did the most damage. As a result he has suffered some nerve damage. We don't know how extensive the damage is and we won't know until we run some more tests. Right now he's being admitted to the critical care ward and you'll be able to look in on him shortly. Be prepared. He looks pretty bad, but he's alive and we'll do everything in our power to make sure that he stays that way."

Doctor Thayer got up to leave and Rat rushed from his seat to shake the doctor's hand.

"Thanks a lot, Dr. Thayer," Rat said gratefully. "Thanks for taking care of my man. We really appreciate that."

"You're all very welcome," responded Dr. Thayer. "The next few days are going to be the hardest, but hopefully the worst is behind him. I'll be the physician in charge once he's admitted, so I'll know everything that is going on with Mr. Collins. Right now I have to get cleaned up. Goodbye and good luck."

Champagne, Rat, and Shaunna returned to the emergency room waiting area to wait until the nurse informed them that JC had been admitted to the critical care ward. Champagne had stopped crying and appeared to be optimistic, but the minute JC's mother showed up with Ronald, her hysterics started all over again.

CHAPTER 14

Shaunna removed the few pictures and personal items from her locker and dumped them in her bag. Her toilet articles she kept out until she returned from the shower and got dressed. Once she was ready to go, she took a moment to look around the dressing room. She heaved her bag onto her shoulder and started to leave, but she stopped herself. She took a seat and decided to wait for Champagne to come off the floor.

Champagne came into the dressing room laughing and joking with one of the girls, a dancer named Kitten.

"I think that nigga just nutted on hisself," Champagne told the other dancer.

Kitten was wearing shiny silver thigh high boots with a silver thong and garter that looked absolutely brilliant in contrast with her smooth dark skin. "Why you say that?" Kitten asked.

"Well, when I finished dancing for him, he had a wet spot on his pants and he looked like he wanted to put his thumb in his mouth and go to sleep."

Kitten laughed and she went to her locker. "That's yo fault. You put that thang on that nigga. Now he got to go to the bathroom and use the wall dryer to dry up his pants."

"I don't care," Champagne said. "Just as long as he don't get none of that sticky icky on me. What's up, Shaunny? Did you have a good night? Them niggas was throwing their money away tonight."

Shaunna looked up at Champagne. Her fierce green eyes seemed to take in every detail of her friend and then her eyes softened.

"Get dressed, Chammy," Shaunna told her. "I'm gone wait on you. I need to talk to you."

"Huh, what's up, girl?"

"Get dressed, I'll wait."

Champagne gathered her toiletries and towel and went to take a *shower. As she showered, she wondered what the look on Shaunna's face meant and what she wanted to talk about. Silently she prayed that her friend wasn't going to confess that she was gay and in love with her or anything like that. She would just have to lose a friend if that was what Shaunna was planning, because she didn't flow like that. Thinking about what Shaunna wanted to tell her plagued her, so she purposely took as long as possible showering and drying off. When she went back to her locker wrapped in her towel, she hoped that Shaunna would be gone and she wasn't there. With a slight sigh of relief, Champagne dressed and said goodbye to the other girls.*

As she went out the back door of the club to the parking lot, she caught sight of her car—her new car. It was a champagne colored Corvette with dark tinted windows. Shaunna was sitting on the rear of the Corvette.

"Gotdamn, Champagne, you taking all day."

Champagne walked to her car and unlocked it. She put her gym bag in the rear and took a seat. Shaunna came around and climbed in. She just sat there looking at Champagne until Champagne grew uncomfortable.

"What Shaunna?"

"I don't know how to tell you this. I didn't think the day would ever come that I would feel like this, but..."

Champagne put her hands up. "Stop please, Shaunna. Please don't say what I think you about to say. I just couldn't take it. You're my friend and I love you, but I just don't go that way. I'm sorry if that's what you're feeling, but I'm not gay."

To Champagne's surprise, Shaunna burst into laughter. She laughed until tears rolled out of her eyes.

"What the hell is so funny?" asked Champagne.

"What, you thought I was about to tell you that I'm in love with you and I want you?"

"I didn't know, that's why I tried to head you off at the pass."

Shaunna shook her head. "Girl, this dancing shit got your head messed up. You need to get away from this shit."

TRIPLE TAKE 2: CHAMPAGNE'S KISS

"My head ain't messed up," Champagne protested. "That's what's going on around here. I was hoping it wasn't that, but the way you was looking all strange and shit, I didn't know what to think."

"Well, my problem is that I'm not really good at what I've got to do and that's say goodbye. I've always hated saying goodbye. Usually I just leave in order to avoid that, but because I said that I was gone change and start at least letting my friends know what was up with me, I stayed tonight to tell you that I was leaving."

"You leaving the club?"

"Not just the club, I'm leaving town. I'm going home to Chicago. My grandmother that helped raise me is real sick and she doesn't really have anybody there for her. My brother is there, but I think he's getting high. My granny is telling me that things is coming up missing out of her house, even her medication."

"What you going to do for money in Chicago? You thinking about dancing there too?"

A look crossed Shaunna's face like she had a bad taste in her mouth. "Hell no. I'm through with this shit! I'm going to get a regular job. I've got more than enough money saved to hold up for quite awhile. That's why I drive a Corolla, not a Corvette. This part of my life is over. If I never see another man with a handful of singles thinking he's purchasing my soul it won't be long enough. I hated doing this and I'm not dumb enough to think I can do it for the rest of my life, like some of these bitches. That's why I wanted to talk to you before I left. I actually like you, Chammy. I like you a lot. I don't think you're like the others here, but you're not far from them. I almost wish that you would leave with me because I'm scared to leave you behind."

"Scared?" asked Champagne in total awe. "You scared? What you heard something or something?"

"No. Just listen. I've been dancing for years now. I've seen what this world can do to a beautiful girl like you. To them, you're just a body, a beautiful body, but a body none-the-less. This world will chew you up *and spit you out. They love to take your spirit and make you into what they want to, and then when they've used you all up, they cast you by the wayside. I think of places like this as Sodom and Gomorrah. That's why when I leave I'm never looking back. The reason I wanted to leave without saying goodbye is so you would be easy to forget. I don't want to be in Chicago wondering what you're doing and if you're alright."*

"I'm gone be alright, girl. I learned my lesson about how far to go and you taught me that, Shaunna. I'm going to continue my self-defense training and I'm not going to fall into the traps that I've heard the other girls fall into. I know that I'm going to do this for awhile, but believe me I'm going to have my eyes open looking for my opportunity to get out of here too."

"Well, I'll be checking up on you from time to time. And you better remember that I might be a Chi-town girl, but Chocolate City is my city too, so I'll hear if you ain't acting right out here. Now give me a hug."

Champagne obliged and they held on tight for a few moments. When they finally broke their embrace both women had tears in their eyes.

"Now take me to get some tacos in this fast ass car before we both get to blubbering," Shaunna said.

Champagne wiped her eyes and nose and then fired the ignition on her American muscle car. "None for me," Champagne said. "You just quit. Me I'm still a dancer." They both laughed as the Corvette roared out of the parking lot.

CHAPTER 15

Rat tossed his towel on the bench beside the penthouse's deluxe hot tub out on the terrace. He used the controls to turn on the water jets as he shivered slightly in the chilly early evening air. He checked his inventory before he climbed into the heated water: cell phone within reach, cigarettes, beer, a blunt, and a music industry magazine. Satisfied that he had his Jacuzzi survival kit together, he submerged himself up to his chest in the water. The jets of heated water on his weary body forced a sigh from him. For the past few days he'd been at the hospital with JC, taking turns sleeping in chairs and on the floor, but he'd finally decided that enough was enough and went to the penthouse to relax for a few hours before returning to the hospital.

He'd tried to suggest to Champagne that she was the one who needed to go home and rest, but she wasn't hearing it. Champagne had pretty much taken up residence at the hospital, even showering there. Shaunna had taken to running the business with Ronald while they stood watch over JC. JC's injuries were doing surprisingly well by the doctors' accounts and soon they would be bringing him out of his coma. Rat wanted to be there when JC woke up, but for now he needed to unkink the muscles in his back and then stretch out across his bed for a nice long nap.

Rat smoked his blunt and thumbed through his magazine as he drank his beer. The magazine held his attention though it was mostly filled with ads for car rims and clothes. Soon he found himself getting sleepy and he put his head back on the Jacuzzi's headrest and closed his eyes. He thought that he was just closing his eyes for a few moments, but it was actually two hours later when the incessant chirping of his cell phone awakened him. He sat up and grabbed for his phone almost knocking it into the Jacuzzi. He caught it though and looked at the caller ID. It was Big M.

Rat flipped open his phone and held it to his ear. "Yo, M what's up?" The news that Big M gave him made Rat sit straight up.

"For real? You kidding, right? How many of them is it? That's all, I got him... I'm headed that way just keep a eye on that nigga and I'm there... Don't touch him, I got him... Follow him wherever he go... I'm on the way."

Rat closed his cell phone and catapulted out of the hot tub. He dried himself extra fast and ran to his bedroom to get dressed. In his bedroom, he dressed in a pair of black jeans, a black hoodie, and all black Air Maxes. In his walk-in closet, he pulled a Timberland shoe box off the highest shelf and put it on his bed. He then went to his dresser and opened one of the drawers. Taking a pair of black leather gloves from the dozen or so pairs there, and also a pair of chalk-less surgical gloves too, Rat then sat on the bed and opened the shoe box. From it, he extracted two nine millimeter handguns. Into one of them he fitted an extra-long 30 shot ammunition clip. The other was loaded with a regular clip. Both guns were loaded to capacity with hollow-point ammunition—bullets that expanded from the air rushing through the head before it hit the intended target.

He shoved his equipment into a book bag and left the penthouse, taking the private elevator to the underground parking garage. In the rear of the garage was a pale blue late model Ford Taurus. The four door sedan, though it was rarely driven until times such as this, instantly purred to life the minute Rat turned the ignition key. While letting the engine idle for a few moments, Rat tucked his weaponry into the Taurus' stash spot. He took out his cell phone and called Big M back. "What that nigga doing?" asked Rat the second Big M answered. "Okay... Yeah, so he up there trying to impress some bitch, huh? Well, I hope she was worth it, 'cause she just got my man snuffed... Don't do nothing, M... Even if they leave just follow them... Nall, I'll be there in a minute... That's right on Sibley ain't it... Yeah, I know exactly where that's at... Alright."

TRIPLE TAKE 2: CHAMPAGNE'S KISS

Rat tossed his cell phone on the seat next to him and put the Taurus in gear. He glided out of the parking garage and headed for the expressway. Twenty minutes later he turned onto Sibley Boulevard and after that he pulled into the parking lot of the strip club. The club was obviously popular because the parking lot was packed. Rat parked his car near the rear of the lot and made sure that he could make a speedy exit if necessary. He removed his 30-shot from the stash spot and then cut the engine. He picked up his cell phone and called Big M back.

"I'm outside in the parking lot. Tell Ty to stay in there watching that nigga and you come out here."

Minutes later from his vantage point, Rat saw Big M come out of the club and look around. Rat blinked the headlights twice to catch M's attention--it worked and Big M hurried over to the Taurus. He slipped into the passenger seat.

"Damn, R what the fuck is that?" Big M asked as he noticed Rat's gun. "That motherfucka look crazy!"

Rat grinned and rubbed his weapon with his gloved hand. "This is what I like to call a dirty thirty. Now what that nigga doing in there?"

"Dude in there with his people playing heavyweight. Popping bottles and throwing around his little cash. What's the plan? We got thumpers in the car."

"Ain't no plan, M," Rat said. "I don't want y'all to do nothing, but what y'all been doing."

"What you say, we ain't on this?"

"That's what I'm saying. No disrespect young homie, but I do my dirt all by my lonely. That way I know if something go wrong then I got to take the weight and I don't have to worry about no rappees on my case. And I know I ain't gone tell on myself."

"What you saying we tricks?" Big M asked slightly offended.

"Damn, Rat it's nice to know that's what you think of us."

"M, that ain't what I'm saying. Don't even take it that way. Look at it like this. If you had to handle some business like this who would you want with you, your man you been down with for years, Fly Ty, or some dude you just met? My man that I be on shit like this with is laid up in the hospital in a coma 'cause of that little nigga in there. My whole crew is killers and I know what they gone do in a pinch and they know what I'm gone do in a pinch. Like I said I ain't trying to front on you, but I'm gone handle this by myself. I appreciate y'all help though. Y'all got me on this nigga's ass, now I'm gone put him in the dirt."

Big M was silent for a moment. "I understand, R. I see where you coming from. I would rather be with my man than with a stranger. I know this is personal 'cause these niggas stretched yo man out, but just know me and Ty will ride with you if you want us to. Nigga, you feed us and this nigga, Con, tried to pull it with you. So if you need us, we on it."

"I take it these niggas is in this big ass van right here with Concrete Click written all over," Rat said. He nodded toward a black and gray high-top conversion van covered with huge stickers emblazoned with the logo "Concrete Click".

"That shouldn't be too hard to follow."

"Idiots."

"What you want me and Ty to do?"

"Go back inside and just chill. Keep an eye for when them niggas leave. I don't like it up here, so I ain't gone pull it here. Plus, I don't know what the niggas he with is on. I ain't gonna underestimate them niggas. I ain't got no time to be trying to win no shootout with two, three niggas in the middle of the suburbs at night. I don't want to have to get nobody but Con. When they leave here, I'm gone see where they go and when I get a chance, I'm gone jump down on him."

Big M opened the car door and got out. "I'll let Ty know what's happening, but he ain't gone like it no more than me. We'll keep our phones clear and the minute it looks like you need some help, just hit us up."

"Got it," Rat said. "And thanks for finding this nigga for me." Rat watched Big M go back inside the gentlemen's club and he prepared himself to wait. As he waited he smoked cigarettes and answered his cell phone in intervals. Almost three hours later, he received a call from Fly Ty letting him know that Con and his men were leaving. He sat up quickly and stretched as best he could before he started the Taurus. Sure enough Con and his followers walked from the club into the parking lot. They were laughing loudly and appeared to be quite drunk. Con had his arm around a tall, light-skinned girl's neck that dwarfed him. The girl had an athletic build and was wearing a skin-tight mini-skirt. They all climbed into the van and it left the parking lot heading east on Sibley.

Half a block behind the van, Rat followed them slowly. He wasn't worried about losing such a large vehicle covered in decals in the late night traffic. He followed them to a J and J's Fish restaurant and parked across the street. From his car, Rat easily continued his surveillance as Con and his boys ordered their food in the well-lit small fish and chicken place. Half an hour later they all climbed back into the van carrying white plastic bags containing their food. The van pulled off and two miles later, it stopped in front of a small motel.

The motel wasn't in the best of shape and the entrance to the office was on the street, but the rooms were split into two floors. The doors to each room opened facing the parking lot which was only a few steps from the first floor room doors. The girl got out of the van and went into the office. Minutes later she exited the office carrying a room key.

Boldly Rat pulled into the parking lot past the Concrete Click van. He found a space near the rear exit of the parking lot and slid into it. He cut the engine and killed the lights and watched as Con got out of the van. The van kicked rocks onto several cars as it swerved out of the parking lot. Con carried the bags of food as he followed the tall girl up the concrete steps to the second floor. The second they were out of sight in the stairwell, Rat slung wide his car door, leaving it wide open as he ran from the car to the back stairwell. He took the steps three at a time to the second floor. As he came out on the second floor, Con and his girl were half the length of the tier away and standing in front of a room door. The girl was trying to unlock the door, but Con was grinding on her butt making it difficult for her. Rat sprinted toward Con, who looked up when he heard Rat approaching. Con saw the man running toward him dressed in all black wearing a mask, and sobered up real quick. He threw his food in the man's direction and turned to run back the way he'd come up the stairs.

Rat dodged the food easily and gave chase to Con. As he passed the unsuspecting girl, he smacked her in the back of her head with the pistol. The blow sent her crashing through the room door and into the motel room. Rat continued past her and raised his weapon. He fired several shots into Con's back just as he was reaching the stairwell. The impact of the slugs slapping into Con's back made him flip down the stairs. Rat ran to the stairwell where he saw Con crawling through filth and urine on the first level trying to make it to the next level of steps. He jumped down the stairs two at a time until he was on the level with Con. In the brick stairwell ten more shots rang out as Rat blew large holes into Con's head and torso. Knowing that Con was done, Rat descended the steps and headed for the parking lot.

As he made for his car, a security guard stuck his head out of the office. Rat aimed and fired several shots at the brick wall by the office, not near enough to hit the guard, but close enough to send the guard back inside scurrying for cover. With the headlights off, Rat glided out of the parking lot and turned down the first available side street. He went up, down and around on the side streets, but made sure that he was always heading west as he made his way back to the expressway.

On the expressway, he expelled the 30-shot clip from the murder weapon and slowed down as he crossed the bridge that spanned the Calumet River. After peeking into his rearview mirror to make sure he didn't see any police, he flung the gun out of the window and into the river.

Back at the penthouse, Rat went onto the terrace and poured some charcoal into the large barbecue grill. They owned a gas grill, but he would need the heat from the charcoal for what he planned to do. He stripped down to his boxing shorts, putting every article of clothing, even his shoes into the barbecue pit and then doused them all with lighter fluid. He lit the fire and a cigarette with the same match and smoked while he watched the clothes burn. Rat noticed that the sun was just beginning its' journey into the sky over Lake Michigan as he picked up his cell phone and dialed a number. Dipping back into the penthouse, he poured himself a healthy shot of Remy, grabbed a bottle of water, and returned to the terrace. He didn't expect his party to answer as he climbed back into the hot tub, but Big M answered after four rings.

"You sound like you sleep," Rat commented.

"I'm good," Big M grunted.

"I ain't gone hold you. Tell Fly I disconnected dude's service. I'll check for y'all tomorrow. Thanks again."

He hung the phone up and picked up a blunt from the lip of the hot tub and lit it. Lost in a swirl of thoughts, weed, and Remy, Rat lounged in the hot tub and watched the sun climb into the sky.

CHAPTER 16

In the garage behind Nat's house, Nat and Dale faced off with one another in the middle of the floor. Nat had pulled his car out of the garage so they would have room. Each of them was holding a pitbull by the collar while making noises to goad the dogs at one another. They let the dogs lunge close enough to one another to almost touch and then they pulled them back. The battle scarred dog Nat was holding was especially ferocious, snapping and slobbering trying to get at the dog that Dale was holding. Several times when the dogs got too close to one another, Nat's dog almost succeeded in grabbing hold of Dale's dog.

"Watch that shit!" Dale yelled. "You doing that shit on purpose, man."

"What?" Nat asked innocently.

"You know what the fuck you doing! You trying to let yo dog hit my puppy on the slide, nigga!"

"I don't know what you talking about. If I wanted to let my bull hit that sooner, then I'd just let her go. Quit whining nigga. That's why yo dog is soft now, 'cause the owner soft. Can't no pussycat raise no pitbull."

Dale pulled his dog back and rubbed the puppy's chest. "Fuck what you talking about. You acting like I'm a new nigga. I know what the fuck Widow will do to a full-grown dog, so I know what the fuck she would do to my puppy."

Nat laughed. "I don't know why you keep calling that big grown ass shit-eater a puppy. You ain't got to worry, I won't let Widow get hold of Fido there. You said that you wanted some help training that pooch, so that's what I'm doing."

"Get the fuck outta here, Nat. Nigga, I know you. I done seen you do that shit to other motherfuckas. Act like you just gone let the dogs bump into each other and then the next thing you know Widow is ripping they

106

dog in half. You won't get mine like that. I just look stupid."

Leaving Nat behind laughing, Dale led his dog out of the garage. He let his puppy get a drink of water from the water hose in Nat's backyard and then he walked him up and down the alley until the puppy relieved himself. When the puppy was through doing his business, Dale placed him in the rear of his customized high top conversion van parked in the vacant lot alongside Nat's house before returning to the backyard. In the backyard, Nat was watching Widow jump and hang from an old car tire that was suspended from a tree branch. She would catch the tire in her mouth and lock on it. Nat was sitting on an old van bench seat, smoking a blunt. Dale took a seat beside him and waited for him to pass the weed.

"This regular weed?" Dale asked after inhaling the blunt.

"Yeah that's reg-o," Nat answered lazily.

"I noticed you been smoking a lot of reg-o lately. What's that about? You done gave up on the 'dro?"

"Man, fuck that loudpack shit," Nat said. "I been hearing that that shit got all type of chemicals and spray and shit on it. A nigga was telling me that shit got PCP or LSD on it. He say that some of the hillbillys that be growing that shit be spraying roach spray and shit on it, knowing that niggas gone be smoking that shit. They be trying to fuck us up on some subliminal shit. That's why I switched back to regular old weed."

"I did hear that some niggas get high off that loud and lose they mind," Dale commented as he handed the blunt back to Nat. "And that shit be too damn high anyway. Ten, twenty dollars for a fucking blunt. Shit, I'll stick to smoking regular weed too." The pair of men fell silent as they passed the blunt and watched Widow swing back and forth on the tire. Widow was as happy as a pitbull could be locking on the tire and swinging back and forth. One time she jumped for the tire and miscalculated the arc of the swing, missed it and landed on her head. She scrambled to her feet to look around and then jumped up and caught the tire. Nat and Dale laughed their asses off at Widow's miss. Soon they fell silent again as the haze of the drugs captured their minds.

Dale spoke first. "Nat, tell me you got some beers in the fridge. That fuckin' weed gave me cottonmouth like a motherfucka."

"It's a couple in there. Bring me one too."

Dale went and got the beers. He handed Nat one before retaking his seat.

"Where's Mar and Julie?" Nat asked after taking a swig of beer.

"Them niggas went to the boat to gamble. They been spending more and more time out there throwing away they money. That's why them niggas always need more cash 'cause they blow so much dough."

"Man, fuck that gambling shit," Nat said. "I used to gamble 'member. Don't nobody know that that gambling shit is the reason I'm a stickup man to this day. I 'member after my dad left me the house when he ran away with that funky crackhead bitch of his, I had enough money to pay the mortgage and shit, but my stupid ass tried to get in the dice game and pump up my cash. Them slick rolling niggas took every cent I had. I went home and thought about it. I got the gun my daddy left and went back and took everything them niggas had. I had to shoot two niggas, but I didn't care 'cause I needed that mortgage money back. After that I said I'll cut out the middle man, let other niggas gamble and then I'll take what they got. I ain't never lost since." Dale belched long and loud. "I feel like you. I ain't never giving no gambling motherfucka my cash. I save my dough for a rainy day. Shit, me and Mar been taking care of each other all of our lives so I know what it feel like to not have shit and I don't ever wanna feel that shit again, if I can help it. Whatever happened to that big stain that you said you had for us?"

"Oh that's in the works," Nat answered. "That shit is being worked out as we speak. I'm telling you this is the one that's going to put us over the motherfuckin' top. This shit is huge!"

"It must be big. I bet it ain't bigger than the shit we took that stud Peno for. That nigga damn near had a hundred and thirty in cash. Now that's the kind of shit I'm talking about. That's that big money. I need another hit like that."

"That wadn't shit," Nat scoffed. "I told you, on this one, I'm trying to walk with six figures off of. And this one is gone be so sweet. We ain't gonna have to do none of the footwork that we had to put in on the other jobs. This cash is just gone walk into our hands and all we got to do is hold out our hands to catch it. This is gone be the sweetest one yet."

"Get the fuck outta here. Ain't no cash just gonna walk up and jump into our pockets. You must got this shit set up pretty sweet if you saying it's like that."

"Nigga, I'm telling you it's like that and Nat don't lie 'bout no money."

"So what we gotta do?" Dale asked. "Come on Nat, wire me to the shit. This shit is killing me trying to figure out what you got planned."

"Curiosity kilt the cat nigga. Just lay back and let me take care of this shit. When it's time to move on the shit I'll fill you all in on what the play is. Until then just think about the way you gone spend all that money. Now quit asking me all them questions and go get that mutt out yo van and let Widow teach her a few tricks."

Dale laid back and sipped his beer. "Hell nall, nigga. That fuckin' crazy dog of yours ain't finta eat my puppy. You a sick ass nigga, you the one that sold me that damn puppy and now you trying to let yo dog kill him. If anything, nigga, fire up some more of that reg-o, 'cause that shit got me feeling nice."

Nat smiled as he pulled another blunt from behind his ear.

CHAPTER 17

"Rat," Champagne called from the doorway of Rat's bedroom. "Rat, get up man."

Rat heard Champagne's voice calling him through the fog of his sleep and he jumped up. "Don't throw no water on me, Chammy! I'm up, I'm up."

Champagne laughed. "Boy, I wasn't about to throw water on you so you can quit acting like that."

"I'm just making sure," Rat said as he sat on the side of the bed.

"I don't even feel like getting wet, so I got my ass up."

Champagne came all the way into Rat's bedroom and sat on the end of the bed.

"They let JC come out of the coma," she announced with a sigh.

"He woke?"

"Well, he stirred around early this morning, but he hasn't woken up all the way yet. The doctor said that that's normal, and that he will be coming around. They're saying that he's coming along splendidly, whatever that means, but they still don't know the extent of the nerve damage. He should be opening his eyes soon, though, if we're lucky."

"So what are you doing here?" Rat asked. "I would'a thought that they would'a had to drag you away with wild horses to not be there when J opens his eyes."

"Oh believe me I'm gone be there. I just came here to get myself cleaned up. I didn't want my man waking up and seeing me looking like this. That would probably have sent him back into a coma."

"You ain't lying, Chammy. You is popped. I ain't never seen you looking this busted. You done had that scarf tied down on yo head for days now." Champagne self-consciously fingered the silken scarf tied around her hair. Then she seemed to think better of it and punched Rat in his arm. "Hey you popped!"

TRIPLE TAKE 2: CHAMPAGNE'S KISS

Rat grabbed his arm. "Ouch, Chammy. You better keep yo damn hands offa me."

"Well, you better shut up then. I got the right to be looking busted, I been at that damn hospital for days. That's alright though because when my man see me he gone see me looking like a star. So don't you worry about it. I'm headed for the shop to get right right now."

"Before you leave make sure you get fifty dollars from me."

"For what?" Champagne asked.

"To tip them at the beauty shop for taking you and doing us all a favor."

After that quip, Rat had to jump up and run into the bathroom to avoid being socked by Champagne. After a few minutes of her berating him from the bedroom side of the bathroom door, Rat begged for a truce. She agreed so he came out the bathroom.

As he moved towards his walk-in closet, he said, "I think I'll get dressed and run down to the hospital. I'll sit with J just in case he wake up while you gone. I had actually planned to get up this morning and come down there, but I was tired as hell. If you wouldn't have woke me up, I'd still be out."

"Shaunny called me earlier and let me know you were here getting some sleep. She wanted to wake you, but I told her to let you sleep and that when I came home I'd check in on you."

Rat laid a pair of jeans and a track jacket on the bed. "I didn't even hear her come in. I know that I was all over the bed. She probably slept on the chaise lounge. I know she been complaining about the bed, talking about it hurt her back. Well, I'm finta hit the water so I can get up outta here."

Before leaving the room, Champagne acted like she was going to punch Rat again, but instead she gave him a hug and kiss on the forehead. "See you later, you crazy fool. I'm going to get my hair done."

Behind her back, Rat wiped his forehead. Champagne was almost to the bedroom suite she shared with JC when Rat appeared at his bedroom door.

"Chammy," he said softly.

"Yeah?"

"Dude that did that to J... I took care of that."

"Thanks, Young Gun," Champagne said. "I knew that you would. There wasn't a doubt in my mind. I knew you wouldn't rest until you did, that's why I never gave you no lip about JC being hit."

Feeling less guilty about JC's plight, Rat showered and dressed. On the way out of his room, he grabbed his .40 caliber and tucked it into the back of his jeans. He yelled out to Champagne that he was leaving and left the penthouse in the private elevator. His Infiniti truck was still in the shop getting the bullet holes removed and being painted so he drove his black Mercury Marauder. He stopped at a Wendy's for a couple of burgers, fries, and some chili and then he drove to the hospital. At the hospital, he didn't check in at the nurses' station; he went straight to JC's room.

JC was sleeping peacefully. They had removed the feeding tube from his throat and Rat had to admit that he did look like he was just taking a nap. He opened the food bags and put a burger and fries on JC's tray table. He knew it was a stretch that his best friend would be ready for a burger, but if he did wake up and he wanted it, it would be there for him. Before he sat down to eat, Rat took his Playstation Portable out of his pocket and popped in a movie. With the PSP's headphones in his ears, he settled down to watch The Longest Yard and eat his meal.

When he was finished eating, Rat went outside to have a smoke. As he smoked he chatted it up with a few people who were also in the small space outside the hospital allotted for smokers. He left the smokers and went to check if the hospital gift shop had any new music industry magazines. There were several new magazine issues on the shelves, but he only liked one. He purchased the magazine and went back upstairs to JC's private room. As he was reading an interesting article about the Southern movement in the rap industry, he heard JC moan.

TRIPLE TAKE 2: CHAMPAGNE'S KISS

Rat put his magazine down and went over to JC's bed. To his surprise, JC was lying there with his eyes wide open. Instantly a wide grin broke on Rat's face.

"My nigga," Rat said happily. "My nigga, Killa J. I see you with us, baby. You here ain't you?"

JC didn't respond, he just kept staring straight ahead.

Rat leaned down by JC's ear, as he did the back of his track jacket lifted up enough for the handle of his gun to be exposed. He put his hand on JC's forehead to shield his eyes from the fluorescent lights. In JC's ear, he whispered, "That's alright Killa J, you ain't got to say nothing. Just as long as I know you here I'm good. I'm glad that you still with us. I'm sorry how this shit turned out, man. You gotta know that I would trade places with you. You my brother and I love you man. The nigga that started all this bullshit, I popped his motherfuckin' balloon for him. That nigga is done, so don't you worry about it none. You just take your time and get better. Concentrate on getting better, J. Soon you'll be playing with the twins and bossing them Mexicans around that work on yo buildings. Champagne gone be happy as hell too. Man, that woman love you, she been here every minute. She just left to go..." JC's hospital room door opened and the attending nurse strode in the room. The short, middle-aged Black nurse was carrying several items and didn't initially see Rat. When she noticed him leaning over her patient she almost dropped the things she was carrying in her arms.

"What are you doing?" she exclaimed as she took in the scene. "Who are you and what are you doing to my patient?"

Without straightening up, Rat peered at the nurse. He had never seen this nurse before, though he'd been here almost every minute since JC had been here.

"I wasn't doing nothing," Rat said slightly defensively. "This is my man and he just woke up and I was talking to him. Who are you? I ain't never seen you before."

"This is my patient now," the nurse stated, "and I've never seen you before. You're saying that this is your boyfriend?"

Rat stood up. "What did you ask me?"

"You said that this is your man. Does that mean that he's your life partner?"

"Saying this is my man means that he's my friend, my homie, my brother. You sure ask a lot of questions? Where's the other nurses that usually be here?"

The nurse came forward to put down the items she'd been carrying on JC's nightstand on the opposite side of the bed from Rat and her eyes bugged almost out of her head. She put the things down and swiftly backed toward the door.

"What's wrong with you, lady?" Rat asked with a puzzled look on his face. "What happened? Did I do something wrong?"

"No, no I'll be right back I forgot something," the nurse said hurriedly as she slipped out the door.

"J, you see this shit," Rat said. "Damn, she watch too much damn TV. They got this shit where you can't even say you love yo homie without people thinking that's your life partner. Well Chammy better get up here quick, 'cause I'm in the rap game, a rumor like that will kill my record label. Just kidding, man fuck that broad. I got crazy love for you. I'm glad that you're coming around. It sounds like here come some doctors or shit to check you out."

Rat had heard a commotion in the hallway outside of JC's room and he went to the door to check it out. When he opened the door there were several armed members of the hospital security staff and two Chicago Police officers. The nurse who left the room minutes ago was talking to the officers and when Rat opened the room door and looked out, the police and security officers all drew their weapons and pointed them at Rat.

"Get on the fucking ground!" One officer yelled. "Put your hands on your head and get down on the ground!"

"What?" Rat said as he raised his hands. "What happened? What did she tell y'all?"

"Get down on the ground and I'm not going to tell you again!"

Rat weighed his options and knew instantly the situation could only go bad or worse. "Alright, alright, I'm getting down. Don't fucking shoot me."

When Rat lowered himself to his knees and eventually to his chest, several of the officers rushed forward and secured him.

"Gun! Gun," one of the policemen shouted as he snatched the gun from the back of Rat's pants. Quickly the other officers cuffed his hands behind his back, drug him to his feet and searched his person. They held onto his money, keys, and cell phone when they forced him into a chair by the nursing station.

"Watch that shit!" Rat snarled. "Ain't nobody resisting so y'all can cut the bullshit. Loosen up these cuffs too. I can't even feel my fuckin' wrists!"

"Shut the fuck up!" an officer snapped. "You'll get them off when you get to the station." The police officer walked back over to the nurse who was cringing in fear by the nurses' station. The tall, dark-skinned officer looked down at her with a kindly look.

"Now tell us again what you saw," the officer told her.

"That man was standing over my patient and it looked like he was holding his hand over my patient's nose and mouth," the nurse stated averting her eyes from Rat. "It didn't look right when I walked in the room because he jumped and acted nervously."

"Bitch, you lying!" Rat shouted causing the nurse to flinch. "Ain't no fucking body jump, bitch! I had my hand on his forehead and when you came in the room I was talking to my man!"

"Shut it up," the officer growled, before turning back to the nurse.

"Now what were you saying, Ma'am?"

"Like I said he was acting suspiciously."

"Have you ever seen this man before?"

"No, my patient had three visitors in the last two days. Two African-

American women and one clean-cut African-American man. He wasn't dressed anything like this thug here."

"Bitch, fuck you!" Rat snapped. "Just 'cause I ain't clean cut then I'm a thug! Fuck you!"

The other policeman grabbed Rat by the collar of his jacket. "We've told you several times to watch your gotdamn mouth! This is a hospital! Show some respect you asshole! Now shut the hell up!"

"Man, fuck you! That bitch is lying on me! You better let go of my damn jacket!"

"I said shut up!" the policeman repeated an inch from Rat's nose.

"Whatever man," Rat said, turning his head. "That bitch is lying and she bullshitting. I ain't trying to hear this shit."

"Get him out of here!" the policeman interviewing the nurse commanded.

The policeman holding Rat's collar dragged him roughly to his feet and propelled him toward the elevator. The security guards backed up the officer.

"Sorry about that Ma'am," the other officer said. "Please continue."

"He looked like he was trying to kill my patient," the nurse said.

"That bitch lying!" Rat fumed. "How the fuck I look trying to kill my best friend! Stupid lying ass bitch!"

When the elevator opened, the policeman shoved Rat into the car. He had tears of frustration in his eyes as he rode down to the lobby. Outside the hospital's entrance, he was placed into the rear of a blue-and-white police cruiser. Ten minutes later, the other officer walked out of the doors to the cruiser. He shook hands with the hospital security guards before getting in the police car.

The officer turned to Rat. "You're under arrest. You have the right to remain silent. Anything you say can and will be used against you in a court of law. You have the right to an attorney. If you cannot afford an attorney, one will be appointed to you."

"What am I under arrest for Barney Fife?" Rat asked.

"For starters, attempted murder and carrying a concealed weapon. That and any thing else we can think of."

As the police cruiser was exiting the hospital parking lot, Rat saw Shaunna and Ronnie pulling into the parking lot in Shaunna's Infiniti. "Gotdamn!" Rat exclaimed as he slumped back against the seat.

CHAPTER 18

Champagne's Porsche zoomed into the owner's parking space behind the sex toy shop she co-owned with Cocaine in Georgetown. She left the car and keyed herself into the back entrance of the shop. The store had several employees and they were busy taking care of customers, showing them various toys and costumes. She watched her favorite employee, an ex-dancer named Tonya make a particularly hard sell of French ticklers, massage oils, and edible underwear to a silver-haired couple who were obviously tourists.

Georgetown had been the perfect place of Champagne and Coke's Toy Store. It attracted a wide variety of patrons from the straight-laced tourists out for a night of carousing to the shifty-looking perverts wearing raincoats. The staff made sure they handled all of them with care and any problems were solved by the beefy security guard named Big Stoney. Their Toy Store had opened its' doors two years previously and had instantly became a hit. Its' location, right next to a gentlemen's club and a bar and grill, had worked in the Toy Store's favor from the very beginning. Restless patrons from either place would stop in the Toy Store and purchase items for their wives, husbands, boyfriends, girlfriends or whatever. Soon the buzz was all over Georgetown, and Champagne and Cocaine had a real moneymaker on their hands.

It had been four years since Shaunna left town and almost three since Champagne stopped dancing at Misty's. A lot of the girls she'd formerly danced with often came in to buy the custom costumes her in-store tailor designed for them, so she saw them often and was kept abreast of the goings-on at Misty's. A few of the girls, like Tonya, who didn't do so well at dancing had ended up working for her. The tailor used to sew them all outfits out of her small apartment, but Champagne had appealed to her business sense by letting her know that she was making pennies compared to what she would make at the Toy Store. With the success of the store and her other endeavors, Champagne didn't miss dancing at Misty's at all.

Over the telephone since she'd left D.C., Shaunna and Champagne's friendship had grown stronger. Shaunna's grandmother had lingered for two years before passing after Shaunna returned home. Shaunna had decided to stay home and Champagne was glad that she did, because she didn't want her best friend looking down her nose at her for what she'd become in Shaunna's absence.

Three years prior, Cocaine had come to Champagne with a proposition. She suggested that they put together an escort and private party service. The hook was they would have men invite them to events like bachelor parties and retirement parties. They would then get the men in compromising positions while the happenings were being videotaped or photographed. The incriminating evidence would then be sold back to the victim for a reasonable price. In the beginning they were taking more risks than was justified by their profits until Champagne took the reins of the operation from Cocaine.

She totally revamped their image making them available to upscale, affluent clients only. Cocaine feared that they were cutting themselves out by catering only to the rich and powerful, but after several successful stings she was convinced. Using some of Misty's' contacts, they plugged into men and women alike with sensitive government positions and rich and powerful spouses. Champagne tailored the requests for money and gifts to look more like compensation for services than plain extortion. Most of their clients accepted this as par for the course, and kept on using their services as long they remained discreet. There was a steady stream of clients and some of them were so outright generous that they didn't have to extort them. If that happened they merely kept the evidence of that person's infidelities or sexual oddities on file for use in case that person ever became stingy.

It had been critical to their survival that they stopped following Cocaine. They would have probably been dead by now at the hands of *some local drug dealer or thug if they had kept following her directives. The people they were involved with now didn't like making messes, so it was almost assured that they would pay quickly and quietly to make any problems go away. Sexually some of the customers were a bit past Champagne's realm of expertise when they first started catering to their private tastes. She had to quickly become versed in S&M, bondage, and any other aspect of sexual deviation. The powerful men and women of the nation's capital rarely, if ever wanted to have normal sex.*

The women, Champagne left to Cocaine. Her partner didn't have any problem with pleasuring a woman. Actually she seemed to rather enjoy it. Champagne didn't mind dominating women, but she had cold feet when it came down to plain sexual intimacy with females. Depending on just how much the customer was paying and if they needed pictures or video, Champagne would let women lick between her thighs, but one of the benefits of being a dominatrix was that she never had to return the favor.

Men however were a horse of a different color. Champagne had almost entirely lost all respect for men. The men they encountered were even worse than the strip club patrons. These men were no better than the drug dealers, car thieves, and stick up men who crawled out of the ghettos. Some of them were the decision-makers for the country; they were CEOs of huge companies, lobbyists, and public figures. Most of these men had several things in common, they were almost always married, they were rich and powerful, and the sight of Champagne in her dominatrix costumes drove these men out of their minds.

In her stiletto heels, Champagne stood an inch or so over six feet making her tower over her clients. She wore provocative costumes made of leather and rubber with or without masks. The men would beg for punishment and she would dish it out, and they would beg for more. They liked to be bound, gagged, beaten, whipped, humiliated, paddled, choked, pinched, scratched, have body parts clamped, you name it. Champagne drew the line at scat sex, she considered herself too much of a lady to empty her bowels on anyone no matter how much they begged for it or offered to pay. She just wouldn't engage in shitting. She felt that that was just beneath her, but if she knew that it would help one of her good customers get off, she didn't mind peeing on them too much.

Cocaine on the other hand liked to be dominated and if the price was right, nothing was out of bounds with her. She didn't mind crawling around on all fours wearing a dog collar while some man sniffed her behind and then mounted her like a dog. There was never any shortage of customers that requested Cocaine. The women really loved her. She became the object that these women's husbands sought when they delved outside of the marriage and Cocaine would let these women have their way with her to stick a finger in the eye of their husbands.

Sometimes the sight of the men made Champagne want to puke. Their pale, soft wrinkled skin and sagging balls was a nuisance, but on the other hand dealing with these men had driven her bank account into the high six figure bracket. Some of them offered useful information too, like about off-shore banking, real estate, and stock tips which Champagne soaked up. She had built herself quite a nest egg, not counting her lavishly appointed condominium, several expensive automobiles and all the clothing, shoes, and jewelry she desired.

Besides the Toy Store, they had purchased a small warehouse and had it totally refurbished with bedroom suites, regular and steam showers, a huge hot tub, and a complete torture chamber. That was just what the clients could see. They never saw the state-of-the-art video surveillance that covered almost every square inch of the warehouse—just the results. They had even hired a video tech, a girl named Kelly. Kelly had tried her hand at dancing to pay her way through film school but quickly found that it wasn't for her. Right now Kelly was at the warehouse making sure that all of the equipment was up to snuff because Champagne had a whale of a date that evening.

The crazy thing about their scam was that the people they stung would still recommend Champagne and Cocaine's services to others in their circle. Maybe it was the age old adage, "Misery loves company", and they wanted to get their kicks by seeing their peers get stung too. Whatever it was they kept sending others. Tonight Champagne would be catering to the needs of a certain conservative U.S. Senator from Texas. This senator sat at the head of several committees and was a force to be reckoned with in Congress. He had been recommended to them by the senator from Arkansas who had taken their blackmailing in stride and still continued to see Champagne and lavish her with gifts.

Tonight she knew that she would have to be at the top of her game and hopefully this would be the beginning of a long profitable relationship with Mr. Senator from Texas. She had stopped by the Toy Store to pick up a few items for the warehouse, including her studded paddle, a huge black strap-on dildo, and the new outfit the tailor, Jean, had made her. In the luncheon interview she'd had with the Senator he'd already let her know that he was open for anything, and he just didn't know that she'd taken that literally. He had no idea just how open he was going to be.

CHAPTER 19

Champagne and Shaunna stood outside of the courtroom at 26th and California watching the steady stream of people going into the various courtrooms. They were waiting for the proceedings that would determine Rat's immediate fate. Champagne glanced at her wristwatch and then over at Shaunna. Shaunna was wearing a particularly peculiar look on her face.

"Girl, what's wrong with you?" Champagne asked.

"It's this place. It stinks so bad I want to throw up. You don't smell that."

"Girl, that's your hormones. Remember when I was pregnant I had hypersensitive senses too. I used to could stand on the terrace and smell the onions on the polishes all the way in Jew-town. That and that damn Lake Michigan. I didn't even want to go outside for the smell coming off the lake. It used to feel like it was in my clothes."

"Chammy, you ain't lying. I can smell everything. And at first I couldn't hold down any food, now I want to eat everything in sight. The other day at the mall I was about to snatch one of them big salty pretzels from a little kid in a stroller and run. I done already started the crying shit. Here we go now..."

Shaunna walked away from Champagne and over to the windows that looked out over the County jail in the rear of the courthouse. Quietly she sniffled a few times and wiped the tears away that were falling from her eyes. Champagne joined her at the window.

"Shaunny," she said softly. "This is just the beginning. I found myself crying once because some idiot at the restaurant forgot to put mayo on my sandwich. Just like the morning sickness this will go away too."

"I can't stop thinking about my man," Shaunna squeaked.

"I already miss him and I'm scared, Champagne. I still never found the right time to tell him. He just had so much going on and then JC got shot. I didn't want anyone thinking that I couldn't hold it together you know. And now this. I want to know what's happening with my man and these people aren't telling me shit. I was sick of throwing up and the minute that was over, now I can't seem to go a whole damn day without crying over something. If I'm not crying then I'm eating. This is really frustrating for me."

Champagne rubbed Shaunna's back. "I know, Shaunny. Believe me, I know. Even this came at the most inopportune moment. Since J has been awake he's been asking for Rat. Them two know they love each other. I don't have the nerve to tell J that Rat is locked up. Hopefully we can get in this courtroom and Rat'll get a bond and from there he can go home."

"You think he will?" Shaunna asked hopefully. "You think they'll give him a bond?"

"Well, it ain't like he killed nobody. I know that's he's got a bad background, but he should get a decent bond. Unless his bond is ridiculously high then he'll be home tonight."

Champagne's cell phone vibrated in her hand. She answered it and held a quick conversation with the caller.

"That was Ronnie," Champagne said after she ended the call. "He said that he's on the way up and the lawyer is with him. They better hurry up because court is going to be starting in a minute."

"They better come on. I'm already tired of waiting. I want to find out what's going to happen to my man…"

Again Shaunna's tears started as Champagne did her best to console her. Minutes later, Ronald and the lawyer, Arnold Showenstein, walked up to them.

"How are you ladies holding up?" Showenstein asked as he greeted the ladies with a handshake.

"As well as can be expected under the circumstances," Champagne said.

"Okay, I'm going to go in and see where we're at with the proceedings,"

TRIPLE TAKE 2: CHAMPAGNE'S KISS

Showenstein said.

Following the lawyer into the courtroom, Champagne, Shaunna, and Ronald slipped into seats on the benches at the rear. They watched Showenstein converse briefly with the court clerk before handing her a slip of paper. He stood off to the side as the clerk pulled a file from a stack of folders and handed it to the state prosecutor.

The prosecutor and Showenstein exchanged a few words and then Showenstein came to the rear of the courtroom and motioned for the three friends to follow him out to the hallway.

In the hallway, Showenstein popped a fresh piece of Spearmint into his mouth. "I've got bad news and worse news," he quipped.

Shaunna's hand trembled as it came up to her mouth. Champagne held her up as her body swayed.

"The bad news is his bond is going to be pretty high. Not exactly a king's ransom, but not far from it. The worse news is that even if you pay the bond he won't be going home any time soon."

Shaunna burst into tears again and Champagne gave her shoulders a tight squeeze.

"If we pay his bond, why can't he come home?" Champagne asked.

"Seems that they have a "violation of parole" hold on him."

"But he finished his parole," Shaunna wailed. "I know for a fact that he isn't even on parole."

"All I know is what the State is telling me. The prosecutor didn't want to give me too many details, but it seems that he had a failure to comply with the conditions of parole. He'll be in the jail here until his preliminary hearing and then if they find probable cause while he's awaiting trial, they'll ship him back to the penitentiary that he paroled from. I won't know the severity of his non-compliance until he gets in front of the parole board."

"So he's going back to prison?" Ronnie asked.

"Yep. I should be able to get him loose, but it's going to take awhile. Since he hasn't been in any trouble during the actual time that he was on parole that's in his favor. More than likely its restitution or a simple failure to comply, something like not getting a job. The state hired plenty of new parole officers and some of them can be pretty overzealous, so it may be nothing."

"What exactly are they charging him with?" Shaunna asked.

"Possession of a firearm by a felon and attempted murder. The attempt I can beat all day. From what I've seen so far it's a stretch. I can't even understand how the State is trying to prosecute that one. The possession of the firearm..."

"What?" Champagne asked. "Give it to us straight."

"The possession is going to be a hard one to beat. A really hard one. I don't really see him catching a break on that one. I'm going to have to see how the police wrote it up, but it seems like it's pretty cut and dry. We're putting the cart before the horse, but on that one it may be better for him to take a deal. But like I said, we're not to that point and it may be quite a ways off, but we've got to know that it can happen."

"What about today?" Champagne asked.

Before Showenstein could answer her a Cook County Sheriff's deputy stuck his head out of the courtroom.

"The judge is on his way to the bench," the deputy announced to the people standing in the hallway.

Quietly they filed into the courtroom and took their seat. Showenstein went to the front of the courtroom and took a seat with several other lawyers in the vacant jury booth. Everyone in the courtroom stood as the judge entered the courtroom a few minutes later. Once the judge was on the bench they all took their seats. Rat's case was the first one called by the clerk. As they watched the proceedings, Rat was escorted into the courtroom by two sheriff's deputies. He flashed Shaunna, Champagne, and Ronald a sickly looking smile before turning to face the judge.

From there the events went with lightning quick speed as everything went the way that Showenstein had predicted. The judge gave Rat a

TRIPLE TAKE 2: CHAMPAGNE'S KISS

$400,000 bond of which he would have to have ten percent posted, but he put a "parole violation hold" on him as well, so that he couldn't bond out. A date was set for the preliminary hearing and that was it as the deputies took him back to the cells behind the courtrooms. Showenstein received a piece of paper from the court clerk and whispered something in the state prosecutor's ear, before walking to the rear of the courtroom and signaling them to follow him.

In the hallway, Showenstein said, "Well everything pretty much went the way I said. I didn't think the State would agree to it, but he's gonna put it through so you can visit him before he goes across the street."

"Across the street?" Shaunna asked.

"It's a maximum security division, because he's been to prison they'll send him there until they put him on the bus back to the penitentiary he paroled from. Right now, though, you can visit him in the back in the attorney/client meeting rooms. It's really not a room, it's a cell. Now if you'll follow me."

They followed Showenstein to a door a little further down the hallway. He knocked twice and when a sheriff's deputy opened the door, Showenstein handed him the note from the prosecutor. The deputy read the note and waved his hand for them to follow him. He led them to a cell like room and nodded his head for them to enter. The deputy left and a few minutes later he returned with Rat. He allowed Rat to enter the room before he swung the cell door closed but didn't lock it.

Shaunna rushed over to Rat and flung herself into his arms. When Rat was finally able to loosen Shaunna's grip, he gave Champagne a hug, Ronald a pound, and shook hands with Showenstein.

"I'll give you some time to talk," Showenstein said as he looked at his watch. "Anything over ten, fifteen minutes is really pushing it. I'll take a walk downstairs and get a coffee and a newspaper and then I'll be back."

127

Showenstein left the cell and let the guard know that he'd back in a while. Champagne started to leave too, but Shaunna put her hand on her arm.

"Stay with me, Chammy," Shaunna said. "I don't think that I can do this by myself."

Champagne looked at her and saw the tears welling up in Shaunna's eyes. She knew without saying that her friend needed her. She took a seat across from Shaunna and Rat at the table that was provided for the attorney and clients. Ronald remained standing.

"What's popping y'all?" Rat asked trying to remain upbeat. "Y'all sure are a sight for sore eyes."

"Let me get this business stuff out the way first, then I'll let you women talk to him," said Ronald. "Well, the thing went through with the tow truck company so we've got that. When the insurance company pays for the damaged equipment at the studio I'll use that money to get the studio built in the yard. You still want the studio right?"

"Hell yeah, I want my studio. Plus I want you to tell Big M and Ty that this ain't shit, finish what they was doing. Let them know what's going on with me too 'cause them little dudes is some real cats. Tell them that I'll be in touch as soon as I get situated. As for my receptionist and engineer, tell them its' business as usual. Tell Tina and Berns I said get to work. I can't think of anything else right now, but when I do I'll let you know, Ronnie." Rat stood and gave Ronald a half-hug.

"Rat, I'll take care of everything," Ronald said as he walked toward the cell door. "If there's anything, just let me know and I'll stand on it for you. Ladies, I'm going to catch up with Showenstein. I'll be downstairs in front when you're through up here."

"Alright, Ronnie," Champagne said. "We'll be down in a few."

As Ronald left, Rat sat back down, but not before giving Shaunna another hug and a kiss on the lips. He held her hand as he took his seat.

"Are you gone be alright in here?" Shaunna asked.

Rat looked around the cell room. "Hell nall," he said. "This County shit is for the birds. I can't lie, I'd rather be in the joint than the County Jail. I'm gone be counting the days until they send me back to the joint."

"I thought you did everything you were supposed to do to get off your parole," Champagne said. "How did you violate your parole?"

Rat dropped his head. "I fucked around and bullshitted off my last two appointments, but I thought because I ain't get into no trouble they was just gone terminate my shit without fucking with me. That's that bitch ass parole officer of mine. That stud could've terminated my shit with no problem, but he was on some bullshit. Hopefully when I go back in front of the board when I get to the joint, they won't trip too hard and terminate my shit satisfactorily. They can't trip on this pistol case I don't think because technically I wasn't on parole. I don't know. We gone have to see. Enough about me, how is J doing?"

"The doctors keep saying that he's out of woods," Champagne said. "He's been staying awake more and more now. He's been able to talk, but he's not able to say much. The doctors said that he isn't in danger of infection that much any more. There's still the nerve damage though. Right now they're keeping a close eye on him."

"That's the best news that I've heard all day. You tell Killa J, I said my fault. I don't know what made that crazy ass nurse think that I was trying to kill him. I'd give my life for that man without hesitation 'cause I know he'd do the same for me. Dumb ass hating bitch was just on some other shit. When she came in the room I was just hollering at my man letting him know that I was there with him. That bitch must have seen my gun and ran straight to get them people. Next thing I know I'm opening the door and there's cops outside talking about get down on the ground. I'm like "Shit" 'cause I know I had my gun on me. Wasn't nothing I could do but let them take me. Enough about me, Shaunny how's our baby?"

"Huh?" Shaunna asked with a look of disbelief.

Rat laughed. "You thought I didn't know. I been waiting on you to tell me. I know you ain't been having your monthly visit. Then you started getting a little wider here and there. How many months are you?"

"Three," Shaunna said softly. "I just didn't know how to tell you. It seems like every time I wanted to tell you something happened. Then the stuff happened at the studio and J got shot..."

"It's alright, Shaunny. Girl, you know I love you. Really I hope that you ain't disappointed in me 'cause I got locked up. Hopefully this shit won't turn out too bad so I can get home to my woman and my baby." Shaunna was now in tears. "I didn't even want to think that you wouldn't be here when the baby was born," she wailed. "I keep hoping that this shit is a bad dream and I'm going to wake up."

"Shaunny, this is real life," Rat said earnestly. "Sometimes shit happen like this. I already know how to take the good with the bad and vice versa. You got to do the same. You think while I'm down in the joint I ain't gone be thinking about my lady and my child? Shit, the twins, my mama, my brothers and sisters, Killa J, Chammy? All y'all gone be running through my head, but ain't gone be a damn thing I can do but my time. Could this be worse? Yeah. Did it happen when we least needed it to happen? Yeah. But all that is besides the point. I'll get back home as soon as I can, but for right now I got to see what these people is talking about."

The deputy opened the cell door. "Time's up," he announced gruffly.

They all stood. Rat gave Shaunna a long, deep kiss and a tight hug. He gave Champagne a hug and peck on the cheek.

"Don't look so sad," Rat said with a smile. "Y'all look like y'all the ones going to jail. I'll be alright, if I know anything it's how to do jail time. Take care of JC, and y'all bet not put no collect call block on the phone."

"You ladies can go back out that way," the deputy said.

They watched Rat until he went through the last door that led to the bullpens. Champagne looked back at Shaunna expecting her to still be in tears, but she wasn't.

TRIPLE TAKE 2: CHAMPAGNE'S KISS

"What you ain't crying?" asked Champagne. "I don't believe this."

"I'm sick of crying," Shaunna said. "My man would want me to be strong and that's what I'm gone do. All that crying isn't going to help him any. Pretty soon people will be thinking I'm a softy if I keep up all this blubbering. I know you got to be tired of hearing me boo-hooing anyway. Let's get out of here so we can go to that Popeye's chicken across the street. I want some chicken covered in hot sauce and honey and one of them big peppers. I want some rice and mashed potatoes. I can taste them now." With their spirits slightly lifted, Champagne and Shaunna left the courthouse building with Ronald and headed across the street to Popeye's.

CHAPTER 20

Champagne sat up in the chair she'd been sleeping in and looked around. She rubbed her eyes and looked over at the other bed in JC's hospital room. Shaunna was curled up in that bed. Champagne had insisted that she take the bed. She had tried sleeping in the bed with Shaunna, but her pregnant friend slept so wildly she ended up pulling the room's chairs together to make a bed. She stood up and stretched to get the kinks out of her neck and body and then went to the bathroom.

As she freshened up and brushed her teeth she looked at her reflection in the bathroom mirror. The sight of her face scared her. Her eyes were puffy and red from the less than peaceful sleep she'd had. Her hair was a mess because she'd taken it down so she could go get some kinky twists, but she hadn't had time to get them done yet. The stress of the recent events could be seen in her face and she could feel it in the knots in her neck and shoulders.

"When this shit is over I'm taking a long ass vacation," she said to the mirror. "Matter of fact, make that two vacations. I'm gone take them kids down to Universal Studios for about a week. When I bring them back then I'm gone head for somebody's island. I don't want to do shit but swim and get drunk for a whole week. Whew."

Champagne made a face like she could feel the island sun on her face already. She was smiling when she exited the bathroom. Shaunna was still asleep so Champagne didn't turn on the television. She decided to go get them something to eat and some coffee. She knew that Shaunna would greatly appreciate any food. She had a taste for a blueberry bagel with strawberry cream cheese herself. Quietly she slipped her feet into her shoes and left the room.

In a nearby Dunk'n Donuts, she ordered herself a medium coffee and a bagel. For Shaunna she picked a steak, egg, and cheese breakfast sandwich and several donuts with a carton of orange juice. Back at the hospital, she purchased a daily newspaper from the gift shop newsstand before going back to the room. When she pushed open the door to JC's room, she received a surprise that almost made her drop her coffee and bags. Shaunna was sitting up talking to JC like nothing had happened.

"Bout time you got back," Shaunna said with a huge smile. "I was just telling JC that I hope you went and got some food. I'm so hungry I don't know what to do right now."

Champagne smiled like a kid on Christmas morning as she approached JC's bed.

"How you doing, mama?" he croaked.

"I'm fine baby," she gushed. "How long have you been awake?"

"For a while now. I've been woke off and on for what feels like two or three days. I wanted to say something, but I just wasn't ready to talk. When I woke up today, I was feeling better. I looked around for you and saw Shaunny, so I waited until she woke up."

"He scared the hell out of me too when he said "Good morning"," Shaunna commented. "I almost peed on myself."

"She was looking crazy," JC rasped after making a sound somewhere between a chuckle and a gurgle.

Shaunna climbed down off the hospital bed she'd been occupying and took the Dunk'n Donut bags from Champagne's hand.

"Forget you J," Shaunna said as she hopped back up on the bed and opened the bag, pulling out her sandwich, which she promptly opened and took a huge bite from. "Damn, Shaunny," Champagne said before turning back to JC. "So how are you feeling? Are you hungry? Thirsty?"

"I'm alright. Shaunny gave me some water. I don't think that I'm ready to eat anything solid just yet."

"Are you in any pain?"

"Not what I would exactly call pain. It's more of a uncomfortable feeling. Shaunny was explaining that I been in a coma. She told me what happened to Rat too."

Champagne's smile instantly disappeared. "Yeah that was messed up. It's actually kind of crazy. That nurse is sticking to her story that he was trying to kill you. We haven't been able to get to her as of yet, but Ronald is working on that. He'll get to her and explain the whole thing and put a few bucks in her pocket. That should make her see the whole situation a bit differently, and then they'll have to drop the attempted murder charge. He just have to fight the pistol case and see what's going on with his parole violation. He said to tell you that he took care of that when you woke up. He wouldn't say exactly what that was, but he said you'd know."

"Yeah, I know," JC said. "If I know anything, I know that he would take care of what needed to be took care of."

Champagne leaned down and gave JC a soft kiss on the lips.

"Get off me woman," JC said. "Man, a dude can't even come all the way out of his coma without you trying to get you some."

"You better get out of here," Champagne said with a laugh. "Boy don't nobody want you like that."

"Oh it's like that huh? Boy, sisters shole know how to kick a brother when he's down, I'll tell you." Even Shaunna laughed as she pulled a jelly donut from the bag. "Y'all don't mind me. I'm not paying y'all any attention as long as I got some food."

"Even if you was, so what," Champagne said as she leaned over JC's bed and gave him another hug and kiss. To him, she said, "How do you feel really? Are you okay?"

"I feel much better than I did. The pain doesn't bother me so much and I can feel all of my parts. It hurts like hell when I do, but I can move my arms and legs. My back feels strange though, like it's not mine or something. Did I have a back transplant or something?"

"Stop acting silly. You haven't had no back transplant. The doctors warned us that you would have some nerve damage, that's probably what that is. They don't know what the extent of the nerve damage is, but it wasn't their main concern..."

The room door swung open and the two doctors walked in the room followed closely by a male nurse.

The shorter of the two doctors came over to the bed where he saw JC was awake.

"Ah Mr. Collins, you decided to join us," said the doctor jovially.

"We're all so glad that you could be here, aren't we ladies?"

"Most definitely," Shaunna said thickly through a mouthful of the chocolate éclair she'd started on. "You are so right."

"Jonathan, I'm Doctor Thayer your attending physician. I must say that you're an exceptionally strong individual, spirit wise and physically. Also we were quite lucky."

"Well, I didn't feel lucky," JC croaked. "I know how those targets at the shooting range must feel."

"At any rate," Dr. Thayer continued. "Your luck held out to get you this far. Now my colleague and I are going to examine you and this afternoon we'll run some pretty extensive tests."

"Excuse me Dr. Thayer," Champagne intervened. "Tests? Extensive tests?"

"Don't worry, JoAnn. It's more poking and prodding than anything. At this point our biggest enemy would be infection, but so far there's been no sign of any. The tests will let us know the extent of the nerve damage, and give us several possible options to treat it, both long and short-term. There won't be anything too invasive, but Jonathan will be quite exhausted by this afternoon. Now that his condition has been updated to 'Stable' we can take a look at getting at the bullet that is the source of our problems. Barring complications we should be able to remove it now that the body has started the regeneration process on its' own."

"So we're talking more surgery huh Doc?" JC asked.

"A few more procedures, some more tricky than the others, but no more than necessary. Now, JoAnn and Shaunna you're going to have to excuse us so we can give him a quick going over."

Shaunna climbed down out of the bed clutching her donuts and juice. Champagne gave JC one more kiss on his forehead and left the room with Shaunna. They took a seat in the small waiting area next to the nurses' station as they waited for the doctors to finish JC's exam. Half an hour later, Dr. Thayer walked into the waiting area. Champagne jumped to her feet.

Dr. Thayer patted her hand. "Everything is alright, JoAnn. Like I said, his wounds are looking good and he's in surprisingly good spirits for everything that has happened. That will make our job ten times easier. The orderlies are on their way to retrieve him now so we can take him downstairs for an MRI. If you want to wait with him that's no problem, but once we get started with our poking and prodding it's going to be quite awhile. If you have any errands to run, now would be a good time because Jonathan will be busy for the next five or six hours. After that we'll probably give him something so he can sleep without any discomfort."

"Thanks a lot Dr. Thayer," Champagne said. "I'll go let him know that we'll be leaving for awhile."

As Champagne went to JC's room, Dr. Thayer couldn't help but notice for the thousandth time that she had a body out of this world under the jogging suit she was wearing. In his mind, Jonathan Collins was lucky in more ways than one.

In JC's room, Champagne gave him one last hug before leaving.

"So, me and Shaunny are going home and clean up. I'm going to take me a long soak in the hot tub to try and relieve some of this tension."

"Why don't you stop downstairs in the building at the spa and get a massage?" JC offered. "You sure look like you could use one."

"I might at that," Champagne answered. "I sure could use a nice pounding."

"Well if you give me a day or two I might be able to give you that pounding."

"I ain't talking about that kind of pounding, man. Though that would be nice."

TRIPLE TAKE 2: CHAMPAGNE'S KISS

"Unnn, y'all two is nasty," Shaunna said. "Y'all got to stop talking like that around me. My man is locked up so I ain't got no pounding coming no time soon."

"Sorry, Shaunny," Champagne said. "We weren't thinking about you. My fault."

"Girl, I'm just bullshitting. You know I'm stronger than that. JC, don't worry about me man. I'm straight."

There was a knock at the door and an orderly stuck his head in the room. "How are you all doing? We're here from transport to take the patient down for his MRI."

"He's ready," Champagne said.

As the orderlies rolled the transport bed into the room, Champagne got her purse and gave JC another kiss. "I'll come back this evening and bring the twins. They're dying to see you."

"You do that," JC said.

"See you later, J," Shaunna called out.

"Later, Shaunny."

Champagne's steps were a bit lighter as she and Shaunna headed for the elevators. She knew she would feel even better after a soak, a massage, and being able to tell her children that their father was going to be alright and that they would be able to see him today.

Shaunna stopped at the nurses' station and got a big cup of crushed ice.

"C'mon girl," Champagne said. "Here comes the elevator. I don't know what I'm going to do with you."

"Just feed me," Shaunna said through a mouthful of ice chips.

CHAPTER 21

Cynthia pulled into a parking space in front of the KiddieHaven Daycare center. As the twins' nanny she had the privilege of driving their station wagon, though by old school standards it wasn't a regular station wagon. It was a nearly new, silver Volvo Cross Country station wagon with factory 19-inch chrome rims, a black leather interior, automatic sunroof, and a nice stereo sound system.

As Cynthia put the car in park, she marveled again at the KiddieHaven building. This place was really a haven for children. Its' surrounding property was fenced off and every inch of the premises were under constant video surveillance. Sprawled on the side of the huge playlot were several swing and sliding board sets. Parents and children had to be buzzed into the building and from there they had to sign in with the armed security guard at the front desk. Inside the building it was decorated with children in mind from the multicolored rainbows and flower murals to the bright alphabet and numbers carpet that covered every inch of the daycare's floors. Out back there was even a small petting zoo complete with chickens, a goat, dogs and ducks.

She left the car behind and buzzed the doorbell in the breezeway. It never took longer than a few seconds for her to be admitted to the building. She stopped at the security desk to sign the visitor's log.

"Hey there Cynthia," the heavyset, gold-toothed security guard said smoothly. "You a little early today. How you been doing, baby girl?"

"I've been okay, Andre," she answered. "I've got some errands to run over this way so I thought I'd pick up the kids a little early seeing as how it's such a nice day. I can let them get some time on their bicycles."

"Well you only been doing okay 'cause you ain't got me in your life. Then you would be doing way better than 'Okay'. When you gone let me come get you and take you bowling or something?"

"How about never", Cynthia was thinking, but she said, "I don't bowl

Andre. I always wanted to learn, but I don't ever seem to have the time."

"I'll teach you how to bowl and anything else you want to learn how to do," Andre the security guard said suggestively.

"Well okay, I'll keep your offer in mind," Cynthia said as she placed the pen on the sign-in sheet. "I'll have to see you later. Can't keep the kids waiting."

Slightly shuddering at Andre's lewd proposal, Cynthia went to collect the twins from their respective classrooms. Though she had to answer a few slightly inquisitive questions from their teachers about the unusual time that she was picking them up, it still only took her a few minutes to get them both.

The twins were full of energy as they grabbed their jackets and book bags and followed Cynthia out of the daycare center to the car.

"Why did you come and get us so early?" Kenton asked. "I wasn't finished playing with my friends. We were going to play basketball after snack and reading time."

"That's okay, we're going to get some ice cream," Cynthia said as she herded them into the car. "After we get some ice cream, then we're going to take your Power Wheels to the lakefront and you two can ride them both as long as you want.

Kenton took off his Spiderman backpack and slung it into the rear of the station wagon. Anaya did the same with her Dora the Explorer backpack. They climbed into their booster seats and waited for Cynthia to fasten their seatbelts.

"When you say as long as we want, you mean as long as we want?" Kenton inquired.

"I mean exactly what it sounds like," answered Cynthia as she buckled their seatbelts. "You can ride them for as long as you want."

"And what about this ice cream?" Anaya asked. "Can we have whatever kind we want?"

"You can have whatever kind you want except for Rum Raisin," Cynthia said. "I couldn't let you two drive your Power Wheels if you have Rum Raisin. The police might pull you over for drinking and driving. We're going straight to 31 Flavors from here. You can even have two scoops because it's so early and that won't ruin your dinner."

"Two scoops of the butter kind is what I want," Kenton said solidly. "I really like that butter kind."

Cynthia closed the rear door and got in the driver's seat. "I think you mean butter pecan, Kenton. What flavor do you want, Anaya? Let me guess, you want Pralines & Cream."

"That's the kind you had the last time that I ate all up, isn't it?" Anaya asked. "It sure was good, too."

Cynthia started the car and backed out of the parking space. "Yes, that's the kind and you gobbled it all up like a little pig. Well this time you're going to get your own so I can enjoy mine."

Anaya giggled. "Well that's the kind of ice cream I want. It was really, really good. I want me two super big, fat old scoops of that kind of ice cream."

As Cynthia drove to the little strip mall where the 31 Flavors store was located, the twins chatted merrily in the rear seat. They were looking forward to their surprise treat of ice cream and a chance to ride their Power Wheels vehicles (as long as they wanted) on the lakefront. In the parking lot of the strip mall, Cynthia didn't have to worry about unbuckling the twins, they were unbuckled and ready to go by the time she cut the engine. She got them out of the car and held their hands as they walked across the parking lot and into 31 Flavors.

"I want my ice cream in one of those big cones, please Cynthia," Anaya pleaded.

"No cones," Cynthia said. "Cones leak and I don't feel like having to clean you two up before we go to the lake. If you're sticky when we get to the lake then the ants and the bugs will follow you all around taking bites out of you."

"Un-unn," Kenton giggled.

"Bugs and ants don't take a bite out of you."

TRIPLE TAKE 2: CHAMPAGNE'S KISS

"Yes, they will," Cynthia reassured him before placing their order. "Bugs and ants love sticky little kids. They say that sticky little kids taste extra sweet."

Cynthia paid the cashier and carried their cups of ice cream over to a table by the window. She placed a quick call on her cell phone and then they spent the next half hour chatting and eating ice cream. Finally the twins were through with their ice cream and Cynthia wiped them off. She took their hands to lead them out the store to the car. When they were halfway across the parking lot, a white Ford cargo van screeched into the parking lot and sped toward them. Cynthia halted the twins to let the van pass, but it screeched to a halt in front of them.

The passenger side door sprang open as did the sliding door in front of them. From the passenger seat and out of the back, two masked men, both bearing guns, jumped out of the van. One gunman put his pistol to the side of Cynthia's head. The other gunman snatched Kenton's hand from Cynthia's grasp and flung him in the van into the waiting arms of another masked man. Next he grabbed Anaya and flung her into the van as well. The masked man in the back of the van, flex-tied their hands behind their backs and put tape over their mouths and eyes. Outside the van, the man with a pistol prodded Cynthia toward the van.

"Bitch get in the motherfucking van or I'm gone leave you here without no fuckin' head!" the gunman growled.

Whimpering slightly Cynthia followed his directions and climbed into the rear of the van. The masked man in the van expertly flex-tied her hands and taped her mouth and eyes. The two men jumped back into the van and it sped off. The driver floored it out of the parking lot and didn't slow down until they were several blocks away from the strip mall.

CHAPTER 22

"I love this place," Champagne said as she pushed open the door to the building's full service spa. "This place is so peaceful that half the time I don't want to leave."

"You got that right," Shaunna agreed as she walked alongside her. "When I'm here I don't know what to get done first, they have so many amenities. Between the pedicures, mud baths, steam rooms, and massages, I don't be wanting to leave."

"Girl, you ain't lying. Give me a mud bath and a steam bath. After that a facial, and then let one of the good masseuses beat the hell out of me, and I'll be as loose as a goose."

The ladies stopped at the front desk to arrange for the various services they preferred. They both opted for manis and pedis, facial treatments, mud baths, and massages. For less than fifteen minutes they sat in the lobby thumbing through travel and fashion magazines as they waited for the spa's attendants to escort them through the facilities. Minutes after a petite male attendant with an almost undecipherable accent escorted them to the rear of the spa they were both immersed in a warm mud bath. Two hours later after pedicures and facial treatments, Champagne and Shaunna, clad only in the spa's extra luxurious towels were stretched out on the massage tables.

A stocky, matronly black woman with incredibly strong hands began working over Champagne, while a small framed white woman kneaded Shaunna's muscles. Pretty soon their moans and grunts filled the massage room as the masterful masseuses expertly worked over every solid inch of their bodies. In the middle of their massage an attendant poked her head into the massage room.

"Ms. Wells?" the attendant inquired.

Champagne lifted up her head. "Yes?"

"I have a package for you. The messenger told the doorman that it was urgent when he signed for it. He buzzed the penthouse several times before someone passing in the lobby mentioned that they'd seen you come in the spa. Would you like me to give you the package now or leave it at the front desk?"

"You can leave it at the front desk. I'll be here for about another half hour and then I'll pick it up on the way out."

"Okay Ms. Wells," said the attendant. "It'll be at the front desk. Sorry about the interruption."

The attendant left and Champagne let the masseuse finish doing her job. When she and Shaunna were finished, instead of putting on their clothes, they decided to put two of the spa's sumptuous bathrobes on their account and wear them out of the spa and up to the penthouse. They were almost out of the door when Champagne remembered the package at the front desk. She went back and got the package while Shaunna keyed the entry for the penthouse's private elevator.

On the elevator, Champagne inspected the package. It was a small bubble wrap envelope without a return address or any distinguishing marks. It was addressed simply to Ms. Wells. She ripped open the envelope and dumped the contents into her hand. There was an ordinary looking cellular phone and a note. She opened the note; it read simply, "This is not a game. Wait for my call."

"What the hell," Champagne said.

"What is that?" Shaunna asked.

"A cell phone and a note talking about wait for a call."

"Who's it from?"

"It doesn't say. That's strange."

"Girl, that thing is probably from your crazy ass man," Shaunna said dismissively. "You know better than anybody that dude of yours is full of surprises. He just woke up for good and knowing him he done already set y'all up some island getaway. I don't know what you tripping for. I should be the one tripping. It's gone be a minute for that crazy fool of mine is able to surprise me with anything."

"You're probably right," Champagne said as she smiled and slipped the cell phone into her bathrobe pocket. "I'll just have to wait for him to give me a call so he can tell me what he's got on his mind. It bet not be nothing freaky 'cause he's going to still need some time to heal, but the minute he's straight I'm gone make sure he remembers what he's been missing."

With barely a whisper the door slid open depositing them into the penthouse.

"I'm going to get something to drink," Shaunna said. "What are you about to do, Chammy?"

Champagne ran her hands through her wet hair. "I'm going to dry my hair and pull it back into a ponytail. Now that I've got time to run over to the shop, I wish I had an appointment, but I know without an appointment I'm pretty much dead. I was thinking about taking a run, but now I'm so relaxed I don't want to do anything but fall across my bed for a couple of hours until the twins get home. Then I'll get dressed and take them over to the hospital. I might even go get J's mama and see if she wants to ride. What about you?"

"I could use a nap too, but first I've got to get me a snack. After that I'll ride over to the hospital, but I'm not staying all night. Tomorrow I'm going to get over to the stores and get back in the thick of things. With my man gone I'm going to have to make sure I occupy my time. Wake me up when you get up."

In the master bathroom, Champagne blow dried her hair and pulled it into a smart, tight ponytail and tied it down with her silk scarf. In the bedroom she discarded the bathrobe on a large ottoman and put on a pair of panties. Next she pulled on one of JC's t-shirts that she routinely slept in and crawled onto the California, king sized bed. Although she turned on the television to catch up with the early afternoon talk shows, she was fast asleep in a matter of minutes.

As she slept she dreamed that she and her family were enjoying themselves as they rode bikes on the lakefront. JC was well and whole and they were all having a good time. Somehow they all ended up at Kiddieland riding the bumper cars just like last summer. Something must have gone wrong with the bumper cars because an alarm started ringing. They tried to keep riding, but that ringing persisted; it stopped and started back just as quick.

Awaking Champagne sat up in bed and realized that the ringing wasn't part of her dream—it was the telephone, but it wasn't any telephone of hers, it was too unfamiliar. Through her sleep clouded mind the image of her opening the envelope on the elevator and finding a cell phone pushed itself to the forefront. She forced herself out of bed and over to the bathrobe on the ottoman. The new cell phone was still in the pocket. As she pulled it out of the pocket, it rang and vibrated again scaring her and almost making her drop it. She looked at the caller ID, but the caller's number was blocked. Smiling she opened the cell phone and put it to her ear, expecting to hear JC's voice.

"JC, hey baby," she said softly into the phone.

"This ain't yo punk ass man, bitch," the voice on the other end said gruffly. "What the fuck took you so long to answer the phone. I see now that you don't follow instructions too good. Well bitch if you want your brats and the nanny to survive this shit you better make sure you listen real careful and do everything I say." "Huh?" asked Champagne dumbfounded at the voice on the phone. "Who is this? What are you talking about?"

"Bitch, that don't matter. I see you ain't as smart as I gave you credit for. Like they say, "Time is of the essence", so shut the fuck up and listen. I've got your kids and your bitch of a nanny. I want five hundred thousand for the kids and a hundred thousand for the nanny. Keep this phone--I'll call back with instructions. Get that money together. Don't put the police in our business neither or your kids are dead. This ain't a game or joke."

"Hello? Hello?" Champagne screamed into the phone, but the caller had terminated the transmission. In shock she sat on the ottoman and looked around the room; her mind was reeling from the call she'd just received. She jumped up and called out to Shaunna.

"Shaunny, get yo clothes on! We're going out the door now! Put on anything!"

As Champagne dressed, Shaunna appeared at the bedroom's doorway, looking sleepy, but she had on a jogging suit.

"Damn, Chammy what's wrong? I thought you was going to take a nap."

Fully dressed, Champagne streaked past her. "C'mon Shaunny, I'll explain on the way. C'mon."

In the car on the way to her children's daycare center, Champagne broke down the contents of the call to Shaunna. She also tried repeatedly to call Cynthia's cell phone, but her calls kept going to voicemail. By the time she pulled up in front of the daycare, she was close to tears. She slammed the car in park and bolted out of it to be buzzed in. Shaunna scrambled to keep up with her.

As she waited for the security guard to buzz them in, Champagne mumbled a prayer that this was just somebody's idea of a sick prank or hoax as Shaunna squeezed her hand. The security guard finally buzzed them in and as they approached the desk, the quizzical look on his face did not bode well. "How are you doing, Ms. Wells, is everything alright with the kids?" Andre asked. "Did Cynthia forget something?"

Champagne's hand flew up to her mouth. Shaunna saw that her friend was speechless and took over.

"Are you saying that Cynthia picked up the children?" Shaunna asked.

"Yes, that was awhile ago, are you sure everything is alright?" Andre repeated.

Shaunna forced a weak smile as she steered Champagne toward the exit. "Oh yes everything's good. We're sorry. She forgot to tell Cynthia that she wanted to pick up the kids today. There's no problem."

Outside Shaunna put Champagne into the passenger seat and ran around to the driver's seat. They sat there in complete and total silence for ten minutes when the kidnappers' cell phone rang startling them both. Shakily Champagne used the phone's speakerphone feature and answered it.

First there was the sound of barking dogs and then Cynthia's frightened voice came over the speaker. "Champagne, this is Cynthia. They have me and the twins. They want 600,000 dollars to let us go. They said if you play any games or get the police in their business then we're all dead. If you don't come up with the money in 48 hours then they're going to kill all of us. They'll call back with instructions."

The phone went dead.

"Cynthia! Cynthia!" Champagne shouted at the phone.

"She's gone," Shaunna said as she took the phone from Champagne.

"They've got my kids," Champagne said as she burst into tears. "What are we going to do?" Shaunna pulled Champagne's head onto her shoulder. "Whatever they say do until we get the kids back. Then we're going to fuck somebody up."

CHAPTER 23

"That was good, bitch," Nat said after taking the cell phone from Cynthia's ear and snapping it shut. "If you keep on doing what you're told you just might make it out of this shit alive. Well, you will if they pay for your ass."

Blindfolded, Cynthia was handcuffed in a standing position to an overhead pipe in Nat's basement. The twins were each shut into dog cages still wearing their blindfolds and flex-ties on their wrists. There were pitbulls in the cages next to them and the dogs were barking and snapping at the unwanted guests. Anaya was weeping wildly, but Kenton had shrunk back to what he surmised was the furthest corner of the cage. There he sat shaking as he took in the sounds around him.

"Bitch, you better hope they pay up for your ass," Dale said. "If they just pay for the kids then that's too bad for you. You better hope that good help is really hard to find."

"Yeah you better hope they love you like Ms. Garrett on Different Strokes," Julius chimed in. "You better hope you real unreplaceable, bitch. It really would be a shame to have to whack a bitch with a body like yours. That'd be a damn shame. That nice ass. Those pretty titties. Shit. I hope they pay for you 'cause that'd be a fucking waste if they didn't."

Julius moved in close on Cynthia from the rear. She tried to shy away from him, but he put his hand around her waist and pulled her back against him, making sure his crotch was firmly against her butt as he sniffed her hair.

"Man, this bitch smell good too," he exclaimed, drawing laughter from his cronies. "This bitch hair smell like some fucking cherry wine candy. Her motherfucking neck is clean too. Whew-wee. I would kill this shit from the back." To demonstrate his lovemaking technique, Julius grabbed Cynthia's breasts from the back and began banging

148

into her rear with hard thrusts. Cynthia gasped and whimpered at his simulation of sex.

"That's enough, FEE," Nat said.

"Man this ain't nearly enough, FEE," Julius said. "I would tear this shit up. I bet it's good. I bet it get real wet too."

"That's enough I said," Nat repeated a bit more forcefully. Julius stopped. "Damn FEE, I'm just having a little fun with this bitch. You act like you catching feelings. Fuck everybody else, remember?"

"Fuck what you talking about, FEE," Dale said. "You is up here acting like you ain't never had no pussy before. Get off that bullshit."

Nat began to tromp up the stairs. "Bring y'all asses on FEE. We need to talk. I ain't bullshitting neither."

Mar and Dale followed right behind Nat, but Julius lingered for a little longer feeling on Cynthia. After one last good squeeze of her ass, he finally let her go. Before going up the stairs, Julius had to adjust the erection in his pants so the fellows wouldn't tease him when he got upstairs. He took care to close the basement door behind himself when he got upstairs. In Nat's living room, they sprawled across the couches, and someone had lit a blunt by the time Julius joined the party.

"Damn nigga, you musta been down there trying to stick yo dick in that bitch," Mar said.

"No, I wasn't," Julius said defensively. "I was just making sure that her cuffs was tight. We wouldn't want that bitch to get away and go get the police and shit. Y'all be trying to act like I don't get no pussy."

"Not none you ain't paid for," Dale quipped. "Either that or you had to get a bitch too drunk to know that she was giving it to you."

"Nigga fuck you," Julius said. "I know you ain't laughing Mar, not with all the cash you be dropping on them bum ass strippers at the club. At least all I got to buy is a bottle and I get me some."

"Nigga, you was gay 'til you met me," Mar said loudly. "I got you your first piece of pussy, fat ass nigga, letting you get some of my sloppy seconds."

"You just mad 'cause you let me hit yo girl and I busted that bitch wide open," Julius retorted. "I had yo bitch begging me for more. She was tired of you shortchanging her."

"That's enough," said Nat. "I don't want to hear about you niggas sick ass sex games. Y'all sound like a bunch of pervs anyway. There's other business on the FEE menu anyway. I haven't quite decided how we gone do the money drop, I know it's got to be some slick shit. I'll figure that shit out real soon."

"I hope so," Dale said. "Cause that's when kidnappings always go bad on the money drop. That shit gone have to be real slick."

"I know," Nat said before sipping his beer. "I know. But we got them now so ain't no turning back. That's our money down there in the basement. That's our big payoff. A hundred and fifty stacks apiece. Now that's cash."

"What if they don't pay up?" asked Mar. "If they don't come up with that cash are we really gone merc a lady and two kids?"

Nat gave him a look. "Hell the fuck yeah. They better come up with that paper. I done my homework on this one. Six hundred ain't no problem for them. If they decide to think that we was bluffing then that's too bad for them downstairs 'cause they shole as fuck dead then."

"I don't give a fuck about blasting no bitch," Dale said. "That ain't even no big thing to me. But I can't even see killing no kids."

Nat took several pulls from a blunt before he said, "Well let's hope that it don't have to come to that 'cause then that means we ain't got the money. But if it do go like that, then fuck everybody else."

CHAPTER 24

Cocaine took a long look at her dress and shoes in the completely mirrored foyer of her upscale condominium. The dress was perfect but the shoes weren't doing it for her. She went back to the huge closet in her room and found just the right pair of shoes to go with her dress. Back in the mirrored foyer, she touched up her lipstick and blew herself a kiss before grabbing her Louis Vutton purse and gliding out the door. A short elevator ride later she was striding across the private parking lot behind the building to her parking space. As she passed her midnight blue Saab she turned up her nose at the car. Though it was expensive and still new it gave her nothing but trouble. She walked past her Saab over to her egg shell colored BMW coupe. It wasn't as new as the Saab, but it was still a classy car.

She keyed the lock and got in. She put the key in the ignition and turned, but the car didn't come to life. She turned the key back and tried again—nothing.

"Damn!" she exclaimed slamming her hands against the steering wheel. "What in the hell is going on? Shit, I can't catch a goddamned break. Fuck!"

She got out of the car and walked around it like that would fix it. She got back in and tried the key again; still nothing. She got out and looked around but she didn't see anyone, at first. Then she saw an elderly couple getting out of their car across the parking lot. She hurried toward them. The man had silver hair but as she drew nearer she could tell that he wasn't as old as his hair made him look. Whatever, she thought, he's a man he'll know what's wrong with my car.

"Excuse me sir," Cocaine said.

"Yes, young lady."

"I hate to bother you and the missus, but I'm having trouble starting my car and I'm wondering if you could take a look at it for me."

The old man scanned Cocaine for any hint of scam or sham and must have decided that she looked on the level, because he turned to his wife for her approval.

"Go ahead, Todd," the man's wife said. "See if you can help her out. She kind of reminds me of Amy a bit. I bet you can get it started for her and we won't even charge you sweetie."

"Why thank you," Cocaine said, but she was thinking yeah right, like I'd pay a man to do anything for me.

She led the man and his wife over to her car. As she opened the door of her BMW, the man stopped and scratched his head.

"Whoa there, sweetie, I didn't know that you were talking about one of these little foreign jobs," said the man.

"I don't know a thing about these hot rods. I'll take a look anyway if you'd like, but I don't know what good it'll do."

"Please just take a look for me. I'd really appreciate it."

"Well okay, but don't expect a miracle," the old man said as he took the key from Cocaine. He played around with the ignition switch for a few moments, but the car still wouldn't do a thing. It took him five minutes to figure out how to pop the hood and another ten minutes to figure out how to open it. When he did open it, he just stood there looking at the engine. Finally he turned to Cocaine with a look of absolute befuddlement on his face.

"Young lady," he said. "It's official. I don't know what in the tarnation is wrong with this hi-tech jalopy. My advice is that you call somebody to come get it and take it to one of them expensive car repair places. After you get it out of there, take it to the nearest car dealership that sells American cars and unload this thing. I'm sorry that I couldn't be of more service to you." The old man closed the hood and left with his wife. He was shaking his head all the while.

"Fuck!" seethed Cocaine. "Piece of shit. Goddammit! I don't need this shit right now!"

She started to go back upstairs to her condo, but just as quickly she *went back into the building and had the doorman call for her a taxi. When the cab arrived, she gave a doorman a tip, blew him a kiss, and hopped in the back of the cab.*

Twenty minutes later, Cocaine got out of the taxicab in front of the warehouse she co-owned with Champagne. She flung several bills at the cab driver and walked away with her high heels clicking furiously on the pavement. She went around the side of the building and looked; Champagne's black Cadillac Allante was parked there.

"Yes!" Cocaine said as she pulled her key ring from her purse. She found the key to the warehouse's side door and let herself in. "Champagne, bitch where are you?"

Champagne came from around one of the wall partitions wearing cleaning gloves, a scarf on her head, and an old jogging suit, carrying a mop and bucket.

"Coke, where you been bitch?" Champagne demanded with a hint of irritation in her voice. "You was supposed to be here three hours ago to help me clean up. This place is a fucking mess. You got this Black shit fucked up if you think I'm your slave. I know you aren't about to clean in that dress and shoes?"

Cocaine looked down at her black silk kimono dress and her expensive black high-heeled shoes. "Bitch, is you crazy! This dress cost seven hundred and the shoes cost four. I'm not about to clean shit. I'm on my way to dinner." Champagne flung the mop and bucket down. "Bitch, you must be losing your mind if you think that I'm going to be here cleaning while you're out there having you a nice time at dinner. You know that we scheduled today to clean this place up. It's really your fault that this place is a pig sty. The sheets need to be washed. The torture chamber needs to be hosed down. The hot tubs need to be cleaned. There's dust every damn where. You need to stop bullshitting Cocaine. I've been here all afternoon trying to get this place in shape."

"I keep telling you to hire a maid," Cocaine said coolly as she looked at her manicure. "I'm not gone even lie, Champagne, I don't be feeling

this spring cleaning shit you be wanting to do every few weeks. I don't be having the time or energy for this shit. We can get one of these half-starved ass college students to bring they ass up in here and clean this place up."Champagne threw her hands up in disgust. "How many times do I have to tell your ignorant white ass that what we do here isn't exactly legal. We don't need some maid or college student up in here sniffing around in our business. If we get our asses in here every few weeks and get the place clean then we won't have to worry about it getting so filthy that it's a major job getting it back together. I swear Cocaine, you're a fucking pig and I'm getting sick of you shifting all the cleaning duties on me."

"Well, if you think you're mad now wait until I ask you this."

Champagne folded her arms and tapped her foot. "What is it? What could you possibly want?"

"Champagne, you know I love you right," Cocaine started.

"Bitch, what is it?"

"Just one little teeny tiny itsy-bitsy thing."

"Cocaine!"

"Did I ever tell you how pretty you are, Champagne?"

"Bitch, what is it?" Champagne exploded.

"Alright, alright. I need to borrow your car."

"Oh hell no, Cocaine. You have got to be joking. You are the only person in the world with two cars and you still need to borrow somebody else's. Hell no. The last time I let you borrow my Porsche, you brought it back with some scratches on it and you swore that you didn't do it but I knew you did. What's wrong with your doggone cars?"

"Girl, my new Saab is making some crazy ass noise and smoking when I drive it. I got to take it back to the dealer and my BMW won't start. It was fine yesterday, but today when I came out it wouldn't start."

"What is it doing?"

"I don't know what the hell its' doing. I'm not no damn mechanic. It's not doing nothing, that's why I need your car. I probably left the

headlights on or something and drained the battery, I don't know. All I know is that I need a ride and it won't go."

"Well why didn't you have your date come pick you up?" asked Champagne.

"Because I don't want to be in the same car as him. If I ride with him that means I've got leave when he wants to leave. I want to be able to go when I want to go. That cuts down on a lot of awkward shit, like me having to get out of his car and explain to his ass why he can't come up for coffee, to use the bathroom, or no pussy. Half the time a man take you out and feed you, then he got you in the car later, that makes him think he's going to automatically get a chance to grope you. I don't have time for that shit. I like to show them what they ain't getting and make them figure out how to get it. Now are you going to let me use the car or not, Champagne?"

Cocaine hit her with her begging eyes and her patented long face and before Champagne knew it she was handing over her car keys.

"Thank you, thank you," Cocaine said as she hugged Champagne.

"Get off me, white girl. Let me tell you. Don't scratch my doggone car. Not one little scratch. If you scratch this one you bought it. I was going to say that you need to come back and pick me up, but I'm not stupid enough to think that would happen. I'm taking a cab home and you need to bring my car there tonight. Not tomorrow. Not the day after. Tonight. Are you listening white girl?"

"Of course I'm listening to you," Cocaine said, but she was already heading for the side door. "Tonight. I'll bring your car back tonight. No scratches. I got it."

Champagne followed her to the door and stood holding it open as Cocaine walked over to her Allante and got in it. Cocaine closed the car door and waved to Champagne as she stuck the key in the ignition and turned it. The car exploded into a massive fireball. As the flames reached the gas tank there was a secondary explosion a split second later. The second explosion wasn't as powerful as the first, but it succeeded in completely engulfing what was left of the vehicle in flames. The concussive force of the first blast made the metal warehouse door slam into Champagne's head. The door knocked Champagne out and she flew backwards into the warehouse. Blood trickled from her forehead onto the floor. Outside the warehouse in the fireball that was once Champagne's Cadillac Allante, Cocaine's mutilated corpse continued to burn.

CHAPTER 25

Ronald walked through the doors of the penthouse talking on the wireless headset to his cell phone. The moment he walked into the living room, he took one look at Champagne's tear stained face and the stressed look that Shaunna was wearing and he cut short his call.

He took a seat on the sofa across from Champagne.

"They took my babies, Ronnie," Champagne said miserably as tears dripped from her eyes. "They got Anaya and Kenton. They even took Cynthia. Ronnie, they got my babies. I'm so scared for them right now."

Who got Kenton and Anaya?" asked Ronald. "What are you talking about, Chammy? Shaunny, what is she talking about?"

Champagne had dropped her head down onto Shaunna's lap. Shaunna rubbed her head and back consolingly.

"Somebody took the twins and Cynthia," Shaunna stated. "We don't know who, but they've been in contact with us already. They say they want six hundred thousand in cash or they're going to kill them. They say if we contact the police they're going to kill them."

"How long have they had them?"

"Near as we can tell since earlier today. Cynthia picked the kids up from school earlier and they must have gotten snatched soon after that."

"When are they saying that they want the money?" Ronald asked.

"We've got two days to come up with the cash."

"Do you have any clue who it is that got them? I mean did they say anything, I mean y'all not really telling me nothing. What about Cynthia?"

"All they said was that we have 48 hours to come up with the cash or the twins and Cynthia are dead. The second time they called, they put Cynthia on the phone so at least we know that she's alright so far." Ronald jumped up.

"Where you going?" Shaunna asked.

"I'm going to talk to JC and let him know what's going on," Ronald said.

Champagne lifted her head from Shaunna's lap. "You can't do that. I know those are his kids too and he has a right to know, but I don't want to tell him something like this in his condition. You know him Ronnie, he'll be trying to disconnect his IVs and shit. There's no way you could tell him something like this without him trying to get out of the bed and see what's happening. At this point all that will do is make things worse."

"How are we not going to tell him about his kids, Chammy? Those are his kids."

"You think I don't know that!" Champagne screamed. "You think I don't know that he would want to know what's happening? His children are somewhere scared and possibly hurt and you think I don't want to run to my man; their father, and let him know? All that will cause is more problems. I have to think about the kids and Cynthia right now and what's best for them. I don't have time to try and talk some sense into their father."

Ronald came back and sat down. He put his head in his hands. "Alright, alright. I get it. I'm sorry. It's just that I know that J is built for this type of shit. With him out of commission and Rat locked up, I don't know what we should do. I vote that we pay them as soon as they set it up and hope that every thing turns out alright. I mean, they're kidnappers so the main thing they want is the money, right?"

"We have to assume that, Ronnie," Champagne said a little less harshly. "We have to hope that they'll take the money and return the kids, but I've got to think 'worse case scenario' too. You can pay off this type of people and they'll still kill them. We have to put our emotions to the side and take a real good look at this. I know that we don't have JC and Rat, but we still have each other. Do y'all understand where I'm coming from?"

TRIPLE TAKE 2: CHAMPAGNE'S KISS

"I understand," said Shaunna. "I understand that we're on our own and if we want to see the kids and Cynthia again we're going to have to get them back."

"Can we at least get some help?" Ronald asked throwing his hands up. "I mean is that asking too much?"

I would love some damn help, but who can we trust right now?" Champagne asked.

"I know the Apostles will help us all they can. They would look at that as a personal favor to JC. Also Rat's guys, his rap guys, M and Ty. I know for a fact that Rat trusts them with his life."

"The Apostles, I don't have a problem with them. I know how they loact with them. I know from what JC and Rat told me about them that they wouldn't have anything to do with something like this. As for M and Ty, well I'm not questioning Rat's judgment, but how do we know that these dudes ain't the ones that have my babies?"

"That's true," Ronald agreed. "I see what you're saying. This shit is crazy. You're right; we really can't trust anybody. What do you want me to do, Chammy?"

"All I need for you to do is get that money together and hang around here for the next couple of days, while we get my damn kids back. I'm going to call the Apostles and see if they can give us some help."

"I'm on it," Ronnie said. He stood up and walked over to Champagne and Shaunna. He gave them both a hug. "The money is no problem, we do have it. I'll be back soon. Call me and let me know if anything changes." Champagne grabbed Ronald's hand. "Ronnie, I'm sorry about yelling at you. I know that you mean well, but this is something that we're going to have to handle. Trust me, it's the only way."

Ronald squeezed her hand firmly but gently. "I don't like it one bit, but I'm going to trust you. I have to remember that you guys were doing this type of stuff when I first met you. I'll be alright, just as soon as we have Anaya, Kenton, and Cynthia back safely."

"Alright, Ronnie. Go head and take care of the busyness."

"That's what I do, Chammy. I take care of the busyness."

Ronald left the penthouse. As he rode the elevator down to the garage, he thought about how he watched the women upstairs transform in minutes from regular women into gutsy, dangerous lionesses. He'd forgotten that's what they were when he met them. Silently he said a prayer for the safe return of the twins and Cynthia before leaving the elevator.

Back in the penthouse, Champagne stood up and wiped her face. "Shaunny, I'll understand if you're not up to this 'cause you're pregnant, but I'm going to call Dante, he's the Head Apostle and then I'm going to get several of my damn guns and I'm getting my kids back."

Shaunna threw down the couch pillow she'd been holding and stood also. "That's what I wanted to hear. I ain't shot nobody in a while neither. You make the call, while I put on me some jeans and some comfortable shoes."

Shaunna went to get dressed while Champagne went to make the call. She started to sigh as she took JC's cell phone from its charger, but she repressed it. Aint' no time to be acting soft, she said to herself as she dialed Dante's number, my kids are depending on me.

...

Shaunna pulled into the parking lot at the Maxwell Street polish sausage stand on 79th and Stony Island. She parked beside a gold Tahoe truck where two young Apostles stood eating polishes. The rear doors of the Tahoe opened and Head Apostles, Dante and Murderman, stepped out. They both took turns hugging the women, though Murderman looked like he hated being touched by human hands any more than necessary. During the hugs, they felt the hardware and bulletproof vests the women were wearing and carrying on their persons.

"Chammy, you can fill in Dante and Murderman while I get me a pork chop sandwich," Shaunna said.

Champagne looked at her. "Really?"

160

TRIPLE TAKE 2: CHAMPAGNE'S KISS

"What?" asked Shaunna defensively. "You're the one that suggested we meet at a polish stand. I'm sorry, but I'm starving."

"Girl, gone head. It don't take both of us to tell them what's going on. And if you hungry then you gone get on my nerves anyway. Get me a Pepsi."

"That's a lot of hardware you wearing," Dante said to Champagne. "What are those?"

"Glocks," answered Champagne. "Old school clips. Sweet sixteen with one up top."

"That's what I'm talking about," Murderman said. "I love a woman that knows her tools. Where did Killah J find you 'cause I want one just like you?"

"He didn't find me, I found him," said Champagne with a smile.

"How's he doing?" Dante said. "I assume this is about the cats that laid him up. Where's Rat at anyway?"

Champagne's smile disappeared. "Well, J's doing much better. He's out of the woods as the doctors say. Rat is locked up. He's in the County on the way back to the joint to see the parole board. This isn't about the dudes that did that to JC, Rat took care of that right before he got locked up. He didn't give me any details, but he said that it was all good. He isn't locked up for that though. He got some bullshit parole violation and he got caught with a pistol. As for the reason I asked to meet with you now, we need to ask for a big favor from you all."

"Anything for my man's woman," Dante said. "What's up?"

"Somebody kidnapped my babies and their nanny. I don't who's got them, but they're asking for money."

"How much?" Murderman asked.

"Six hundred thousand. The money isn't the problem. What we're worried about is us paying them off and they still come up dead."

"How long they been gone?" asked Dante. "And why such an odd number? Who asks for six hundred stacks?"

"The nearest we can narrow it down, they got snatched earlier today.

The kidnappers have been in touch with us twice, but they haven't given us instructions for the drop. They gave us forty-eight hours to get the money together. The number is crazy, but the way they explained it is, five hundred for my kids and one hundred for their nanny. Like they're really giving us a choice. I don't want them motherfuckers to have their hands on my children for that long, but we don't know which way to turn, so that's why I called you. We know that you guys run this city on the down low, so we're hoping that maybe you could give us some info on who or where to look."

Dante thought about what she'd said for a minute. "Damn, Champagne this is some bullshit. I don't have the slightest idea who might have your kids. It's safe to say that it ain't no Apostle, but other than that I can't tell you much. Right now because the drug game is so fucked up, there's plenty of thirsty ass niggas out here who would pull this type of shit. It could take forever to run them down, but like you said don't nobody want they kids in some gutter motherfuckas hands for any length of time. Do Killah J know what's going on?"

"I didn't tell him about the kids. I just don't feel that he's strong enough right now and I don't want him to get all worked up."

"What about the cops?" Murderman asked. "Did y'all tell them what's up?"

"No, the kidnappers were real specific about that. I know you're supposed to go to the cops, but they might get my kids killed. My belief is that we're going to have to do this on our own."

"Pretty much," Dante agreed. "This situation is fucked up enough without some cop trying to get on the news and the kids end up dead. I hate to say it like that, but that's the truth. The only thing I can see us doing is hitting the streets and seeing if we can get a line on the motherfuckas who got them. What you think Murder?"

"Well you know how good I am at getting information," Murderman said. "I know of a couple of crews with the nuts to pull off some shit like this. I keep track of such shit just in case I ever need it. I can roll with y'all and we can check shit out. I need some action anyway."

"As much as I want to say yes to you being with us, I can't let you. Whoever this is knows a lot about us already. They may be watching us and see you and think you're a cop or something and jump the gun. I think it would be more of a help to us if you ran a separate investigation."

"That makes sense," Murderman said. "I'm sorry I wasn't even thinking about it like that. I definitely wouldn't want to be the reason y'all seeds got hurt. Don't worry though, I'll get my top A's straight on top of this. We got a city wide network so if there's info out there we'll squeeze it out of the streets."

"Thanks," Champagne said. "We're going to give the impression that we're going along with everything they've said so it'll look like everything is above board. Me and Shaunna..."

"Hold on," interrupted Dante. "There's something you said. You said it seems like they know a lot about you. What did they say that let you know they had info on you?"

Champagne wracked her brains for a few seconds. "It wasn't anything real big. I guess it was more of a feeling that I was getting than anything. Now that I think about it, they knew JC was my man, they knew that that amount of money wouldn't be hard for us to get; they knew where we live because that's where they sent the cell phone that they're using to contact me. Whoever it is did their homework 'cause they knew enough to get their hands on the twins and their nanny."

Dante had a real thoughtful look on his face. "Think hard. Do you remember being followed or strange phone calls? Anything that may have seemed out of the ordinary but it wasn't a big deal at the time it happened?"

Champagne thought for a moment. "Not really. So much has been going on in our lives with our work and then J getting shot up, and then Rat getting locked up, but I don't remember anything that looked out of the ordinary. I really don't know how they got the up on our kids, but they did. There's no telling how long they've been watching us."

Y. Blak Moore

"It wouldn't be the Concrete Click," Murderman commented. "Right now they're too busy making funeral arrangements and in-fighting. Don't ask. I told y'all I keep my ear to the street. If it was them they'd kill the kids outright, not try to ransom them."

Shaunna walked up to them carrying several greasy paper bags with food in them. She handed Champagne a can of soda. "Sorry y'all," she said. "I was hungry. Them onions was smelling so good, I would have been thinking about this place all night."

"It's cool," Dante said. "What's your next move from here, Champagne?"

"Well, I was thinking the first thing we'll do is check on our people like JC's mom and Rat's mom and brothers and sisters. Just make sure that everybody else is okay. Then from there we got a couple of our people that we have to talk to so we can see where their heads are at."

Dante came forward and gave both Champagne and Shaunna a brief hug. He looked Champagne straight in the eyes. "Look here, Champagne. We gone get right on top of this here, don't worry. We gone put the pressure down like these are my seeds. Mainly 'cause Killah J and Rat is our peoples. That goes for y'all too. Them dudes ain't never did nothing but right by us and made sure we was eating. The Apostles don't turn their backs on their friends. Make sure that you keep in touch with us. I'm turning Murder loose on the city, so we should be able to turn up something. Anything we find out we'll fill you in and you do the same. The kids are gone be alright if we can help it."

"Thanks, Dante," Champagne said.

"We're going to get out of here. I'll call you with anything. Thanks again."

Champagne and Shaunna got back into the Taurus and after Shaunna almost got them killed trying to bite her sandwich and pull into traffic, they went south on Stony Island. Murderman and Dante returned to the rear of the Tahoe. Their driver pulled out into traffic going north on Stony Island. "Tay, what you think?" Murderman asked.

164

TRIPLE TAKE 2: CHAMPAGNE'S KISS

"Right now I'm feeling for them ladies," Dante answered. "This is some real bullshit when a motherfucka got yo kids. I hate niggas who pull this type of bullshit. That's some thirsty ass shit. It's fucked up too that they dudes ain't able to be there for them. They seem like they ready to handle the business though. God got to be with them on this one, I meant every word of what I said. You can go work yo magic 'cause them ladies need some answers as soon as possible."

A smile broke onto Murderman's face. It wasn't warm at all, really more of a cold, evil thing.

"Well you do the praying and I'll do the slaying," Murderman said. To the driver, he said, "Yo, A drop me off over at Yo-Yo's strip on 71st. I've got work to do."

CHAPTER 26

Dale put Kenton back into the dog cage and locked it. From there he went and flopped on the basement couch next to Mar.

"I don't know what the fuck they gone do if they got to use the bathroom again," Dale complained. "I ain't about to be no fucking babysitter. We should have bought they little asses some fuckin' pampers or they better just use it on theyselves in them damn cages."

"You the one that volunteered to take them to the bathroom," Nat said. "I said fuck 'em. Them little motherfuckas would be pissy and shitty waiting on me to take them to the bathroom. I ain't got no kids..."

"That's right FEE, you ain't got no kids," Mar said. "If you had kids then you wouldn't want to see nobody kids pissing and shitting on theyselves. All we got to do is feed them a couple of times and take them to the bathroom and then we gone get that money and they asses is gone."

"What you need to do is shut them fucking dogs up," Julius said. "Them motherfuckas ain't shut up once since we brought them fucking kids here. That shit about to give me a damn headache."

"Let's go upstairs anyway, FEE," Nat said. "They are starting to get on my damn nerve. We need to hang out for a minute too like everything is normal. We don't want nobody guessing that we up to something."

At Nat's suggestion, the four members of FEE left the basement. They went outside to hang on Nat's front porch, something they knew the residents of their neighborhood were used to seeing them do. In Nat's huge front yard was a horseshoe game that they often played. Nat and Mar, constant competitors against one another, began playing horseshoes and betting twenty dollars a game. On the porch, Julius and Dale watched the games and made side bets. They had been out there for close to an hour when Julius got up and went to the screen door.

"Where you going, FEE?" Dale asked. "This nigga Mar about to lose this one too and that's gone be fifty you owe me nigga."

"Fuck you, bet off," Julius said. "I gotta take a shit."

"Yo soft ass, ain't no bet off," Dale said. "When you get back we gone finish this shit. And make sure you wash yo damn hands so you can hand me my money."

Inside Nat's house, Julius went past the first floor bathroom to the inside basement door. He paused and didn't hear anyone following him so he slipped down into the basement. The scene hadn't changed a bit; the dogs were still barking, the kids were still in the cages, and the nanny was still chained to the pipe. Julius listened again to hear if anyone came behind him, but he didn't hear anything. He slid over to Cynthia who began whimpering when she felt him near her. Her whimpering seemed to excite him as Julius' breathing grew ragged.

"You'se a bad bitch," he whispered in her ear as he rounded her. "I wish we could have met under different circumstances 'cause then you would be my bitch. I would love to have a bitch like you. I would give you whatever you want. You wouldn't have to worry about me cheating on you or nothing."

Cynthia stopped whimpering at Julius' soft seductive whispering. He took that to be a sign that she was feeling him so he cupped her breasts from behind. She started to struggle and make noises behind her gag. Julius ignored her protestations and lifted her shirt and pulled her breasts free from her bra. He came around the front of her and ogled her titties.

"Damn, bitch," he said. "You got some motherfuckin' tomatoes. Them motherfuckers look good. Gotdamn. Let me see how they taste. I hope you ain't got no musty ass titties 'cause I know some bitches don't clean they titties. Titties is just like nuts, you got to be careful 'cause they'll get musty."

Julius leaned forward and captured Cynthia's nipples in his mouth. She tried to wriggle out of his grasp, but he was determined to suck her titties.

"These motherfuckas is nice," he said as he stood up and avoided a kick from her. "Ain't no dirt or hair on the nipples. I like them. Clean, pretty titties."

Julius got behind her again. He whispered, "It's okay if you fight. I like it when they fight. If you give it up too easy then I know you're a bustdown bitch. I hate bustdowns. I like a bitch with a little class, the kind that make you fight a little bit for it."

He unbuttoned and unzipped her jeans from behind. He was grunting already as he pulled down her pants. By now Cynthia was yelling into her gag, but the only sound that escaped was a muffled grunt. The sight of Cynthia's form fitting satin panties had Julius going wild. He pulled her panties down around her ankles too. He grinned as he stroked himself through his jeans.

"I knew it, bitch. I knew you had ass like a motherfucka. You got a fat ass booty. That's what the fuck I'm talking about. I'm gone love fucking that fat ass of yours."

Julius unbuttoned his jeans and pulled out his dick. He rubbed it back and forth on Cynthia's buttocks. Roughly he kicked her legs apart and prepared to insert himself into her.

"Nigga, what the fuck is you doing!" Nat barked. He was standing on the last step of the basement stairs. "I told yo fat perverted ass to leave her the fuck alone, Julie! Now I catch you down here about to take the pussy! What the fuck is wrong with you?" Julius had been so into the act that he hadn't heard Nat come down the basement steps. Even now as Nat was hollering at him, he didn't put his dick back in his pants or relinquish his hold on Cynthia's hind parts.

"Come on FEE," Julius said trying to keep his tone light. "I wadn't trying to do nothing but have a little fun with this bitch. This bitch don't mean nothing to us. I wasn't going to damage her, I was just going to put some dick in her. She still gone be in perfectly good shape for us to get that money for her ass."

Nat advanced on them. "No, old dumb ass boy you wasn't just going to put some dick in her, yo dumb ass was going to put some DNA in her. Now put yo dick back in yo pants and get yo ass back outside."

"This is all of our hostage," Julius protested. "How you just gone say that can't nobody fuck her. Until they pay for her this is our bitch to do with what we please and I want some fuckin' pussy."

"Goofy ass nigga, what the fuck is wrong with you? Are you that crazy over some pussy that you ain't gone listen to me?"

"Fuck that, FEE!" Julius pouted. "You always bossing me around. I do everything you say, now I just want a little ass and you talking shit. I ain't trying to hear that. You can't keep protecting this bitch. I'm finta fuck her. You can have her next if you want, but I'm fucking this bitch now."

Julius spread Cynthia's cheeks even wider and attempted to insert himself into her. After pulling his pistol, Nat strode over to him and put the gun to his head. Julius began to shrink from the cold steel at his temple.

Through his gritted teeth, Nat said, "Motherfuckin' bitch ass nigga! Once I give a fuckin' order that's it! That's why I'm the boss, 'cause I'll blow yo fuckin' head off if you don't do what the fuck I said do! Now put yo dick back in yo fuckin' pants, go upstairs and get you a beer to cool off and take yo ass back outside. Do you understand me?"

Julius responded by tucking himself back in and zipping his pants up. He slowly pulled his head away from the gun and after a couple of sidelong glances at Nat and Cynthia, he stomped up the basement steps.

Nat stuck his gun back in his waistband. He bent over and pulled up Cynthia's panties and pants only slightly pausing to check out her assets. When her clothes were righted, Nat took a key from his pocket and unlocked the handcuffs from Cynthia's hands. He led her up the basement stairs to the bathroom on the first floor of his house. In the bathroom, he helped her sit on the floor and handcuffed her to pipe under the sink.

"You should be safe in here," Nat said as he stood up. "Just for safekeeping though, I'm gone lock this door from the outside. I'll check in on you in awhile to make sure that you straight."

Nat closed the bathroom door and locked it from the outside using an ancient skeleton key. Out on the front porch, Nat motioned for his crew to draw near.

"The nanny is locked in the bathroom," he announced. "I've got the only fuckin' key. Now before anybody else acts like they can't control themselves, do I need to lock them kids in a closet or something?"

"Man, I ain't finta fuck with no kids," said Julius looking shamefaced. "Y'all can't trip on me getting no pussy. I'll take me some pussy, that's in the game, but I ain't no pervert, though."

"Well I hope that's the very last time that we have this fuckin' discussion," Nat said. "The very next time I have to tell somebody this shit, there's gone be hell to tell the captain. Everybody got that?" Everybody nodded. Nat sat up and looked around the basement. He knew without looking at his wristwatch that it was pretty late. He looked over at the cages the kids were being kept in—they were asleep. He'd had Dale feed them some chips and sandwiches and then take them to the bathroom and they'd finally dozed off. The dogs were finally asleep or lying down so it was finally quiet. Dale, Mar, and Julius were asleep on the different couches and easy chairs from the effects of all the weed they'd smoked.

Quietly Nat slipped from the couch and up the basement stairs. He took the skeleton key from his pocket and let himself in the bathroom. Cynthia was asleep on the floor, curled up like she'd tried to get as comfortable as possible on the small mat in front of the sink. He locked the door behind himself and knelt on the floor beside her. The moment she felt someone near she started to wriggle around. As gently as possible, Nat removed the tape from her mouth and eyes. Next he removed one of her handcuffs and helped her stand up.

"You alright?" Nat asked.

TRIPLE TAKE 2: CHAMPAGNE'S KISS

Cynthia shoved him. "Am I alright? Am I alright? Besides the fact that I've been handcuffed, gagged, and blindfolded? Besides the fact that you're supposed to be watching out for me and that fucking, nasty, fat ass friend of yours almost raped me? Where the hell was you when he was trying to rape me?"

"He didn't rape you did he?"

"Damn near. That nigga had my panties down about to stick it in. That was too fucking close for comfort. Now you've got me laying in the gotdamn bathroom chained to a fucking sink for hours. You better hurry up and get that damn money because I can't take this shit anymore. I'm telling you I'm ready to leave now." Nat leaned against the sink and pulled Cynthia into his arms. "He didn't rape you did he? I stopped him before he could. It took everything I had in me not to kill him for putting his hands on my girl."

"Whatever nigga. I couldn't tell when that nigga had my fucking pussy in his hand about to put his damn dick in me. I didn't feel like my man was looking out for me then. I didn't sign on for all this. I didn't know that it was 'sposed to be like this. All you were supposed to do was kidnap me and them brats and hold us 'til they came up with the money. I told you now was the best time 'cause JC is in the hospital shot all up and Rat done got locked up. Ain't nobody left but them two sadity hoes and that half fag ass business manager of theirs. This shit is 'sposed to be easy and quick, but here it is I got to be handcuffed to pipes and shit in that foul ass basement while some fat ass, little dick, nigga trying to take some pussy."

"That's enough," Nat said. "I done told you that I was sorry bout Julie almost raping you. That's really a good thing 'cause it shows that they is still sleep to the beat that you'se really my girl."

"How the fuck is it a good thing that I was almost raped? Nat, you got a fucked up way of looking at shit. I don't give a fuck about how sleep they is to our plan, you should have made sure that they keep they damn hands off me."

"What I was trying to say was that this worked out for the best. Since I got you up here in the bathroom away from where anybody can see you, I can give you the key to the cuffs. When I go back downstairs, you can climb out the window and gone to the crib. From there be ready to hit the road. I'll tell they dumb asses that you escaped and then I'll tell them that I'm going to look for you and then I'll meet you at your house. The money we're still sending that out to Richmond by Fedex. By the time we get to Virginia, the cash will be waiting on us and we'll be able to kick back. All we got to do is follow the plan from here out and everything will be cool."

Sensing that she was still angry even after his apology and explanation, Nat began to kiss her. At first her lips were unyielding, but as he kept kissing her and letting his hands roam over her figure, she began to give in. She opened her mouth and allowed Nat's tongue to explore her mouth. He slipped his hands under her shirt and lifted her bra. Tenderly he manipulated her nipples until they were hard to the touch. He lowered his head and took them in his mouth, gently nipping and sucking until Cynthia let go of a light moan. As he bent, Nat unbuttoned her jeans and worked them down over her hips. Leaving her panties up, he used his hand to massage between her legs as he continued to suckle her breasts. He slid his hand into her panties and slipped a finger into the wetness he found there. Cynthia moaned louder and began rubbing Nat's head. He maneuvered her over to the sink to let her butt rest on the sink's lip. He knelt in front of her and pulled her panties to the side. She put one leg up on the edge of the tub to allow him easy access as Nat began flicking her pussy lips with his tongue. He seized her clitoris with his lips and sucked gently while flicking it with his tongue. Cynthia's leg began shaking as she gripped his head tighter. Sensing her excitement, Nat began to alternate between sucking on her clit and sliding his tongue up and down her slit. Suddenly Cynthia's grip on his head turned to iron as her legs began shaking uncontrollably. He shifted his hands to support her weight, but he didn't stop as she gushed a sweet orgasm onto his lips and chin.

When she was finished quivering, Nat stood and wiped his mouth. He turned her around and placed her hands on the sink. He placed his gun on the back of the toilet and pulled her panties down to her thighs. Next he freed his dick from his pants. She reached back and guided him into her wetness. Both of them looked at one another in the bathroom mirror over the sink as Nat pumped her from behind. As his thrusts grew harder and stronger, Cynthia's eyes closed and she let her head sink back onto Nat's shoulder. He held her hips tight and continued to bang away at her. Cynthia rose up on her toes and ground herself back against him. She started working her hips clockwise as he pumped drawing a look of pure pleasure on his face. He released her hips and reached around to capture her jiggling breasts. Minutes later, he began to moan and buried his face into her neck as he climaxed.

"I'm coming in your wet pussy!" he whispered fiercely. "I'm coming!"

Cynthia reached back and grabbed Nat's butt and helped him pump her. "That's right, baby," she whispered. "Come in Mama's pussy. Let it all go. Put that nut deep in me."

With a grunt, Nat spent himself and stopped pumping. He smothered Cynthia's neck with kisses before withdrawing from her. He took a face towel to wipe himself off and gargled a shot of mouthwash. Cynthia had pulled her pants and panties back up and stood back watching him. Once he was cleaned up, Nat opened the small bathroom window and turned to her.

"Now look baby," he said. "Gone straight to the crib and lay low. Be ready to ride the minute I get there. I'll be there as soon as I get hold of the dough. Gone head."

Cynthia climbed out of the window and made the short jump down to the ground. She was on the side of the house. Carefully she picked her way through the side yard and out into the alley. Making sure she stayed in the shadows, Cynthia began jogging toward home.

Nat watched her until she was out of sight. He knew that it wouldn't take her more than five minutes to make it to her small town home several blocks from there. Silently he thanked the stars for the day he'd met her and she'd told him about her job as a nanny to the kids of some rich Black people with questionable backgrounds. It hadn't taken him long to formulate his plan of kidnapping the kids. He had even let her think it was her idea. She was lucky that he'd fallen in love with her or he would have cut her out of the equation too. He'd let her stick around for awhile longer, plus she was good at setting up marks for his schemes.

The double-cross that he had planned for the other members of FEE didn't have him losing the slightest bit of sleep. To him, they should have seen this coming. Really, he was tired of carrying them. He had to come up with the schemes and victims for everything they did. He made all of the plans, took care of their expenses, and kept them with weapons. He knew that it was just a matter of time before one of them got caught and told on everybody else. He wasn't sticking around for that. By the time they figured out what happened, he'd be long gone. He was tired of holding their hands anyway. They all claimed FEE, but he didn't think it was really in their hearts. When he said, fuck everybody else, he meant it. It wouldn't be hard for him to leave his house and he'd already put everything of value of his in storage. The only thing that he would really hate leaving behind would be his dog Widow. The other members of FEE hadn't noticed, but long ago he'd removed anything from that house that could give away his identity to the authorities. That was the main reason that they only robbed those that made their fortunes outside the law, because they were less likely turn to the authorities for help.

He wasn't worried about Dale, Mar, or Julius finding him once he relocated to Virginia. They were hood niggas so he wouldn't have to worry about bumping into them unless he came back to the hood. It wouldn't be a big deal for him to move up and down the East coast once he got to Richmond. He would do the same thing there: find a group of fools to follow him around as they robbed the rich to make themselves richer. The next group he would pick the same way. They didn't have to have too many brains, just enough to follow orders. If they were like the fools he was leaving behind and blew all of their dough, that was cool too because it kept them hungry. Either way it went, shit don't stop.

This scheme had come at the perfect time because he was sick of the Chi. Chicago was so full of fake ass dealers stunting like they was getting it, it had become too much of a task determining whether these actors really had some big paper before robbing them. The fact that the twins' parents were really supposed to have a nice amount of bread was a blessing. This was his chance to leave Chi-town behind and take the show on the road. The fact that he would have a bag full of money and a slick bitch on his arm when he set up base in Richmond would definitely make things very interesting.

Nat took one last look at his face in the mirror. Satisfied that he was clean, he left the bathroom, taking care to lock the door behind himself. Back downstairs in the basement, he retook his place on the couch amongst his sleeping friends.

CHAPTER 27

"Shaunna, it's me Champagne," she whispered into the telephone. "I didn't know who else to turn to. I need your help, Shaunna. I don't know what to do. Please help me. Cocaine's dead! She was in my car and it blew up. Help me, Shaunna, please. I need you. Get here as soon as possible. Don't worry about money, I'll take care of everything. You've got to get me out of here. Please come right now."

Champagne hung up the telephone and looked around her condo for the millionth time. After the car had blown up, she'd lain unconscious in the warehouse for what seemed like forever. She was finally awakened by a member of the fire department. They took her to the hospital and bandaged her head. After that several detectives questioned her for an hour, but were forced to let her go because she couldn't and didn't tell them anything. When she signed out of the hospital, she spent close to two hours changing cabs before making it to her condo. She was sure that no one could have followed her here because of the many times she'd switched cabs. Whoever had put a car bomb in her Cadillac couldn't know about this place. It wasn't in her name so she wasn't worried about that, but she wasn't taking any chances. She owned a gun, a .380, and she kept it in her hand from the moment she walked in the door.

She called Shaunna because she knew Shaunna would know what to do. She always knew what do. She knew that she had to get out of D.C., this city had gotten too small real quick. As tired as she was she hadn't closed her eyes because every time she did, she saw Cocaine waving to her before the car exploded. She was hungry, but she hadn't eaten. She didn't even trust going into the kitchen—she just wanted to sit there on the floor with the gun and her eye on front door. It was the only point of entry to her condo and she was going to guard it with her life. A piece of paper on the corner of her coffee table caught her eye. On the paper was her father's telephone number. Her stepbrother James had given it to her two *weeks ago during one of his so-called 'just check on her' calls. She didn't want to, but she was at her wits' end so she decided to call her father. Taking care to stay low, she crawled over to the table and got the number. She returned to her vantage point so she could watch the door. She dialed the number and waited for someone to pick up on the other end.*

"Master Sergeant Wells," her father said into the telephone.

"Daddy, this is JoAnn," she said in a voice barely above a whisper.

"What do you want?" he asked after a long pause.

"Daddy, I'm in trouble," she managed to squeeze out.

There was another pregnant pause. "What's going on, JoAnn?"

"Somebody tried to kill me and they killed my friend by mistake. I've got to get out of here and I need your help."

"Are they trying to kill you because of all those expensive cars and things you've managed to get your hands on?"

"Huh?" she asked, dumbfounded.

"You don't know what I'm talking about or didn't you understand the question? I know about all of the stuff you've got. James told me."

Mentally JoAnn cursed James' name for being such a suck-up to her father.

"Daddy, somebody is trying to kill me," she whined. "I don't know what to do. I haven't asked you for anything in years. I need your help now though."

"Humph. Why is someone trying to kill you, JoAnn?"

"I don't know," she said, trying hard not let her frustration leak into her voice. "It shouldn't make a difference should it?"

"What do you do for a living, JoAnn? Or better yet what did you do to get all the things James told me you that have?"

"I used to run an escort service," she replied softly.

"I knew it, you are a whore just like your mother," he stated bitterly. "Just like I always said you'd be. Now that you're in trouble because of your sluttish ways you want to call me. Well I'd take it as a personal favor if you never called me again. I hope you survive long enough to change

your whorish ways, but other than that I don't have anything to say to you. Good luck."

With a click the telephone went dead in her hand as she shook her head in disbelief. She hung up the receiver and prepared herself for the tears at her father's lack of concern for her life, but surprisingly they don't come. She had known not to expect any help from him—it would have been nice though if he could have even hinted that he cared. Gun in hand, she resigned herself to waiting for her only real friend.

Fifteen hours later when Shaunna had the doorman buzz her condo, Champagne was still sitting on the floor watching the front door. She gave the doorman permission to send Shaunna up and ran to the door to have it open so Shaunna could come straight in when she got off the elevator. She tried to smooth her hair down a bit as she stood at the front door, but she knew she had to look like a mess because she felt the swelling in her face and head.

Shaunna stepped off the elevator and looked at her friend. Champagne hurriedly escorted her into the condo. She double-locked the door and looked out the peephole before taking Shaunna into the living room.

"Champagne, what have you gotten yourself into?" Shaunna asked.

Champagne pulled Shaunna onto the floor and sat down beside her. In a whisper, she told Shaunna everything that had happened in her absence, up to Cocaine being incinerated by a car bomb meant for her. Shaunna's head was whirling at the lurid details of the things Champagne was telling her. When Champagne was finished, she sat in total silence for moments.

"What do you think I should do, Shaunny?" Champagne asked desperately.

"There's only one thing you can do. Get the hell out of here. But to do that safely, you're going to need some help and there's only one person I know that can or would help you."

"Who?"

"Misty."

...

TRIPLE TAKE 2: CHAMPAGNE'S KISS

In Misty's' office at the club, Champagne was still nervous even though she still had her gun. They had been waiting on Misty to come upstairs to the office for twenty minutes already. Shaunna had already outlined to her what she needed to do to get Misty's' help. Champagne didn't care at this moment, she would have even given Misty some head at this point if it would oil the old girl's sense of fair play. Misty's' office looked like it could have been the set of an old pimp movie. It was supposed to be an office, but actually it was a fully furnished suite, decorated with enough fake leopard skin print here to upholster a fleet of Coupe DeVille's. Several large, evil looking electric eels swam in a humongous aquarium in the wall behind Misty's desk giving Champagne even more of the shivers. "What's taking her so long?" Champagne said impatiently as she paced the office, taking care to stay away from the fish tank. "What the hell is she playing at, a waiting game?"

"She's coming," Shaunna said. "You need to calm down and sit down. She'll be here."

"But when?"

"Now," Misty said as she swept into the room. "I'm here ladies of mine."

Misty still dressed like a grade school teacher, but she'd had her white gray hair cut into a severe page boy hairdo. She looked as spry and timeless as ever, as she glided into the room, her customary walking cane barely touching the floor. She gave Shaunna a light, quick hug, but when she hugged Champagne she almost buried her face in Champagne's breasts. When she released her, she lightly patted Champagne on the butt, but Champagne wasn't complaining.

"Have a seat, ladies," Misty said. "Anything to drink?"

"Nothing for me," Shaunna said.

"I'll take a Jack and Coke," Champagne said.

Misty went to the bar and poured Champagne a nice slug of Jack Daniels and Coca-Cola. She made herself a Cosmopolitan and then took her seat behind her desk in a large leather chair that dwarfed her diminutive frame.

Now tell Misty what she can do for you, my girls."

Champagne sighed and looked at Shaunna.

Come on now, don't be shy," Misty said. "Believe me, there's nothing you could say that would shock this old bird. I've seen and heard it all."

"I don't know where to start," Champagne confessed.

"Begin at the beginning," Misty said.

Champagne looked over to Shaunna with a questioning look. "Tell her everything you told me," Shaunna said. "The only way she'll be able to help you is if she knows what she's dealing with."

With a mighty sigh, Champagne began to fill Misty in on the details of her double life leading up to Cocaine's death. During her story, Misty didn't blink once no matter how explicit or illegal their activities seemed. She was perfectly still and quiet until Champagne was finished.

"So basically you're trying to get out of town in one piece?" asked Misty once Champagne was through.

Champagne nodded her head and took a gulp of her drink.

"That shouldn't be too much of a problem. I'll have to make a few calls first. You know relocation could get pretty expensive."

"I'm aware that nothing in life is free," Champagne said. "I have twenty thousand dollars for your help to make sure that I make it safely to Chicago. I'm also prepared to make sure that you're more than compensated for the help you'll be giving me. I'm also willing to make you the deal of your lifetime."

Misty used her desk lighter to ignite the tip of one of her Salem cigarettes. "Just what is this deal, sweetie? Are you offering to take me with you?"

"Nothing as earth-shattering as that," Champagne said. "But I am willing to sell you my condo, my toy store, and the warehouse for pennies on the dollar. The only thing I want to leave with is some of my furniture from the condo, my cars and truck, and my clothes. I don't want anything from the store and you can definitely have everything at the warehouse."

Misty sat forward in her chair and put her elbows on the desk. "Are *you sure that you want to stick your neck out to get your things?"*

"I'm not going to stick out my neck. I'm going to be with you for safekeeping while Shaunna oversees the removal of my things. I won't be coming out of hiding until it's time to go. Here's five thousand to hire the movers and get the ball rolling." Champagne tossed a tightly bound roll of money onto Misty's desk, before finishing her drink. She sat her empty glass on Misty's desk and waited for her to pick up the money, but she didn't.

"So, what if I said 'no' to all of this Champagne? And how do you know that I won't sell you out to the Senator that wants to kill you?"

"That's simple," Champagne said with way more confidence than she felt. "I know your motto. Money talks, but it also keeps the best secrets. You wouldn't have lasted all these years in business if you were stupid. I know about all the different pieces of property that you own all around this town, so the things I'm giving you for a steal would be a sound investment on any day. Besides the cash I'm paying you, you won't take actual ownership of the properties until I've reached Chicago safely with your payment."

Misty exhaled smoke from her nostrils in two smooth streams and laughed. "I knew that I hadn't lost my eye for talent when I met you. Everybody thinks I'm getting old, but I'm like an old horse trainer who's handled thoroughbreds all of their life. I know horseflesh and I can still pick a winner. Of course, I'll help you out, but it's not just for the money. I like you Champagne. You're one of the smart girls, you've just got learn to keep better company. When you get to Chicago, don't go too fast. Take your time and most importantly learn from your mistakes. Now if you want you can climb into the bed over there and get you some rest while I make the necessary calls. I promise that I won't climb into bed with you. We're partners and I never try to screw my partners."

As Champagne looked across the room at the circular leopard skin covered bed, she realized that it'd been quite a while since she'd felt safe enough to close her eyes and sleep for any amount of time. She slipped her pistol to Shaunna and got up from the chair to semi-stagger over to the bed. Whether it was from the drink, the lack of sleep, or the relief at having Misty's help, soon after crawling into the bed Champagne was fast asleep. Shaunna turned on the big screen television and took a seat. She was prepared to stand guard over her friend if she slept until next month.

CHAPTER 28

Ronald pulled into the parking space behind the Taurus. He got out of his car carrying a large, blue gym bag. As he approached the rear of the Taurus, the trunk popped open. He deposited the gym bag in the trunk and shut it. He got in the rear of the Taurus, taking a seat behind Shaunna in the driver's seat.

"It's all there," Ronald said. "Six hundred thousand."

"Thanks, Ronnie," Champagne said. "I knew that we could count on you to take care of the busyness."

"You sure that you all don't want me to ride with y'all?" Ronald asked. "I'm not scared."

"Ronnie, we need you to be totally clean of this if it goes bad," Champagne said. "There's no doubt in my mind that you're not scared, but what we're doing isn't what we need you to do. We're a team and as long as you play your position we can win. There's no dishonor in the role you're playing. What if something happens when you're with us and we all land in jail or worse get killed? Who's going to take care of things?"

"I know, I know," Ronald said. "But it's frustrating watching my people go through something like this and I can't be a help to them except for running errands. That doesn't feel good."

"It's not that you're running errands," Shaunna interjected. "Look at it as doing what needs to be done for the team, Ronnie. You know we love you, but it's best this way. If it'll make you feel better..."

The cell phone the kidnappers had sent Champagne began ringing, causing her to hush Ronald and Shaunna. She opened the cell phone.

"Hello?" Champagne said into the cell phone.

"This is Cynthia. The kidnappers are moving up the drop to four hours from now. They said if you want to see the kids and me alive, you'd better be ready to make the drop. They'll have me call back in exactly two hours with the exact details. So be ready to go."

The cell phone clicked as the line went dead.

"What did she say, Chammy?" asked Shaunna.

"She said that they're moving up the drop time to four hours from now. Ronnie, we're going to have to see you later, okay baby?" Ronald leaned over the seat and kissed Champagne and Shaunna on their cheeks. "You two be careful, alright? Let me know the minute you hear something."

"Got you," Champagne said as Ronald climbed out of the backseat.

"You don't have to worry, we'll call you."

"Where to Chammy?" Shaunna questioned.

"Any where but here. I need a second to think. Something just didn't seem right about that call."

This time Shaunna watched carefully as she pulled into traffic.

"What do you mean? What seemed different about this call."

"The first two times they called the caller was a man and he put Cynthia on the phone. This time it was Cynthia. During the other calls there was a lot of noise, like dogs barking and I think I could hear the kids crying in the background. The first time they put Cynthia on the phone, she seemed real scared. I could almost feel her fear. Now this time she seemed calm and it was quiet. I can't quite put my finger on it, but this call wasn't as believable as the first two."

"So do you want to pull somewhere and park while we wait out the two hours?"

"No, I think I want to check something out first."

Champagne put in a call to Ronald. "Ronnie, do me a favor. Find Cynthia's exact address for me. I need it real quick. I remember that it was over east, but I can't remember exactly where." To Shaunna, she said, "Ride east, I got a feeling in the pit of my stomach." As Shaunna turned the car around, Champagne scrounged around in the front seat armrest for a pen and paper. Soon her cell phone chirped with Ronald's text of Cynthia's address.

TRIPLE TAKE 2: CHAMPAGNE'S KISS

"What are you thinking, Chammy?" asked Shaunna.

"It may be something, it may be nothing, but I want to check out Cynthia's house. If nothing else it'll give us something to do until it's time to make the drop."

...

Cynthia hung up the cell phone after calling Champagne and went into her small kitchen. She opened the refrigerator; there was only a few leftovers, a jug of water, and a two liter of diet ginger ale. She chose the jug of water. She pulled a Taco Bell Star Wars collectible cup from the dish rack and filled it. She carried her cup of water into her small bedroom and sat in the middle of her bed Indian style. She started to drink the water and ended up spitting it on the wall as she burst into hysterical laughter.

"I'm surrounded by idiots," she said aloud. "These motherfuckers are so stupid. I can't believe this shit. I should have done this a long time ago. Then I would have been rich."

She bounced off the bed, spilling her water and scampered over to her bedroom dresser. On top of the dresser was a single first class plane ticket to San Antonio. She picked up her ticket and fell back onto the bed. She kicked her feet in the air.

"Hell yes!" she yelled. "San Antonio here I come!"

It had been a simple matter for Cynthia to set up the kidnapping scheme with Nat's help. She couldn't believe her luck with how easy it had been to convince the fierce robber to marshal his forces to pull it off. It never ceased to amaze her, the things these dumb ass men would do for some pussy. It was like a form of hypnosis. Give them some, suggest something, give them some more, suggest the same thing; pretty soon they would be thinking it was their own idea. They were all the same from the thug types to the clean cut types—they all thought with their little heads.

This sting would be the sweetest one of them all though. She'd learned a long time ago, guys who didn't trust anyone were really looking for someone to trust and that was what she had appealed to in Nat. So much so that he'd trusted her with close to 70,000 dollars of his own money, that she was supposed to be taking with them to Virginia. She wasn't going to Virginia though. There was nothing to link her back to the kidnapping she had even worked under an assumed name. Champagne's simple ass business manager was supposed to check her references and background, but he was easier to manipulate than Nat had been; she didn't even have to give him any pussy, just promise that one day he would get some.

She didn't have the slightest remorse about doing what she was doing, she owed it to the world to take what she felt she needed, by whatever means. That was the reason she was going back to San Antonio, to show certain people that she'd made it without them. Everything was going according to plan—her plan. Nat couldn't even come up with a decent way to get the ransom money. He kept talking about how hard it was going to be to get the money without complications. How hard could it be to get a bag of money from two bitches and their soft ass business manager? She would have been a little worried if JC and Rat were out and about, but fate had shined on her when JC got shot and Rat got locked up. That was when she'd made Nat put a rush on the plan—her plan. Now she was just two phone calls away from leaving town with damn near three quarters of a million dollars in cash. She planned to call Dale and let him know about Nat's plan to cut out the other members of FEE and run with the cash. She would make that call just to cause confusion among the ranks of FEE, so she could grab the cash from Champagne and get out of town. If those idiots killed the kids, then so be it. They weren't her kids. Her only son was back in San Antonio with his grandmother. That was one of the main reasons she was heading there. The first thing she would buy with her money was her son's love and affection.

Cynthia opened her cell phone and dialed Dale's number. "Dale, this is Cynthia. I'll wait... Damn you're dumb, if I was chained up in the bathroom, I wouldn't be on the phone with you now... My man Nat let me go... Boy just shut up and listen. The reason I'm free is because..."

CHAPTER 29

"It's got to be that house there," Champagne said as she pointed to a small townhouse. "The one on the end."

Shaunna slowly cruised by the house. "What do you want me to do? Park?"

"No, keep going. Go around the block and then up the alley. Come out right there on the side street and park."

Shaunna followed her instructions. "What next? What are you thinking?"

"I'm thinking that for some reason I really don't trust this bitch. Also it just came to me that this bitch Cynthia picked up my kids early from school yesterday. She didn't have any reason to do that and she's never done that before unless one of us told her. So why, mysteriously, did she pick the kids up early, coincidentally on the day they all get kidnapped??? That shit just don't make sense to me. Maybe I'm tweaking and if so then I'll be the first to admit it, but don't that shit seem strange or is it just me?"

"Now that you mention it," Shaunna replied. "That does seem a little bit more than out of the ordinary. That plus the phone calls. I don't know, Chammy. You may be onto something. If Cynthia really is involved, do you think that she'd be stupid enough to be at home?"

"Well, I look at it like this. If Cynthia really is involved then she wouldn't think that we would figure this shit out. It would really make sense if she was in on it because the kidnappers knew too much. Our address. Who my man is and that he wasn't around. That we can even come up with that kind of money. Even where to get our kids from. Maybe she helped unwillingly, but she had to have helped them. I can't come up with any other explanation. Maybe I'm just grasping at straws, hoping that this will turn out alright, but I know that I'll feel much better once I've got a chance to talk to Cynthia face to face. I don't see no harm in checking out her crib. If she isn't there, then we at least know that they do have her, but if she's home she's got some real important decisions to make that will affect the rest of her damn life."

...

Dale closed his cell phone and looked across the basement at Nat who was sitting on the couch watching ESPN Sportscenter. He whipped his gun from his waistband and pointed it at Nat.

"Man, what the fuck is wrong with you?" Dale shouted. "What type of nigga is you?"

Mar was asleep on the end of the couch, but he awoke when he heard Dale shouting. Nat looked away from the television, surprised at having a gun pointed in his direction. "Nigga, you better quit pointing that heater at me," he said calmly. "I don't know what the fuck you talking about, but you better quit playing."

Dale stood and advanced on Nat without lowering his gun.

"Nigga, this ain't no fucking game. I just got a real interesting call on the telephone, nigga. Guess from who."

"What?" Nat said, now showing signs of anger. "Nigga, do I look like the fuck I would sit here and try to guess who you done talked to on the phone? You better sit yo ass down and get that damn pistol out my fuckin' face!"

Julius came bounding down the basement stairs with several slices of pizza on the cardboard circle from the pizza box.   "I told you niggas that I was gone get the last of that pizza. Don't ask for shit neither 'cause I coughed all over it."   When he saw Dale pointing the gun at Nat, Julius froze. "What the fuck y'all doing? Dale, what the fuck you doing?"

"Shut up Julie," Dale ordered. "I was just getting to what the fuck is going on. This nigga Nat is trying to fuck us. Our own fuckin' homie is trying to beat us out."

The loud voices of the men woke the twins, who had been dozing in the dog cages. Anaya started crying while Kenton sat up and listened.

Dale hit her cage with his gun hand. "You better shut the fuck up little bitch 'fore I pull you out of there and kick yo little ass! Shut it up right now!" He swung the gun back toward Nat. "I ain't never think you would play us like this nigga. I just got off the phone with your little girlfriend Cynthia. Yeah nigga, yo bitch just called me and let me know what the fuck you was planning."

Momentarily a look of surprise slid across Nat's face, but he quickly regained control of his emotions and placed a scowl on his face. He laughed coldly as he turned to Julius.

"Julie, you hear this shit? This nigga, Dale, done finally lost his entire mind. How the hell did he get a call from Cynthia? He knows that I just met that bitch when we snatched her up. That's some bullshit. One of his bitches he done pillow-talked around is calling him playing tricks with his mind. You better stop talking to them bitches and letting them in yo business, they'll mess you up every time."

"Nigga, I don't tell no bitch my business," Dale said. "You just trying to flip this shit around, but I ain't trying to hear that. How the fuck did Cynthia just call my phone? I don't know that bitch and I ain't give her my number. The bitch is 'sposed to be upstairs locked in the bathroom."

Speaking for the first time, Mar asked, "What's up Nat? This shit can be solved real easy the way I see it. Is that bitch still in the bathroom?"

"What? You too, Mar? You niggas is tripping. Hell yeah! She still in the bathroom handcuffed to the sink. Man, you niggas better chill the fuck out. That's just jitters from pulling a big job. There's so much money on the line that it got you niggas tripping. That's alright though, I'm gone let this shit ride one time and one time only, but you niggas better get y'all minds right."

Nat took his seat and used the remote to flick channels on the television, all the while hoping that his bluff had worked.

"Nigga, you musta forgot who you talking to," Dale stated. "Did you just try the Jedi mind trick on us? What, just 'cause you say that it didn't happen, then the shit didn't happen. I know for a fact that a bitch calling herself Cynthia just called my fuckin' phone and told me about y'all plan to run off with the ransom money to Virginia. The bitch say y'all been planning this shit for a minute. She knew my name. Ain't no way she should'a knew my name. Ain't nobody never said my name 'round this bitch so how she know me?"

"I don't know nigga," Nat said. "How the fuck would I know how a bitch that I don't know, know yo name? Maybe you said yo name around this bitch. Whatever, that shit don't mean nothing."

Not liking what he was hearing, Mar pulled his gun and sat it on his lap. "Like I said Nat. This shit is real easy to prove. All we got to do is go up them stairs and see if the bitch is in that bathroom. If she there, everything is good. If she ain't, then we got some issues. So why don't you throw me the key that goes to that door."

"Nigga if you don't believe me, fine, that's on you. But I'll be gotdamned if I give you the key. I can't believe that you niggas don't trust me. Fuck that, I ain't giving you shit. I know that bitch is in the bathroom. I ain't got to prove shit to you niggas." "Oh that's where you wrong, nigga," Dale declared. "You wrong about that one all the way. Mar go upstairs and check that bathroom."

"He won't give me the key."

"It's a bathroom door, not a bank vault," said Dale. "Kick that motherfucka off the fuckin' hinges."

"Oh, y'all gone disrespect my house like that?" Nat asked in a last ditch effort to deter them.

"Nigga, if she still in there with the money we got coming we buy you a new door," Dale said.

Gun in hand, Mar took the basement steps two at a time. At the bathroom, he used his shoulder as a battering ram to bust open the door. No Cynthia. He dashed back downstairs to the basement and aimed his gun at Nat too.

"She there?" Dale asked.

"Nope. Nothing in the bathroom but towels, rugs, soap, and tissue," Mar answered. "Nigga, you got some real explaining to do."

"Ain't nothing to explain," Dale said fiercely. "This nigga was gone pull up. Just like Cynthia said, he was gone get the whole six hundred stacks and run off with the shit to Virginia. Man, fuck this nigga. Let's kill his bitch ass and we gone get the cash."

Julius set down what was left of his pizza. He walked between Nat and the two brothers with his arms up. "Hold on now y'all," he said. "This shit is moving too fast. We been through too much together to let a bitch and a couple of dollars fuck up our flow. Everybody let's calm down. Mar and Dale, y'all put them guns down and let's talk this shit out."

Using Julius as a shield, Nat pulled his gun and sent shots in the direction of Dale and Mar. One of the bullets slammed into the back of Julius' head showering the ceiling with blood and brain matter. Julius pitched forward and Mar moved to his left to avoid his body. He stepped directly into the path of bullets flying from Nat's gun, catching a bullet right above his right eye and another below his nose. His body lost control of its' motor functions and Mar pitched over onto his side twitching in death throes. Dale sprang into action, dropping to one knee and closely grouping a series of three shots from his gun into Nat's chest. Nat flung his gun over his head as he stumbled over a milk crate and sprawled on his side against the dog cage holding his precious pitbull Widow. He fought to get back to his feet, but couldn't gain footage in his blood mixing in with the water that spilled from Widow's bowl when he fell on her cage. Widow whimpered and licked at her master through the cage as the blood pumped from the holes in his chest and stomach.

Dale ran to his brother's side and dropped onto his knees. He pulled Mar over onto his back and gasped in horror at his brother's disfigured face. The large neat hole over his right eyebrow was barely bleeding, but the shot that hit him under his nose had torn away most of his top lip and broken his jaw which flapped loosely as his body convulsed.

Dale stood and walked past Julius, who was missing the top half of his scalp over to Nat.

"You kilt my little brother, you fucking bitch!" Dale fumed. "You had to try some bullshit! You kilt my brother! Now him and Julie is dead 'cause of you!"

Nat coughed and spat a large glob of blood near Dale's feet. He shuddered and began bleeding more profusely. He tried to bring Dale into focus, but a glaze covered his eyes.

"Fuck everybody else!" Nat declared defiantly, but his words were drowned out by the blazing of the gun as Dale emptied his weapon into Nat and Widow's head. Dale dropped his gun and staggered back over his brother's body. He pulled Mar's head into his lap and wept.

CHAPTER 30

Champagne left her guns in the Taurus with Shaunna as she got out the car. Making sure she looked as inconspicuous as possible she crossed the street and went into the alley behind the address Ronald had given her. There was a small backyard behind the townhouse surrounded by a wooden privacy fence. At the gate of the fence, she reached through and lifted the metal latch. Stealthily she crept into the backyard. There was a small deck in the back and a set of patio doors that led out onto it. She crept along the fence until she came to the deck. Praying that the wood wouldn't creak, she crept up the steps and at the edge of the patio door, she peeked through the small space afforded by the blinds hanging there. She didn't see anyone at first so she stood there with her eyes glued to the narrow opening she could see through the blinds.

Five minutes passed and she was ready to give up when Cynthia came in view inside the townhouse. She came into view from the right side of the townhouse and set a bag down by a table in the front room. There was a large white cat by the couch, which Cynthia scooped and started walking toward the kitchen, directly towards Champagne.

Champagne faded back to the side of the patio doors and reached for her guns—the guns she'd left in the car. "Damn," she whispered. "Shit." On tiptoe, she snuck down the deck steps and sidled off to the side of the yard. She had just ducked down behind a garbage container when the patio door slid open. Cynthia tossed the cat out into the middle of the yard.

"Sorry, Tony you've got to go," Cynthia said. "This way is better for you because Mommy is out of here. You've been trying to get outside; now's your chance. Go find you some cat pussy, pussy cat. Wish I could take you, but I can't, so good luck Tony the Tiger. Mommy will try to send you a postcard from San Antone."

TRIPLE TAKE 2: CHAMPAGNE'S KISS

Champagne heard the patio door close, but she waited a few seconds before peeking around the garbage can. The cat, Tony looked at her curiously as he padded past her to hop up onto the deck. The cat was staring through the patio door so he didn't see Champagne beat a hasty, but silent retreat from the yard, back over the Taurus. She dove into the passenger seat.

"Gimme my gun," she demanded.

"What happened?" asked Shaunna. "What happened?"

"That bitch is in there and she's planning a trip to San Antonio, but I've got news for her. She's not going to make it."

Shaunna grabbed her arm. "Hold on now, Chammy. What are you going to do? Are you just going to go charging up in there?"

"Hell yeah! Let's go."

"Chammy, we don't know who's up in there with her. We don't know if the kids are in there. You charging through the door might get them hurt. We got to take this slow. I know your kids may be in there, but we've got to make sure that we do this shit right. Let's do this right because we may only get one chance to do this right. Let's take our time and get the kids back safely."

Champagne didn't want to admit that Shaunna was right, but what she said made perfect sense. She took a moment to calm down and think her way through this. As she was pulling on her baseball batting gloves it suddenly hit her.

"You're absolutely right, Shaunny, but I just thought of something. I saw Cynthia put a cat out in the yard. It was her cat, that's when she said that she was going to San Antonio. Remember when she called the first time there was a lot of dogs barking in the background and noise. That's what made me want to check out her house because the second call was so quiet in the background. This can't be the place that they were holding my kids because she's got a cat, not dogs. Wherever my kids are there are a lot of dogs there. This bitch knows something. I say that we go up in here and make this bitch tell us where my kids are.

What do you think?"

Shaunna handed Champagne her guns and put on her baseball batting gloves. "Now that sounds much better than just running around half-cocked. Are we going in through the back?"

"Yeah," said Champagne. She led them across the street and back through the gate. On the deck at the patio door, Champagne peeked into the house again and Shaunna shadowed against the wall beside her. She didn't see Cynthia, but they knew she hadn't left the house.

Champagne drew her gun and with her fingers mentally crossed, she tried the latch on the patio door. It resisted a little, but with a slightly harder shove, it slid back out of the way. Using her gun, Champagne parted the blinds and slithered through them. She held them back so Shaunna could come through them too. Softly Shaunna closed the patio door. The townhouse was small with only a kitchen, a small dining area and a living room on the first level. No Cynthia. Champagne pointed toward the ceiling with her gun to indicate to Shaunna the upstairs level. Holding their breath that the stairs didn't creak under the tired carpet that covered them, they started up the stairs. Halfway up the stairs, they heard Cynthia singing. They made it to the top of the stairs and Champagne peeked into Cynthia's room. The twin's nanny was wearing only a towel while she danced around her bedroom singing along with the radio.

A look of total fury contorted Champagne's face as she rushed into the room and upended Cynthia with a flying tackle that would have made a NFL linebacker proud. Cynthia flipped over the bed and landed on her neck, but she sprang to her feet quickly, only to be rushed by both Shaunna and Champagne. The two women flooded her quickly with blows. Cynthia finally passed out when Shaunna clucked her on the nose bone with a handful of pistol. During the struggle, Cynthia lost her towel. Their breathing was a bit heavier as they drug Cynthia naked down the stairs and tossed her on the couch. Shaunna went to check out the kitchen. "Bitch, wake up!" Champagne demanded as she slapped the shit out of Cynthia. "Wake the fuck up right now! I am not fucking playing!" Cynthia opened her eyes and walled them with fear. "Ms. Wells, what happened? Why did you beat me up? I haven't done anything Ms. Wells."

"Bitch, don't call me Ms. Wells. My gotdamn name is Champagne. You need to stop bullshitting in here and tell me where the fuck my kids are!"

"I don't know Ms., I mean Champagne. I don't know where they are. I just escaped the kidnappers myself and I didn't know where to go so I came home." Champagne laughed sharply. "Bitch, you must think that I'm fucking playing with you. Do you hear the stupid shit that you're saying? When we came through the door you were dancing around your fucking room. That didn't look like someone that just escaped from some kidnappers. You didn't call the police or one of us, bitch you went home to take a shower and then dance." Champagne raised her gun hand to crack Cynthia in the head again. "Bitch, you better stop playing with me before I knock your fucking brains out of your head!" Cynthia cowered on the couch, covering her head. "I'm not Cynthia!" she screamed. "I don't know any Cynthia! Why are you in my house?"

"What the hell is going on in here?" Shaunna called out from the kitchen. "This bitch ain't got nothing in her damned fridge."

"This bitch is playing crazy now," Champagne yelled. "You need to get in here with me."

"Get out of my house! Help me someone, there's some crazy people in my house!" Cynthia yelled. "Help! Help me someone! Help!"

To quiet her down, Champagne began slamming her pistol into Cynthia's head and face over and over again, until finally with one exceptionally hard blow to the top of her skull, Cynthia stopped screaming. Her eyes rolled into the back of her head and she began flopping around until she slipped off the couch and banged her head with tremendous force on the sharp edge of the marble topped coffee table.

Shaunna rushed into the room. "Chammy, what did you do?"

"She was hollering so I was trying to make her ass shut up," Champagne said.

When Cynthia stopped flopping around on the carpeted floor, Shaunna went over and examined her a bit more closely. Champagne had beaten her pretty good. There was thick scarlet blood leaking from Cynthia's nose, mouth, and scalp. From one exceptionally deep gash in her head, Shaunna could see what looked like pieces of her skull. She lifted Cynthia's left arm several times and dropped it; there was no resistance whatsoever as her arm crashed to the floor.

Shaunna sat back on the floor and looked up at Champagne. "She still alive, but I don't know for how long. If she do survive her brain is gone be mush. Her skull is all but caved in. You fucked her up pretty good."

"What have I done?" Champagne said as she sank onto the coffee table. "I wasn't trying to kill this bitch, just make her shut up and stop playing fucking games with me. What the hell are we gone do now?"

"I don't know," Shaunna said. "At this point, I really don't know. I see that I can't leave you alone. Give me a second." Shaunna sat with her head in hands for a few moments. "The only thing I could come up with is that we search this place good and hopefully we can find a clue. Also I'm going to call Murderman and tell him to come over here, maybe he's found something out or he can at least give us a clue on what to do next."

"Make sure he comes by himself," Champagne said. She went up the stairs to Cynthia's bedroom to search for clues to her children's whereabouts. Her search of Cynthia's room yielded a cell phone and not much else. She returned to the first level, where Shaunna had found a bag full of money and a Snickers candy bar. She was eating the Snickers.

Champagne shook her head as she opened the cell phone and viewed the recent calls. There were a lot of missed calls from her, a call going to her, and a call to someone named Dale FEE that was placed after Cynthia called her last. She pushed the send button to connect to Dale FEE, but no one answered. She pulled up the phonebook—there weren't many numbers there. The only one that made her raise an eyebrow slightly was the name Nat FEE, but only because he had the same surname as the person she'd called last.

"What did Murderman say?" asked Champagne, her voice heavy with disappointment.

"He wasn't too far from here. He was over on 71st with his guys, so he said he can be here in about ten minutes. He's coming by himself too. I found some money. Looks like about 50, 60,000 in there."

Not even the mention of found money could make Champagne perk up. She flopped on the couch near Cynthia's naked body. They talked quietly as Murderman's ten minutes turned into twenty minutes. Shaunna was just about to call him again when they heard a tap at the patio doors in the back. Gun drawn, Champagne went to check it out—it was him.

In the living room, standing over Cynthia's naked body they explained to Murderman what had happened and how they'd ended up here. He looked up at the two women in admiration when he examined Cynthia.

"She won't be fucking with nobody else kids," Murderman confirmed as he too checked her vitals. "This bitch is pretty much out to lunch for the rest of her life. Now tell me what y'all found out."

"Not a damn thing," Champagne said bitterly. "The only thing we found is her cell phone and some money. It couldn't be this bitch's money, I mean we were paying her, but not enough for her to stack it like this."

Murderman rocked back on his haunches. "It's got to be her nigga's money. She didn't pull this all by herself. Let me see her phone." Champagne handed him the phone and he examined the calls and contact numbers. He whipped out his phone and dialed a number. "Yo-

Yo, tell me do you know a Dale or a Nat FEE that got some pitbulls? Oh yeah. What's to these studs? They stickup men, hunh? Are they brothers or something, they both got the last name FEE? That's what that mean? Are they the real deal or some pretenders? They the same niggas that stuck up Peno rich ass? For real? Where can I bump into them studs at? Yeah? That's not too far from where I'm at right now. Thanks, A. Nall, if I need you, I'll give you a call."

"I got some good news," Murderman said as he slipped his cell phone into the holster on his belt. "I think I may know where your kids are. Let me tell you." As Murder-man explained what Yo-Yo had told them, Champagne began to regain hope that she would be able to find her kids.

"Y'all go get in the car while I finish up in here," he told them.

Champagne and Shaunna took the cell phone and bag and went outside to get in the Taurus. "What do you think he's doing?" Shaunna asked. Champagne just gave her a look.

Inside the townhouse, Murderman took a knife from his pocket and unfolded it. It had a wicked sharp looking blade with a serrated edge. He flipped Cynthia onto her back and spread her legs. He plunged the blade into her right thigh and severed the femoral artery located there. He yanked his knife out and blood instantly began to pour from the mortal wound. By the time he made it to the patio doors there was already a large puddle of blood soaking through the rug underneath Cynthia. He slid out of the patio door and shut it tight behind him, but not before a cat scampered through the patio door. Tony the cat padded into the living room where he found his mistress lying in a pool of blood. Purring, Tony jumped up onto the arm of the couch and settled down to watch her bleed out.

"Follow me and stay close, we're not going far," Murderman instructed Shaunna before climbing under the wheel of his car. "Once we check out the scene, we'll figure out what to do."

CHAPTER 31

Murderman pulled over and waved Shaunna over in front of him. He parked the car he was in and climbed in the backseat of their car. He pointed to a large, old house close to the end of the next block.

"That should be the crib that my man gave me the address to," Murderman said. He pulled his gun from the small of his back and checked to make sure a bullet was on deck. He took the safety off and returned his weapon to the rear of his pants. "Any suggestions lady? I've done this type of thing before but there were never any kids involved that I had to worry about."

"I say first we go check the place out," Champagne said. "We've got to be careful because you remember I told you that I heard a lot of dogs. They sounded like pits too. We can try to get as close as possible to the place without alerting anyone. It's such a big place but it looks old so it shouldn't be too hard to get in. That's how I see it, how about you all?"

Murderman turned his black Atlanta Braves fitted hat to the back. "Sounds good to me. Don't worry Champagne, I put that on my A's if yo kids is in there, we gone get them back."

Shaunna parked on the next street over and they made their way through the side yard of the house directly across the alley from the targeted house. Behind the garage, they switched to stealth mode communicating with their eyes and hand signals. Following Murderman's lead, they crept into the back yard. The back door of the house was open and they could hear barking coming from inside but it was muffled. They stole upon the back porch and Champagne tried the screen door; it was latched from the inside. She peeked through the screen and didn't see anyone. Murderman flicked out his knife and lifted the latch of the screen door. One by one they melted into the kitchen. They searched the first floor—nothing. Upstairs on the second floor, they didn't find anything either. On the first floor, Shaunna walked past the open door to the basement and almost threw up from the smell of unwashed dogs.

With her eyes and gun hand, Shaunna motioned to Murderman and Champagne. Cautiously they crept down the stairs into the basement. Their presence set the remaining dogs off in their cages. They all jumped, but recognized that the dogs were caged. Then they saw the bodies of the members of FEE scattered on the floor.

"What the fuck?" Champagne muttered as she viewed the carnage. Her scan of the room made her notice her son and daughter in the dog cages. She and Murderman broke the small locks on the cages and pulled the kids out of them. She holstered her guns and took the tape off their eyes.

The kids were so happy so see their mother, they couldn't stop hugging and kissing her and trying to explain to her that they knew she was coming to get them.

"Okay babies," Champagne said hurriedly, trying to dislodge the kids from her neck. "Twins, you've got to listen to Mommy. We have to get out of here. Shhh... You guys have to listen now. No talking. Mommy, Auntie Shaunny and our friend are going to get you out of here, but you have to be quiet. Can you do that for me? Nod your heads."

"But you said don't nod our heads when somebody asks us a question," Kenton said.

Champagne put her finger to his lips. "Well now I'm telling you to nod your head if you understand. You're going to have to be real quiet. Let's go."

Led by Shaunna and Murderman, Champagne left the basement holding her children's hands. On the first floor, they were all headed for the kitchen and out the back door, when Dale jumped from the behind the basement door and grabbed Champagne around the neck. He jammed his gun to the side of her head.

"You're not going to take them from me!" Dale shouted, causing Murderman and Shaunna to whirl around. "They're not going anywhere!

We went through all of this to get our money and you're not leaving here without paying me every last cent of it!"

Champagne let the kids hands go and they ran over to Shaunna. Both her and Murderman had their guns pointed at Dale, but they hesitated to take a shot for fear of harming Champagne.

"Get the fuck over here!" Dale slobbered, blood and drool slathering the side of Champagne's face. "You fucking brats get the fuck back over here! I want my motherfuckin' money and I want it right now! My brother died for that money and I'm going to get it!"

"Calm down," Champagne said. "Let's not lose our heads. We have the money right outside in the car. All you have to do is let him go get it and we'll give it to you and leave. We've got the money and we're willing to pay so calm down. Go get the money for him, Murder."

Murderman lifted his gun hand and edged backwards to the kitchen door. "Don't do nothing stupid, man. I'm going to get the money for you. It's right out in the car and it'll only take me a few minutes to bring it back."

"Stay right there!" Dale commanded. "What the fuck do I look like a fuckin' fool! You're not going nowhere! Let that bitch right there go get the fuckin' money! And she better hurry the hell up or I'm going to kill this big bitch right here! Hurry the fuck up and no damn tricks! You've got two minutes, bitch, so hurry the fuck up before I start killing motherfuckers up in here!" "I'll be right back with it, man," Shaunna said to Dale, but she was looking at Champagne for some sort of signal. All she received was a nigh imperceptible head nod from her friend. "I've got all the money and I'll be right back with it so don't do nothing stupid."

Shaunna ducked out the back door letting the screen door slam. She hurried to the Taurus and popped the trunk. Instead of grabbing the big bag with the six hundred thousand in it, she grabbed the lighter bag that they'd taken from Cynthia's house. At a trot, she headed back to the house.

"It's me," Shaunna said, as she slowly opened the screen door, not wanting to surprise the kidnapper holding Champagne. "I told you that I would be right back. I've got the money. I've got your money right here."

"Open the bag, bitch and let me see the cash," Dale directed.

Shaunna opened the bag and held it open for him to see.

"Come closer with the bag, bitch, I can't see that shit. That might be some funny money. Let me see the shit or I'm gone kill this bitch here."

With Dale's attention on making sure there was real money in the bag, Champagne started to make her move. She slid her hand into her jacket and unholstered one of her guns. Slowly she slid her hand out of her jacket clutching the gun and tucked it under her arm with the barrel aimed at Dale's midsection.

Shaunna closed the distance between them holding the bag open. As Dale leaned forward to peek into the bag, the gun he was holding left Champagne's head for a split second. Champagne lifted the arm covering her gun slightly and began firing. In her anger she kept firing the gun until it was empty. Dale never had a chance as he staggered back into the living room and fell onto the coffee table with eleven holes in his chest and torso. The coffee table collapsed under Dale's weight and splintered into a thousand pieces. He died staring at the watermarked ceiling.

Champagne, Shaunna, Murderman, Kenton, and Anaya were out the back door and almost to the car, by the time Dale's soul left his body. Hurriedly they packed into the car and Shaunna drove Murderman back to his car.

Before he got out, Champagne turned to Murderman in the backseat. "Thanks, Murder," she said. "I don't know what we would have done without your help. Thank you so much."

"No thank you, Champagne," Murderman returned. "I told you that I needed some action and you guys provided that, though it wasn't as much as I would have liked. I'm glad that you got the kids back alright.

And if that nigga JC ever mess up, you make sure you give me a call. I could shole use a gangsta chick like you."

Champagne laughed. "JC ain't gone mess up, he knows what he's got. Tell Dante I said thanks. Now that this shit is over, I'll be sure that I let JC know how you guys helped out. When you leave, take that bag with you. We don't need it."

"You sure?" asked Murderman. "'Cause I didn't do this for no cash. Like we said, your dude is our friend and he was real good to us."

"Take it, man. We got that from that crazy bitch Cynthia. It's yours with our blessings. As for us, we're going home and I'm not going to let my babies out of my sight. Thanks Murder."

Holding the gym bag full of Nat's money, Murderman watched them cruise away in the Ford Taurus. He knew without a doubt why JC loved Champagne so much, she was a lady of a different caliber.

"I've got to get me one of those," Murderman said aloud about Champagne. "That's a real woman there." He tossed the bag of money onto the floor on the passenger side of his car and drove away.

CHAPTER 32

Champagne sat on the edge of the bed and tied the laces on her running shoes. She walked across the large master bedroom to the dresser and looked in the mirror. In front of the mirror, she whipped her hair into a ponytail. From her walk-in closet she took the jacket to her running suit off its hanger and shrugged it on. Back at the dresser, she selected a pair of her designer sunglasses from the dozen or so pairs there. She slung her purse on her shoulder and disconnected her cell phone from the charger.

"Shaunny, where are you, I'm ready to go," Champagne said into the mansion's intercom system.

"I'm in the kitchen making me a road trip snack," Shaunna answered on the intercom.

"Well, I'm on my way down."

She walked to the west end of the hallway and went down the stairs that led to the rear of the mansion and its' kitchen. Shaunna was in the kitchen at the enormous island putting the finishing touches on the sack of food she called her snack. JC rolled into the kitchen in his wheelchair with the children following closely behind him. Anaya raced from behind her father's wheelchair and dove into Champagne.

"Mommy, mommy are you going to remember what I told you to tell uncle Rat?" she asked. "'Member that I told you to tell him that I ain't mad at him for missing our birthday. And that I love him. And that..."

Champagne stooped and gave her daughter a hug and kiss. "I remember, I remember," she said. "I'm going to tell him everything you said, okay?"

Kenton gave his mother a hug too. "Tell uncle Rat, that I said hey and that I love him."

"C'mon you guys can walk us out," Champagne suggested. "That is if the pregnasaurus is finished." Shaunna grabbed her snack pack and a bag of Sour Cream and Onion Ruffles she was already eating. "I'm ready," she mumbled with her mouth full of chips. "A girl got to eat don't she? Shoot."

In the rear of the mansion was a cavernous eight car garage and a half block long driveway that dissected the vast backyard. In the driveway was parked Champagne's black Cadillac Allante. She used the car alarm remote to unlock the doors so she and Shaunna could get in the car. Once she closed the car door, JC and the kids came over to the car. She rolled down the window for them to say their final goodbyes.

JC leaned forward in his wheelchair so that his arms were resting on the car door. Champagne offered him her cheek and he gave her a kiss. He sat back in his chair and the kids climbed on his lap.

"Me and these two bums are just going to hang out until my mother gets here," JC said. "Remember take the Stevenson it'll take you straight to Stateville. You can't miss it. Don't worry none neither, the lawyer got Rat a way better deal than I thought he could get. He should only end up having to do sixty-one days since they threw out his parole violation and gave him two years. He'll be out way before that hungry ass baby of yours is born."

"Y'all gone leave me and my little hungry monster alone," Shaunna said.

"Alright, I'm out of here," Champagne said. "Love you all and you two better be good, don't get on Daddy's nerves."

"We'll be good," the twins returned.

Champagne turned the key in the Cadillac's ignition and the car exploded. The initial blast from the car bomb instantly mangled JC and the twins before flinging them, wheelchair and all, clear across the backyard. In the passenger seat, Shaunna all but incinerated. Champagne wanted to scream, but when she opened her mouth flames engulfed her. She closed her eyes to let the searing pain of the fire wash over her and she thought she could hear God calling her name.

"Champagne, Champagne. Open your eyes, baby girl."

Y. Blak Moore

She didn't want to open her eyes, to see her pregnant friend burning, to see her man and children spread all over the lawn.

"Champagne, wake up girl."

She knew that voice, she'd heard it many times, comforting her through dark times, making her laugh, guiding her through her fears, and making her face her demons. It wasn't God's voice, it was JC's.

She opened her eyes. There was no fire, no burning car, no bodies. She was in bed in the master bedroom of the mansion she shared with her man, kids, and friends. JC was standing over her. He used the remote to open the blinds.

"Sorry to wake you, Chammy. You didn't look like you were sleeping too peacefully anyway. I'm about to leave with Ronnie. I've got to go take a look at some of the work that I've got going at the properties. If you ain't around these funky ass contractors will lay their asses down on the job. I wanted to ask you something before I left though."

JC used his cane to accommodate the slight limp he'd gained as he went over to his dresser and took something out of the drawer. He came back over to the bed and sat next to Champagne with a slight groan. Champagne stretched and then propped another pillow under her head so she was a little more elevated.

"I was just wondering," JC started. "Um, if you ain't gone be doing nothing in a couple of months on a Saturday morning. Then would you do me a big favor and marry me?"

"What? What did you say?"

JC held up an open, black velvet ring box. Perched on the little pillow in the box was a four carat princess cut diamond engagement ring.

"I said would you marry me?" JC repeated.

Holding her breath, Champagne took the ring box from him and got the ring out of it. She slipped it onto her finger.

"Oh, hell yeah!" Champagne shouted. "We can go to City Hall today!"

JC laughed. "Not today. I've got to wait for my best man to get out of prison. If I don't I'll never hear the end of that shit. It's only a couple

208

of months and then I can snap the house arrest band around my leg, I mean get married."

Champagne punched him in the shoulder.

"Hey now easy, easy," JC said while rubbing his shoulder. "I'm not healed all the way. I take it that your answer is yes."

Champagne held up her hand so the sun streaming into the room could ignite her massive diamond ring. "It's safe to say that my answer is 'Yes.'"

"She said yes, y'all," JC called out. "Come on in."

The twins, Anaya and Kenton came flying into the room and launched themselves onto the bed. Shaunna and Ronald followed them into the room smiling.

JC held up his hand. "Hold on, y'all. I need one more thing, so your new fiancée can have a good day. It's something that I never thought I'd get again when I was laying in that alley shot up."

"What's that?" Champagne asked.

"Champagne's kiss."

"One kiss coming right up Daddy," Champagne said as she got on her knees and put her arms around his neck.

"Uhhh, Mommy and Daddy are nasty," Kenton said.

Champagne and JC each reached out and covered their children's eyes as they kissed.

"Alright you two, get a room," Ronald joked. "Oh yeah, this is your room."

Shaunna came over to the bed and took the kid's hands and guided them down off the bed. "C'mon 'Naya and Kent, Mommy and Daddy look like they need some grownup time. Let's go downstairs and get something to eat."

"We just ate, Shaunny," Anaya told her. "You're the one that's pregginant. You're not going to ruin my figure."

"Girl, you a mess," Shaunna said. "You ain't figured out that you ain't got no figure."

Champagne had already started removing JC's boots as their friends and children were leaving the bedroom.

"Uh, Ronnie, could you call the contractors and tell them that we're going to be a little late."

"Got you J," Ronald said before closing the bedroom door.

ACKNOWLEDGEMENTS

Always I acknowledge the Creator. If not for the Creator's mercies, I would not have been able to create my body of work. Believe me when I say, it took some prayer, faith, and mercy to get to this point.

My doggone kids Cacharel(Loony), Ciara(Bubba Cow),
and Yanier(Ham).
Sazon (Bun-Bun) and Briana (Bebe) Love you all.
My sister, Tebby, and my nephews Devin, Dwight, and Darius.

My editor Ytteb Martin(yttebmartin417@gmail.com)

To ALL my Elementals, peace and thanks for all the love. It's TOO MANY of y'all to even attempt to try and name. I made that mistake once, I'll never try it again. If you rock with me, this is for you.
I'M BACK.

ABOUT THE AUTHOR

Triple Take 2: Champagne's Kiss is the 4th novel penned by Y. Blak Moore. Blak is a lifelong Chicago Southside resident by way of the Low End. He is also the author of the street lit sensations' Triple Take (Random House/Villard), The Apostles (Random House/Villard) and Slipping (Random House/Villard). This is his fourth book in the series of seven novels he has dedicated himself to penning. Currently he is working on Diesel Dolls and Chill, his 5th and 6th novels. Blak is the CEO and lead designer of Elemental Apparel. He has three biological children, but has been an influence and mentor to countless others.
Word

.

CPSIA information can be obtained
at www.ICGtesting.com
Printed in the USA
BVHW030212280220
573625BV00001B/9